Male Image, Female Gaze

Male Image, Female Gaze

Men in Shashi Deshpande's Fiction

MANPREET J. SINGH

RAWAT PUBLICATIONS
Jaipur • New Delhi • Bangalore • Hyderabad • Guwahati

ISBN 978-81-316-0508-0

Published by
Prem Rawat for **Rawat Publications**
Satyam Apts, Sector 3, Jawahar Nagar, Jaipur 302 004 (India)
Phone: 0141 265 1748 / 7006 Fax: 0141 265 1748
E-mail: info@rawatbooks.com
Website: www.rawatbooks.com

New Delhi Office
4858/24, Ansari Road, Daryaganj, New Delhi 110 002
Phone: 011 2326 3290

Also at Bangalore, Hyderabad and Guwahati

Typeset by Rawat Computers, Jaipur
Printed at Chaman Enterprises, New Delhi

For my daughters
Harnidh and Sukhnidh

Contents

Preface

Shashi Deshpande crystallizes emotions and responses which run through our lives in diffused, unquantifiable strains, defying a clear categorization. She achieves this through a fine detailing of her relational world, which makes us see that we are entrenched into our situations, not necessarily for a lack of options but also because of our own need to be a part of them. She suggests that the only viable course for tackling the contentions arising out of such a situation is to work on them from within. This would involve not just giving an expression to our feelings but also looking into the motives of those who are instrumental in generating them.

This work attempts to analyse Deshpande's detailed inclusion of the male world in her feminist posturing as part of this inclusive approach. It attempts to show how relationships need to be made more workable from a woman's point of view, by involving men in the process. This she believes is possible only if women step out of their alienated spaces and take a proactive stance in finding out ways to make inroads into rigid patriarchal structures. It also attempts to show that the male–female positioning analysed by her is not limited just to the husband–wife relationship. In their cumulative social influence, men as fathers, brothers and sons have an equally important role in defining the spaces allocated to women in their various roles. It is a change in response through all these relational constructs, which can lead to a shift in the paradigms which structure our world. To exclude them from this analysis would be to leave out crucial portions of the world portrayed by Deshpande.

In order to analyse the issues mentioned, this work takes up eight novels by Deshpande, beginning with her first work *Roots and Shadows* (1983) and ending with *In the Country of Deceit* (2008), her latest novel. Between these are six novels which function like a continuum, explicating and portraying various facets of the issues being explored. These are: *The Dark Holds No Terror* (1980), *That Long Silence* (1988), *The Binding Vine* (1993), *A Matter of Time* (1996), *Small Remedies* (2000) and *Moving On* (2004).

Her two detective novels, *If I Die Today* (1982) and *Come Up and Be Dead* (1993) do not form a part of the present work because although there are reflections of the concerns taken up here, the writer's focus is on the construction of a crime thriller and they work out as writings of a different genre. The same holds true for her books for children. Her short story collections, *The Intrusion and Other Stories* (1993), *Collected Stories: Volume I* (2003) and *Collected Stories: Volume II* (2004), are of course replete with some of the issues which the following chapters analyse. However, this study makes only occasional references to these, because they comprise a separate body of work and would entail independent focus. One of her short stories, *The Day of the Golden Deer* (2004), which has been re-published in Namita Gokhale's *In Search of Sita: Revisiting Mythology* (2009) finds a mention because of its focus on the constituents of masculinity.

I have been lucky that the stage at which this work was taking shape I had Deshpande's consolidated opinions in the form of her book *Writing from the Margin and Other Essays* (2003), to fall back upon. It is through constant reference to the views expressed in it that I have tried to corroborate the analysis in terms of the writer's own intention. The essays in this collection, according to Deshpande have evolved out of the lectures given and articles written by her for over fifteen years. They reflect an evolution and revision of her thought processes and offer the most appropriate validation for the views expressed here.

The analysis of feminist concerns, gender constructs and concepts of autonomy used in this book are taken from works from different fields, many times written by writers who do not belong to the cultural context it explores. However, the understanding derived from these works is adapted to the indigenous requirements by integrating them with the insights accrued by Indian writers who are working on various facets of the sociological reality, of the milieu being explored here.

I would like to thank Dr Nilufer E. Bharucha for her help in putting together the diverse components of this work, which has resulted in the elaboration of an important but unexplored facet of Deshpande's writing.

My thanks to my family, who grinned and bore it all! They have almost accepted Shashi Deshpande as an inevitable part of their lives.

1

New Areas in Feminist Analysis

Shashi Deshpande writes of a milieu to which she belongs not just by birth or nationality, but by the fact that it constitutes her lived reality. Her objectivity therefore functions through the social and relational nuances of the life she experiences, rather than through the ideologically dissociated vision of a distanced onlooker. The gender concerns which she takes up are parts of a context, with which she identifies despite its imperfections. Although she is aware of the imbalances in the system, she does not denigrate the importance of the relationships and institutions within it. In fact, even as she explores the problem areas, she keeps moving beyond theoretical assumptions to emotional and relational dimensions outside their purview. The shift which she envisages is an inclusive, rather than a componential one. In the process she brings new areas into the ambit of her study, bringing into focus previously neglected dimensions to the issues she addresses. Among these is the inclusion of male response as a constituent of the feminist endeavour.

Deshpande does not overlook the importance of theory itself. She sees ideas as universal tools for understanding and influencing life, particularly in dealing with disparities operating in systems across cultures. She acknowledges the insights which feminism has provided on the contradictions between a woman's experience and her social roles. Simone de Beauvoir's *The Second Sex* (1949) which questions the secondary status of women, Betty Freidan's *The*

Feminine Mystique (1963) which exposes the psychological distress implicit in female roles, Kate Millet's *Sexual Politics* (1970) with its exposure of the false construction of women in male writings, are an indelible part of Deshpande's world view. However, running parallel to the insights accrued through these is the awareness, that their literary representation could become relevant only if they are merged into and evolved through the working of the particular milieu being represented. Their credibility rests on being "rooted in theoretical paradigms that either organically derive from or are most directly relevant to the objectives of life of the society in question."[1] This, she realizes, becomes even more pertinent while portraying change within that social structure, because proposing a shift which disregards the essential attributes of the society in question could create a disjunction between "the literary and the social text."[2]

Deshpande's contribution lies in coalescing this understanding into her works. It lies in her implicit assertion that unmodified western feminist precepts, advocating an individualized and autonomous female identity, might be incongruent with what women in her own milieu might see as a feasible resolution to their problems. It also lies in her insistence that to judge them by ideological parameters constructed to tackle the discrepancies of a different social order would be wrong. Their options need to be workable in relation to their own context. They need to be aimed at providing an emotional and intellectual comfort level, not necessarily through dissociation from the world to which they belong. She believes that for feminist insights to become functional, by way of initiating the kind of change which suits the needs of the women she writes of, these have to be re-scripted according to the specificities of their own cultural requirements. This involves the daunting task of re-determining the intent of the feminist endeavour, redefining the measures of its success and taking responsibility for establishing its departure from the ideology which gives it birth. In short it involves an assertion of the right to look for solutions which can function through the configurations of one's own context.

Deshpande attempts all this and therefore stands apart, offering a fresh perspective on the way feminism could function in her world.

To study Deshpande's works from this perspective is to go beyond seeing them as feminist critiques in the form of novels, written to expose patriarchal practices, or to place her protagonists in the category of the antagonistic others, bent upon breaking free from restrictions imposed by society and culture. It also implies disagreeing with the view that if her women eventually return to a life within relationships, it is only because they are unable to sustain the rebellious gesture. Deshpande is not trying to create defiant spaces, but mutually acceptable ones, both at individual and relational levels. She is concerned with a world which comprises neither of women, nor men alone but functions through their connection with each other. The breaking of silence by Deshpande's female protagonists has to be seen as the "recognition of the self in the other" by "her male characters."[3] In this sense, her works are as much an effort to re-define masculinity as they are an endeavour to re-structure feminity.

Deshpande herself asserts that because her work is seen as conventional feminist writing, it is not fully understood. It is indeed surprising how there has been an insistent effort to ignore a contemporary writer's own views in order to fit her work into the theoretical grid provided as a research tool. It is time we paid attention to Deshpande's voice which says that she does not want to be seen as a propagandist or to endorse "... a Western concept rejecting the family and home, hating men and waging a war against them."[4] She says, "seeing the fragmentation and chaos that this cry for freedom has let the world into, I think it is time for us to ask ourselves the question – what do I do with this freedom?"[5]

In a viable and culturally relevant personal concept of feminism, she dissociates herself from "empty intellectualism"[6] and instead proposes a change which results from "a gentle and gradual inter mingling, a slow acceptance, a final absorption."[7] For Deshpande, belligerent feminism is not an end in itself. Success of feminism is only a precursor to more balanced relationships for all human beings. Therefore, its utility lies not in its sexist stance, but in its ability to validate its logic and prove its viability, to change male resistance into a willing participation for creating more justifiable gender equations. She says, "How can feminism be anti-men, when it is really working for a better relationship between men and women, instead of an uneasy relationship between tyrants and oppressed."[8] In short, Deshpande does not utilize feminism to perpetuate allegories of gender oppression or to endorse an iconoclastic stance. She uses it as an analytical tool, which works through individual social contexts, in relation to which women stand empowered or disempowered. She advocates the use of the insights of feminism to gain female autonomy, in relation to the society in which women exist.

The entire thrust of Deshpande's world view needs to be explicated primarily in terms of how she contextualizes her women and what she envisions for them in terms of selfhood. First and foremost, her women do not exist in intellectual vacuums delinked from social and cultural effects. Their identities are deeply influenced by their surroundings and there are aspects to their personalities which exceed the individualized notion of self. Significantly, none of Deshpande's novels deal with the life of a woman in isolation. Her protagonists are always placed in relation to the many generations preceding them, to show the slow evolution of change through the institutionalized structures of family histories, which serve as microcosms of social histories. These portrayals bring into focus how female identity has been generated through the premium which society has placed on it's various roles. They also show how the same social order, with its changing tenor and many faceted profiles, has given women the impulse to revaluate those roles. When they metamorphose through those revaluations, they once again have had to incorporate their new profile into the social psyche and sustain it through the hostility towards altered equations. For better or for worse, their context is a part of their lives and cannot be dispensed away with, even if it contributes to the constraints imposed upon them. Therefore, in showcasing the shifting paradigms, Deshpande consciously keeps the context alive, to show that if new perspectives have to be accommodated, the space needs to be created through stretching and pushing the boundaries of this context. There is no breaking out of it, except at the cost of alienating oneself from one's origins, which would nullify the benefits accruing from it. A sustainable change, according to her, can be worked out only in combination with a difficult but vital change in the thought processes evolving out of the social dynamics.

A necessary corollary to Deshpande's socially contextualized perspective on women's lives is the place she gives to relationships. Deshpande does not see her women as super specimen desirous of maintaining selfhood in absence of human relationships. Instead she sees them as inextricably entwined with their relationships. There is awareness that "... they are produced through these very relations and implicated in forming these relations."[9] Even as she explores the relational paradigms and their construction to suit the patriarchal set up, she constantly remains aware of the fact that there are human spaces within these lopsided arrangements, which hold in themselves a potential for expansion. If they have their misaligned aspects, she does not consider that as a reason for negating them in entirety. She understands that relationships exist over a subliminal play of power paradigms, but she also sees that they carry within themselves the essential bonds of connection and commitment without which one would lose one's focus. Deshpande does not allow herself the liberty of existing in an intellectual bubble, deliberately oblivious to these aspects, because they jut out uncomfortably through theoretical symmetries. That is why her representation of relationships is never contrived to become an agenda. Talking of relationships she says, "It's needed. It's necessary for women to live within relationships. But if the rules are rigidly laid ... then one becomes unhappy."[10] Her works therefore deal with the need to change these rules. They depict the desire to modify the social notions of a woman's capacity and inclination for roles assigned to her, not to break out of them. Her protagonists wish to alter the organization of familial structures, not to dismantle them. They do not seek an individualized separateness in the false belief that they are atomistic agents capable of living self-sufficient, isolated and independent lives. Rather they wish to invest their relationships with honesty, so that the connectedness is not threatened by underlying currents of hostility.

Perhaps Deshpande's clarity on the need for relationships and equal surety on the need to change the paradigms in which they operate, can be explained in terms of an aspiration for relational autonomy, i.e., autonomy in relation to the social world, involving both connection to and differentiation from it. It accrues to the idea that "persons are socially embedded and the agents' identities formed within the contexts of social relationships and shaped by a complex of intersecting social determinants."[11] Her conception of autonomy does not see the feasibility of an autonomous agent's capability of maintaining a sense of self in the absence of human interaction. Therefore, she does not see autonomy for women in terms of their escaping social influence, "... but rather that one is able to fashion a certain response to it."[12] This would of course involve questioning the discourse which delegitimizes their desire to know themselves and developing competencies which would aid in establishing them as persons. However, this changed profile needs to be integrated into their social and relational world instead of causing alienation from it. Deshpande's feminist endeavour thus envisages autonomy from within social and familial structures, rather than assuming that pursuit of personal goals can be isolated from social aims and involvements.

Deshpande's stance towards men, who form the social as well as personal world, through which her women traverse in pursuit of a more adequate positioning, emerges as one of the most important features of her work. Since her world is primarily relational, she moves out of the polarities constructed by divisive precepts, which place the inhabitants of this relational world in two opposing categories. She agrees to the idea that "women in our society are not readymade specie in antagonistic relationship with homogenized specie, labelled male."[13] Even when her women find male attitudes detrimental to their need for autonomy, the focus is directed towards the cultural determinants which shape these attitudes, rather than the individuals themselves. The men themselves are average, carrying their own individual psychological burdens and trying to fit into the designated roles for which they are, more often than not, inadequately equipped. They are not insensitive but they do get subsumed by social demands and many times unwittingly stake valued relationships by internalizing the conditioned impulse to assume power as the logical privilege of their sex. The resulting dichotomy between what they are and what they become is portrayed in almost sympathetic terms.

As Deshpande's perceptive gaze penetrates through aggressive male facades, she lays bare the insecurities arising from a threat to the only identity which men have known. Her female protagonists are invested with a similar understanding of constraints which concepts of 'masculinity' impose upon men and how these strain relationships. Deshpande implies that men need to be made aware of the need to move into roles more suited to the demands of changing times. Her later novels in fact introduce male characters who relinquish these redundant masculine mores, and nonetheless emerge as strong, balanced and dependable individuals, who mean more to the women in their lives, than their earlier ossified counterparts. Through portraying such a change, Deshpande shows the possibility of eventually drawing men into supportive roles without threatening their identities and by providing them positive returns in lieu of the control they relinquish.

Significantly, Deshpande's approach synchronizes with views emerging from sociological concerns attempting to locate practical recourses to facilitate the movement of the gender related impasse. Mary E. John, in her introduction to *Women's Studies in India: A Reader* (2008) says that while dealing with women's issues we need to break through the frameworks provided by isolated theories and form an integrated perspective, in relation to our own lives. Among vital new issues, she proposes for future studies, "the question of men and masculinities."[14] Sociologist Radhika Chopra feels that "If autonomy, empowerment and equality are anchored in everyday lives, then we need to understand how men can become players and partners in women's lives and in the process of empowerment. If their resentment to change could be modified into an understanding of its necessity, they could become those 'critical others', who could support and help sustain that empowerment."[15] This becomes particularly relevant with reference to the Indian women's experience of autonomy and agency, "which is grounded in the context of their everyday lives, their connection with care and commitment as well as their relationship with others."[16]

Deshpande thus delimits feminism from the restrictive practice of merely proving and re-proving its findings. Instead of making it a basis for validating female alienation or even belligerence, she advocates its use as a proactive tool to influence social attitudes. Sita's thoughts before her impending exile, resulting from Rama's inability to free himself of the masculine persona in Deshpande's short story "The Day of the Golden Deer," reflect her views on the course women need to adopt. She says, "I have to fight now; the demons of fear, hate, self-pity and bitterness. Yes, and anger too. Only when I have vanquished these will I emerge out of the forest of exile once more."[17] Deshpande's women do exactly this. Their anger and alienation is eventually directed towards changing the structures which give rise to them. Their awareness is utilized for eliciting a social response. It looks towards generating the accrual of the saner section of the male counterparts, to build up intellectual pressure upon the male intelligentsia, and to diplomatically project its secondary benefits to those among men who look for personal benefits.

It is thus not coincidental that Deshpande's works are replete with relationships in terms of husbands, fathers, brothers and sons. These are not vague sketches, lurking in the background, incidental in importance to the actual concerns. Rather, they are sharply delineated as part of these concerns. There are vast tracts of works devoted to their backgrounds, psychological motives, individual predilections and social personas. Equally spaced out are her portrayals of the varied male responses to the female attempts at changing the power paradigms which give men their privileged status. Her depiction of their resistance to change, the emotional upheavals involved in it, the mellowing down of their attitudes and the gradual realization of the inevitability of the process, carries us through the unexplored labyrinths of the male world. Deshpande makes us understand where the impediments to feminist overtures originate, why they need to be addressed and how appropriate and requisite approaches could soften the rigid stands in which they are couched. In the process, she also constructs an alternative approach to radical feminism, where change in the gender hierarchy could become the common concern of men as well as women. If male resentment to change could be modified into an understanding of its necessity, one could perceive men as allies who could participate in the empowerment of women, rather than as antagonists who oppose it.

For those who feel that this position is dangerously close to relinquishing agency, by subordinating women's condition to the very factors which generated it in the first place, it would do good to remember that Deshpande's literary world is positioned from a woman's perspective. It is the female gaze which assesses the modalities of maintaining balance, in contrast to the male gaze, which acted as a means of control. The gendered relation to the gaze here is no longer a product of patriarchy or a way of reinforcing male dominance. The female gaze is a means of resistance to "entrenched singular form of authority."[18] It is the returned gaze, working from that critical juncture where the impossibility of stasis becomes the locus of change.

Notes

1. Chidi Amuta. "Introduction." *The Theory of African Literature*. London and New Jersey: Zed Books Ltd, 1989. pp. 5–6.
2. Susie Tharu and K. Lalita. "Introduction." *Women Writing in India, 600 B.C to the Present, Vol. II: The Twentieth Century.* Ed. Tharu and Lalita. New Delhi: Oxford University Press, 1993. p. 39.
3. Nilufer E. Bharucha. "Shashi Deshpande." *Dictionary of Literary Biography: South Asian Writers in English*, Vol. 323 (2006). p. 106.
4. Shashi Deshpande. "Why I am a Feminist." *Writing from the Margin and Other Essays.* New Delhi: Penguin Books India, 2003. p. 82.
5. Shashi Deshpande. "A Toppling World-View." *Writing from the Margin and Other Essays.* New Delhi: Penguin Books India, 2003. p. 207.
6. Ibid., p. 208.
7. Ibid.
8. Shashi Deshpande. "Why I am a Feminist." *Writing from the Margin and Other Essays.* New Delhi: Penguin Books India, 2003. p. 83.
9. Chandra Talpade Mohanti. "Under Western Eyes, Feminist Scholarship and Colonial Discourses." *The Post-Colonial Studies Reader.* Ed.

Bill Ashcroft, Gareth Griffiths and Helen Tiffin. 2nd ed. Routledge: Oxford, 2006. p. 245.

10. Shashi Deshpande. "A Woman's World ... All the Way." Interview by Vanmala Vishwanathan. *Literature Alive* 1: 3 (December 1997). pp. 8–14.
11. Catriona Mackenzie, Natalie Stoljar. "Autonomy Refigured." *Relational Autonomy: Perspectives in Autonomy, Agency and Social Self.* New York: Oxford University Press, 2000. p. 4.
12. Diana Meyers. *Gender in the Mirror: Cultural Imagery and Women's Agency.* <http://www.philosophy.uconn.edu/department/meyers/meyers.html.> 9.
13. Chandra Talpade Mohanti. "Under Western Eyes, Feminist Scholarship and Colonial Discourses." *The Post-Colonial Studies Reader.* Ed. Bill Ashcroft, Gareth Griffiths and Helen Tiffin. 2nd ed. Routledge: Oxford, 2006. p. 245.
14. Mary E. John. "Introduction". *Women's Studies in India: A Reader.* Ed. John. New Delhi: Penguin Books, 2008. p. 16.
15. Radhika Chopra. *Reframing Masculinities: Narrating the Supportive Practices of Men.* New Delhi: Orient Longman Pvt. Ltd., 2007. p. 2.
16. Ibid.
17. Shashi Deshpande. "The Day of the Golden Deer." *In Search of Sita: Revisiting Mythology.* Ed. Malashri Lal and Namita Gokhale. New Delhi: Penguin Books, 2009. p. 208.
18. Jean Paul Sartre. "Theories of Gaze." Quoted by Jeremy Hawthorn. *Literary Theory and Criticism.* Ed. Patricia Vaugh. Berkeley: University of California Press, 1993. p. 514.

2

Retracing Masculinity

A willingness to understand the attitude of those whom radical feminist studies have situated in the other camp, requires a deliberate shift in perspective. One could begin by substituting antagonism with objectivity, in trying to understand the processes which have gone into formulating traditional notions of masculinity. This would provide an insight into the creation of an image, which over time has been naturalized through social consent. The dichotomy between the person and the image makes male experience a difficult traversing ground between the complexity of emotions and the unrelenting demands of personas and social patterns. The hardened male identity which resists change, on closer analysis might reveal a fear, not just of a loss of privilege but also of the only available notion of the self. The inflexibility of male attitude could therefore be rooted in reasons other than hostility against female self-hood alone. Deshpande explores all this to analyse the multi-dimensional facets of issues which one tends to see from a simplistic one way stand. In the process she also suggests the possibilities inherent in approaching them more realistically, so that the shift in gender roles is a mutually acceptable and comprehensive one.

Anthropologically speaking, gender attributes are rooted in biological distinctions, which at one time validated the demarcation of roles based on different physiological abilities of the two sexes. By virtue of the peculiar division of work, men became the procurers of resources and hence the providers, while women came to be associated with female gender roles like child birth, raising children, nurturance etc. The two roles gradually came to be identified with two different sets of characteristics which constructed masculinity and feminity in broadly opposing categories. For both men and women, success in their gender role became the central component of their identity, and those activities which fulfilled these roles began to be given high value. Over time it led to hardened gender identities, on which esteem and ego began to depend. To assert this gender identity, both men and women began to dismiss other aspects of their make-up as unimportant, thus diminishing the full range of human and sex differences.

The surface of normalcy and permanency of this gender demarcation, the balance of which seemed unassailable, has had complex dichotomies operating through it. It has comprised of an unequal arrangement, where one sex has had access to the outside world; hold over economic power and a consequent control over the family it sustained. The other sex has been confined to home, deprived of outside influences, and made economically and thus personally subservient. However, as times have changed, mental capabilities have replaced physical prowess as the requirement for generating economic resources. An obvious corollary to this change is women's demand for new roles concurrent with their abilities in the changed scenario. What follows is a desire for a simultaneous change in their positioning in the gender hierarchy. Inherent in this desire is the requirement that existing notions of masculinity and feminity undergo a change.

However, this change is resisted by the entrenched male-oriented system because apart from threatening the superior male status, it also threatens the very constituents of the identity by which men define themselves. There is a socially constructed image which defines masculinity. The patriarchal system which emphasizes that men should control resources as well as decision-making, also dictates the attitudes and qualities which men must have, for perpetuating this system. As a control tactic, the system associates male sense of self with his ability to live up to these requirements. The undercurrent of ridicule directed at any diversion from the prescribed persona elicits derision, at what is condescendingly described as effeminacy. This ensures that men have no option, if they want to survive in the gendered male community. If we look at the equivalents of 'masculine' in Thesaurus, we find an almost unreal set of attributes including virile, macho, muscular, resolute, strapping, vigorous, etc. The problem with this attributive process is that "... it naturalizes masculinity, thus making it inevitable and non-negotiable."[1] This kind of a non-negotiable participation in a hegemonic gender stereotyping, makes men its prisoners, because the system hinges their sense of worth to it.

As a result, patriarchy negatively influences minds, imaginations, psyches and behaviour of men. In context of the critical necessity of maintaining ones superiority in the absence of superlative skills, the only alternative is to create a comparative situation which produces an inferior 'other'. Thus, the larger than life male image requires a diminished female image for its sustenance. The superior position of the provider needs to be maintained against female incapability to assume the same role. The posture of the aggressive male initiative needs the timid dependency of the female to be played off against. To ensure that this suitable index of comparison is sustained, men have eulogized and highlighted those aspects of women's personalities which construct them in the required diminutive dimensions. They have not only dismissed all other parts of the female personality as aberrations, but have also resisted with full force, any attempt by women to repudiate this.

Contradictory as it might seem, this skewered process of self-enhancement has debilitated men no less than women. It has placed them in the position of colonizers, perpetually in fear of losing their power. Their justifications, like that of a colonizer are misplaced. The truth seeping out of the chinks leads to insecurity, with which they deal through denial. The rigidity implicit in their posturing, dents their own personalities. It also dissociates them from those aspects of their personalities which interfere with notions of masculinity. Defending their gender identities becomes a taxing proposition for men. Sarah White rightly says, "Unlike their imagery of established patriarchal power, most studies show masculinity as being rather fragile, provisional, something to be won and then defended, something under constant threat of loss .... Manhood certainly does not appear to be self-reliant and autonomous. On the contrary, masculinity seems to depend chronically on the estimation of others, to be highly vulnerable to attack by ridicule, shaming, subordination, or 'dishonourable' female action."[2]

What makes this seemingly irretrievable situation a matter of interest, not only to feminists, but to anyone who hopes for a more justified system of existence, is the fact that masculinity like any other human attribute, is fluid. In fact, it is constantly reconstructed in response to changes in economic patterns, intellectual inputs and cultural shifts. This can be witnessed in the gradual but phenomenal change in the male image from that of a cave-man, to a suit and tie wearing one. The same flexibility can also be made operative in man–woman relationship. One reason is that masculinity does not occur in isolation, but is embedded in a patterned context, and has functional meaning only in terms of that context. This context in turn is maintained by the continuity of culturally sanctioned vehicles, of social interaction among sexes. "Changes in these traditional practices and the new interactions result in commensurate modification in functional sex difference."[3] This is also aided by the "the profile of psycho-sexual androgyny consisting of male and female type elements,"[4] present in each human being. Men might have pushed back the secondary characteristic of receptivity, but it remains a part of their personalities and can be elicited in aid of transforming the relationship between men and women.

Significantly, in Deshpande's portrayal of male response, men are the objects and not the subjects of study. It is amply clear, that it is her women who will determine the change and the redefinition. It is their lived experience which will form the material, the energy for action and for change. It will deal with the contradictions they discover between their defined roles and the perspective which feminism gives to them, on those roles. Men form part of the analysis, the agents of the structures to be transformed. She makes sure, that attempts to involve them in the change do not get subordinated to the same implications of domination and appropriation which need to be changed. That is why, in the vast time span covered in most of Deshpande's works, till the women are unsure and apprehensive of their own contradictory responses, they can at best elicit hostility to their confused overtures at selfhood. It is only when they become sure of what they want, that men too are forced to look at the feasibility of the new equations. In other words, it is the controlled reaction of feminism, to what is obviously a complex psychological issue, which according to her can lead to a change in perspective among men. It is from a point of self-assured understanding of the roles they wish to assume, that women can initiate the shift from hostile antagonism, towards willing participation. With a surety that arises out of belief in one's correctness, and the acquisition of competencies which equip one for independence, Deshpande's women use their perceptions to make inroads into male hostility. Implicit in the process, is the stress on the benefits that would accrue to men as well, if they work in tandem with women for implementing the process of change.

It is interesting to note that even when Deshpande portrays hostility among men as they try to safeguard their privileged domain, she does so with the skill and insight of a psychologist. Underlying it is her opinion, "... what is he, but a victim of his own idea of himself?"[5] What comes across is not just the plight of the female trying to stand up to the privileged sex, but also the insecurities of the privileged male. Deshpande understands, that for men, masculinity is the core around which their personality takes shape, and that in compromising with it, they would be playing with their self-esteem. Her approach and understanding is close to the precepts evolving through contemporary gender studies, which explicate that "the gender schema becomes a prescriptive standard or guide and self-esteem becomes its hostage."[6] Therefore, there exists among men, "an honest sense of the wish to save at whatever cost, a sexual polarity, a vital tension, and an essential difference, which they fear might get lost, in too much sameness, equality and equivalence."[7] Feminism threatens not just this polarity, but also the privileged status which it entails. The psychological dislocation it involves, gives rise to knee jerk responses, some of which display the desperation of a person driven to the wall. Among these is the "classification of the disruptive and disturbing information as non-data."[8] Men respond suspiciously to alteration in status arrangements. Deshpande's men too respond with anxiety, resistance, and a loss of a sense of order when they find themselves face-to-face with the inexorable change in gender equations. Mohan in *That Long Silence* and Som in *Small Remedies* repeatedly attempt at establishing their own image as providers with simultaneous attempts at constructing their wives as a homemakers, although in both the cases the women involved are intelligent individuals in need of recognition for their abilities. As they find their women attempting to step out of the phallocentric structures, these men exercise designs of mastery, and try to coerce them back into predefined roles, which they insist are the only true imperative of their gender. While Mohan reacts strongly to Jaya's attempts at establishing herself as a writer, Som reduces Madhu's attempts at writing to nothing more than a hobby. In more aggravated forms, this culminates in patterns of domination which translate into cruelty. Manohar in *The Dark Holds No Terror* turns to sexual cruelty, as Saru's professional success diminishes his status as the provider.

More interesting are Deshpande's insights, on what she feels could eventually compel men to tide over their egos, to acknowledge the inevitability of change. We find her male characters, returning to retrieve relationships from the brink, because beneath the bravado of their initial hostility lies their need for those relationships. Here again, Deshpande's opinions are validated by studies on gender. Stephen Heath in his book *Male Feminism* (1987) clarifies that men have a "socio-sexual stake in feminism."[9] Despite their attempts to dismiss female discontent as non-data, "relations cannot be magically free of the given terms of male-female positioning."[10] The growing resentment and the desire for dignified options have made women averse to being used as "a looking glass possessing the magical ... power of reflecting the figure of man at twice his natural size."[11] This in turn has dislocated the falsely magnified identity by which men have existed all these centuries. In other words, "feminism has decentred man – which means that there is no simple position, only a shifting marginalia ... the collective identity of man is no longer available."[12] In such a context, moving closer to feminism would provide men with a scope of regaining something of the male/female security. It would give them an opportunity to renegotiate their identity against the crumbling structures of patriarchy. Deshpande's men too seem to be inching closer to this renegotiation. Mohan deserts Jaya when she asserts herself. Yet, he eventually returns to her in full awareness of the impossibility of retrieving the old equation in their relationship. Manohar follows Saru to her father's house faced with her resolute refusal to reply to his letters. Som asks Madhu to return to the relationship she has rejected for its inflexibility. Implicit in all these examples is man's attempt to renegotiate a place for himself, once it is clear that the old paradigms have dislocated him from his former secure positioning. It becomes imperative for him as well, to participate in the formulation of new equations.

Looking beyond these surface implications, Deshpande also implies that as resistance loses its full throttled thrust, it might make way for a more integrated personal core for men too. In accepting new equations, they would also be availing the right to dispense away with the inflexible gender codes, which dwarf them in comparison to the image they need to live up to. This in turn would help them reconcile their attributive and optative identities. Male position as the provider might have arisen out of a comparatively greater suitability to the demands of a particular time. However, the consequent economic and social edge it has given to man, has led to an insistence that those particular attributes are the sole constituents of his personality. In doing so, he validates the continuity of his position of power, but in the process also diminishes the full range of his experience as a human being. He relegates to the background the individual differences, weaknesses and psychological peculiarities which formulate him as a person. This results in an awkward positioning in the prescribed grid, so that notions of masculinity interfere with realistic expectations from the self. For example, Gopal in *A Matter of Time* acknowledges that the responsibility of marriage is not for everyone. He however recognizes it too late, thus leaving his wife and three daughters in a lurch. Jaya's brother Ravi in *That Long Silence* does not have that element of responsibility, which is required for living up to the role of a husband and a son. Devious, manipulative behaviour thus becomes his strategy to wriggle out of the expectations others have from him. The most touching portrayal is that of Dhruva, Saru's little brother in *The Dark Holds No Terror* who is made a victim of these role formulations. His mother makes him sleep alone because he is a boy and must live up to his masculine role, notwithstanding the fact that he is morbidly scared of the dark.

Explicating upon the dichotomy which this induces, Patrick Lee says, "males are viewed as competitive, achieving, risk taking, and invested with environmental mastery among other things. All one has to do is to look briefly at random samples … real men who live longing for love and approval, counting their accomplishments on the fingers of their one hand, and hedging all risks with the preoccupation with security."[13] This gap between the attributive and optative identities makes the male perpetually vulnerable. Deshpande implies that aligning themselves with the changing impulse would give men an opportunity to dispense away with this stress. It would aid in rectifying the larger than life image which they have construed for themselves. It would also help them in coming to terms with their own limitations without suffering a loss of self-esteem.

In agreeing to participate in the new equations, men might also discover how their attributive identities have, in many social situations, been exploited and utilized by other power structures operating within society. The value judgments, exposing them to ridicule at the slightest deviation from their prescribed roles, might then emerge as part of the covert control tactics used by society in a shrouded reversal of roles, to sustain its own economic agendas. Deshpande portrays this through the unresolved undercurrents of resentment, especially in those male roles, where the surface privileges get translated into responsibilities, with no consideration for desires and aspirations which lie beyond those roles. Among these are Chandu Mama in *That Long Silence*, whose ambition to go abroad to study is thwarted by his mother, who refuses to risk her future security, thus reducing him to a small time doctor, venting his frustration through petty affairs. Jaya's father's Gandhian aspirations are similarly trampled upon by his mother. Those who escape these social constraints to pursue their own aspirations are looked upon with disapproval. Jaya's uncle Makrand is never forgiven by his mother for leaving home to become an actor. There is the underlying authorial sympathy in the portrayal of Dada, Jaya's elder brother, who forgoes his responsibilities as the eldest son, in order to pursue his own ambitions. Shripati in *Moving On* is also an example of a frustrated man whose professional and personal aspirations are sacrificed at the altar of responsibilities and obligations, inherent in the male role. Deshpande seems to be suggesting that the claustrophobia inherent in such situations could find a solution in alternatives, which regard gender as a fluid concept and believe in the possibility of redefining privileges and responsibilities, for both women and men.

Deshpande implies that participation in female empowerment might also reward men in terms of honesty in relationships, which otherwise has been sacrificed at the altar of power equations. Time and again, she shows that the compulsion to maintain a subordinated posture to suit male requirements causes resentment among women. The disparity between their inner experiences and the lives they are forced to live, corrodes into commitment. Deshpande's women find other avenues, intellectual and emotional, to cater to their true identities, while the men in their lives continue to revel in the false belief of their ability to control them. Indu's attraction to Naren in *Roots and Shadows*, Saru's bent towards Padma in *The Dark Holds No Terror*, Jaya's leaning towards Kamat in *That Long Silence*, Urmi's attraction to Bhaskar in *The Binding Vine* are all examples of intelligent women veering towards relationships outside marriage, because they do not find recognition of their potential as thinking individuals within it. These are juxtaposed with relationships like those of Joe and Leela, Tony and Rekha, Hari and Lata in *Small Remedies*, where men recognize and respect the woman's individuality and in return get unalloyed loyalty and a love untarnished by secondary considerations. Deshpande thus advocates recognition of women's individuality, a regard for their right to find satisfaction through what best suits their temperament, and an acknowledgement that they are more than the roles society has imposed upon them. In return, men might find themselves participating in relationships tempered with mutual regard, intellectual rapport and companionship, which do not flounder upon the volatile foundations of a power struggle. Once again the writer's views are in congruence with those emerging through gender studies, which draw conclusions based upon empirical evidence. Patrick Lee, for example says, "there are human benefits in not having one's self-esteem dependent upon compulsive assertion of authority, dominance, ambition, initiative and the other ulcer producing prerogatives of traditional masculinity."[14] The freshness and wholeness of the new experience would probably help men in transcending their own misplaced defences.

If Deshpande portrays these benefits for the discerning male, she also depicts changing attitudes among men who see the rigidity of opinions negatively impacting those whom they care for. Her works also showcase a new set of opinions among the younger generation of men, to whom the new, more balanced equation comes quite naturally. Deshpande sees this as an obvious progression and implies that if help comes from quarters which have had the privilege of being in positions of power, it should be availed. In fact, at many places there are sequences and situations in her novels where male contribution to female empowerment is welcomed and willingly accepted. It not only brings the power of social sanction to the aid of women's issues, but also finally culminates into a joint effort, which works towards a more habitable world. We see this attitude portrayed among men of every generation. Saru's father supports her decision to study medicine, Jaya's father trusts her literary abilities, Urmi's father recognizes her as more competent than her brother. Ever Shripati, the aloof patriarch advises Sumi to focus on her daughter's education rather than their marriage. We also have men like Amrut in *The Binding Vine* who is clear about the equal status he wishes to share with his future wife. Raja in *Moving On* displays a large-hearted flexibility in adapting to Jiji's clarity on what she wants.

In a world where boundaries limiting a woman's life to home are fast fading, how men in the outer world react to the female overture at selfhood becomes equally pertinent. Deshpande depicts these as mixed attitudes, undergoing the same slow change, as the familial ones. Indu's employer in *Roots and Shadows* represents the old attitude which expects a woman to toe the line. He takes it for granted that Indu would write what he wanted her to, irrespective of her own sense of right and wrong. The magazine editor in *That Long Silence* slots Jaya's woman oriented work into peripheral literature, fit only for women's magazines. However there are others who respond more positively and show a slow but certain change. In most cases, this change derives from a recognition of a woman's right to decide for herself, and in deference to her persistence in doing so. Nagaraj, the property dealer in *A Matter of Time*, begins with disdain for Sumi's decision to look for a separate house. However, he eventually recognizes her resolve and decides to help her. The image of Nagaraj riding the scooter with Sumi on the rear seat becomes representative of male help coming from the most unlikely quarters. After Sumi's death, he comes to have one last look at her and goes back carrying with him the image of a woman, who brings to him an understanding of something beyond his own perceptions. There is also the striking image of the unknown boy who steps in to help, when Aru finds herself literally and metaphorically lost after venting her anger against her father for having deserted the family. Later when she thinks of the figure on the motorcycle riding ahead of her, heedless of the pouring rain, leading her out of confusing lanes, there is something in the image which reflects a new breed of men to whom the role of supporter comes naturally. The ones who continue to use their twisted gender orientations for exploitative ends abound even in the changing times. The property sharks who try to usurp Jiji's father's house in *Moving On* by threatening and playing upon her fears as a single woman, reflect that section of men. But along with them are men like Iqbal in *In the Country of Deceit*, who recognizes Devayani's need to pick up the threads of her life after her break-up with Ashok, and invites her to join his law practice. He also ensures that she knows that he is making this offer in recognition of her potential and capability, not out of pity.

Here too Deshpande's views are ratified by sociological findings. Radhika Chopra, an Indian sociologist working on women's issues talks of this "... self-reflexive agency among ordinary men, a reflection that has emerged from engagements with gender."[15] This according to her is different from the earlier men's reform movements, where women were merely objects in the debates among men. The twentieth century sees a different sense of men's understanding of gender relations. Perhaps this results from the fact that their lives correspond to autonomous women's movements. Understanding these movements makes enlightened men realize the suffocation of normative strictures, particularly when they relate it to the effect they have upon women for whom they care. Just because certain trends have evolved out of a collective impulse, "... it does not imply that the individual is thoughtless, uncreative, and inflexible ... is blind to contradictions that may be inhering knowledge or acculturation."[16]

Issues of personal experience persuade individual men to engage with issues concerning gender. This becomes the motivation for them to "take apart gender identities, which masquerade as cast-iron monolithic formulations."[17] Stephen Heath, in his book *Male Feminism* provides the missing dimension to the concept of feminism when he says, "Feminism is also a subject for men, what it is obviously concerns them; they have to learn to make it their affair."[18] He further adds, "Feminism speaks to me, not primarily, not equally, but *too*. The definitions and images and stories and laws and institutions oppressive to women that it challenges, ends, involves me, since not only will I find myself playing some part in their reproduction, but I too am caught up in them, given as a 'man' in their reflection, confined in that place which is represented as mine."[19]

Deshpande's analysis of male response is thus underlined by a positive belief in its potential to respond. It demonstrates her faith in the reality of a more integrated future for man–woman relationship. It is to this that one could attribute the pattern of growth in her works. Individual works trace how rigid responses become malleable and make way for better relational overtures in subsequent generations. The work as a whole shows how the dominant theme of resistance of the earlier novels is replaced with a new, dynamic response of the later ones. The anger and insecurities inherent in unequal, claustrophobic relationships stand contrasted to the dignity and honesty generated by attitudes which respond to change.

Notes

1. Kamla Bhasin. *Exploring Masculinity.* New Delhi: Women Unlimited, 2004. p. 13.
2. Sarah. C. White. "Men Masculinities and the Politics of Gender Development." Vol. 5, Number 2, June (1997). Quoted by Kamla Bhasin. *Exploring Masculinity.* New Delhi: Women Unlimited, 2004. p.36.
3. Patrick C. Lee. "Introduction: *Sex Differences, Cultural and Developmental Dimensions.* Ed. Patrick Lee and Robert Susan Steward, New York: Urizen Books, 1976. p.31.
4. Ibid.
5. Shashi Deshpande. "The Day of the Golden Deer." *In Search of Sita: Revisiting Mythology.* Ed. Malashri Lal and Namita Gokhale. New Delhi: Penguin Books, 2009. pp. 201–08.
6. Sandra Lipsitz Bem. "Masculinity and Feminity Exist Only in the Mind of the Perceiver." *Masculinity/Feminity: Basic Perspectives.* Ed. June Machover Reinisch, Leonard A. Rosenblum, Stephanie A. Sanders. New York: Oxford University Press, 1987. p. 308.
7. Erik H. Stephen. "Inner and Outer Space: Reflections on Womanhood." *Sex Differences: Cultural and Developmental Dimensions.* Ed. Patrick Lee and Robert Susan Steward. New York: Urizen Books, 1976. p. 108.
8. Mary Daly. "Towards a Feminist Poetics." Quoted by Elaine Showalter. *The New Feminist Criticism: Essays on Women, Literature and Theory.* Ed. Showalter. London: Virago Press Ltd., 1986. p. 127.
9. Stephen Heath. "Male Feminism." *Men in Feminism.* Ed. Alice Jardine and Paul Smith. New York: Routledge, 1987. p. 18.
10. Ibid.
11. Shoshana Felman. "Women and Madness, the Critical Phallacy." *Feminisms: An Anthology of Literary Theory and Criticism.* Ed. Robyn R. Warhol and Diane Price Herndl, 3rd ed. New Brunswich, New Jersey: Rutgers University Press, 1996. p. 16.
12. Stephen Heath. "Male Feminism." *Men in Feminism.* Ed. Alice Jardine and Paul Smith. New York: Routledge, 1987. p. 24.
13. Patrick C. Lee. "Introduction". *Sex Differences, Cultural and Developmental Dimensions.* Ed. Patrick Lee and Robert Susan Steward, New York: Urizen Books, 1976. p.24.
14. Ibid., p. 21.

15. Radhika Chopra. *Reframing Masculinities: Narrating the Supportive Practices of Men*. New Delhi: Orient Longman Pvt. Ltd., 2007. p. 8.
16. Vinay Kumar Srivastava. "Male Bias, Matrifocality and Family Dynamics." *Modernity, Feminism and Women Empowerment*. Ed. Abha Avasthi and A.K. Srivastava. Jaipur: Rawat Publications, 2001. p. 58.
17. Radhika Chopra. *Reframing Masculinities: Narrating the Supportive Practices of Men*. New Delhi: Orient Longman Pvt. Ltd., 2007. p. 9.
18. Stephen Heath. "Male Feminism." *Men in Feminism*. Ed. Alice Jardine and Paul Smith. New York: Routledge, 1987. pp. 8–9.
19. Ibid., p. 8.

3

Surviving the Broken Myth

In order to understand the process which has dislodged men from their secure gender positioning and led to a crumbling sense of identity, one has to delve into the power tactics which sustained their supremacy, and the shift in female perspective which eventually began to dent into it. This leads us to the study of those myths and images which have been constituted by regimented discourses and used by men as micro-practices of power. It also involves a study of the overt and covert measures with which these have been "lodged into the cognitive, emotional and connotive infrastructure of women's minds,"[1] thus paralyzing their impulse for self-determination. This chapter proposes to trace the shift in terms of the reclamation of the individual beneath these debilitating images and the parallel disruption of the male hegemonic order. Deshpande's women dissociate themselves from stereotypical images and become thinking questioning characters. "... the ability to think for oneself, the power to reason logically, the urge to discover the truth,"[2] become the essential precursors to their demand for self-hood in relation to their social world. It empowers them to initiate the process of integrating their true identities into the institutions through which they function. For men, this amounts to a loss of ideological control, an uncomfortable shift in the convenient status quo. To re-settle into differently defined relational identities is a daunting task, not just with respect to the privileges lost or gained, but in terms of the emotional upheavals it causes.

To understand the connection between feminine stereotypes and the myths from which they originate, one needs to go back to their socio-historical origins. A myth is defined as "a traditional, typically ancient story dealing with supernatural beings, ancestors or heroes that serve as a fundamental type in the world view of a people as by explaining aspects of the natural world or delivering the psychology, customs or ideals of a society."[3] Myths about men and women originate from the roles once allotted to them on the basis of their biological differences. This eventually resulted in a system where man as the provider, also became the one to control economic power. The once logical allocation of roles became a lopsided arrangement where one sex became subservient to another. The double incentive of a position of power in economic terms and gender superiority in interpersonal relationships, became the underlying impetus for the search of institutionalized props, to maintain and perpetuate the status quo. Individual differences which could be radically different from the stock characteristics and various other facets of feminity and masculinity, which did not fit into this unilinear division of the role and prerogative system, began to be summarily dismissed. A hegemonic system of information was constructed so that power could operate through it. An entire system of carefully drawn opposites validated the logistics of inequality. This resulted in frozen identities for both the sexes where women were portrayed in terms of "angelic beauty, sweetness, passivity, docileness and selflessness."[4] Men, on the other hand, were constructed as assertive, competent and invested with environmental mastery. Both thus became definable beings, the definition being commanded by the logic of resemblance to socio-sexual stereotypes.

Apart from such generalized mythic images conferred by the anthropological evolution of gender, every culture has its own specific myths to contend with, and these have their origins in ancestry, scriptures and epics, etc. MSN Encarta defines these as "idealized and glamorized ideas and stories surrounding a particular phenomenon, concept or famous person."[5] Perhaps in the Indian context, the vast plethora of epic writing became a source of innumerable myths, due to our colonial status. The colonizer's utilization of the women's issue as a crucial tool to justify colonization, led to the reformists' search for an exalted image of Indian womanhood, as an apt counter argument. They looked into the glamorized Aryan background, searched through the Vedas and epics, and with their patriarchal orientations always intact, came up with a mythic embodiment of accomplishments and virtues which according to Vijaya Ramaswami became "both a shackle, and a rhetorical device,"[6] for the Indian woman. This mythic woman was intelligent like Maitreyie, efficient like Draupadi, devoted like Sita and faithful like Savitri. Her unreal euologization is described in terms of "ardent piety", "complete abnegation", "unlimited emotion" and "ascetic tenderness."[7] These attributive traits embodied the entire gamut of a woman's life, from her childhood to her conjugal life, always demanding supreme sacrifice as the only course to be true to the imperatives of her gender role. As Uma Chakravarti puts it, "reaction to the attacks by colonial writers ensured those Indian women were built up as superwomen."[8] Thus, Indian women were caught in a complex image which Kumkum Sangari aptly describes as "emblems of continuity and objects of reform."[9]

Subordination to these myths, universal as well as cultural, has affected women in strange ways. For instance, the emphasis on 'womanliness' has induced in her a self-destructive narcissism. The desire to appear docile and angelic has led to an infantilization, "turning her from an autonomous person into a character in search of an author."[10] In the process, she has forfeited her right to be the agency. She has been made to believe that she can imagine a future identity only through an external male presence, and is unable to realize it on her own. This has led to the internalization of a necessity for constant diminishing of the self. She has been required to bury away the recognition of her own potential, beneath a deliberately dwarfed identity, to make man look larger than life. The passivity and selflessness ascribed to woman are potent tools for perpetuating her subordination. They have ascertained control in all aspects of man–woman relationships. Within this self-limiting frame, Indian women have been further subordinated to self-abnegating mythic identities. Prabhati Mukherjee says that if we look at the eternal triumvirate of Sita, Savitri, and Parvati, we find that, "their lives are remarkable for the absence of any interest outside domestic affairs."[11] The careers of these paragons of Indian womanhood demonstrate that for them, nothing matters more than their husbands. Women like Kunti and Draupadi have been used as poster images when it suited the requirement, but it is clear that they could never measure up to the haloed status of the others because they dared to transgress the boundaries, to step into the outer world. The mythic image and its endorsement have come from every available means. Social and religious mediums like ritualistic blessings to commemorate the triumph of fidelity, literary medium like works of classical poets and dramatists, cultural mediums like group recitals, etc., have all enforced these images through a collective process of "condemnation and commendation."[12]

What made women ascribe to these myths and exist with a less valued status? What were the tools of subjugation that men used to establish the necessity to do so? According to Toril Moi, the patriarchal system, through its systems of knowledge, emphasized that the chosen standards for feminity are natural and a woman who refuses to conform can be labelled both "unfeminine and unnatural."[13] Thus, hitting at that aspect of the ego which derives sustenance from the gender identity, the patriarchal institution ensured that woman herself became an instrument for perpetuating the myth. Literature constructed by man repeatedly emphasized that if a woman became an agency, she transgressed the limits of feminity. The angel became a monster, a witch, a demon. In India, the 'pativrata' had only one opposite, the 'kulta'. Woven into this were the subtle, unspoken instruments of subjective emotions like promise of love/withdrawal of love, cherishing/abhorring, protecting/banishing, etc. The psychological pressure coupled with more practical considerations of a society that offered minimal avenues to a woman, helped in the entrenchment of images imposed upon them.

The difficulty in such unification is that there is no fit between the specific patriarchal practices, the symbolic ideality and women themselves. Thus, as and when women got a voice, they spoke of the dichotomy between their own experiences and the mythic identities imposed on them. As they discovered the multiplicity of their feelings they began to recognize the psychological distress and frustration inherent in role playing. What emerged was a vast tract of buried emotions, where resistance took varied forms, collided with the system, and exposed the chasm between myth and reality. Deshpande says, "The point is that all the women in myths have been created by men to fulfil their various needs. There is the eternal child to be protected and controlled, the self-sacrificing mother to nurture and cherish the child, the chaste partner to guarantee exclusive rights of the man over her body as well as undoubted paternity of children ... and finally the goddess to provide morality. What place does a real, thinking, feeling woman have in this agenda? Women are bound to have those doubts."[14]

Deshpande's women, not surprisingly then, are individuals who belong to the teeming educated middle class, who are nevertheless unique in the enhanced faculty of feeling and perceiving. Even before the moment of crises pushes them into a crystallization of their beliefs, they are aware of the discrepancies between their own experiences and the halo they are supposed to see surrounding social structures like marriage, family, motherhood, etc. All of them are aware of another 'self' beneath the roles of the wives, mothers, daughters, and sisters they are playing. They are acutely aware of the suffocation of this self, in a setup which denies its existence. Sooner or later they all show dissociation with the arched eyebrows, painted lips prototype of feminity, which seems to be the primary burden on this self.

These women eventually stand up against the myths supporting the constraints against their individuation. They declare that though the ideals imbibed in these myths might be lofty, they cannot and will not approximate to the pictures of ideal womanhood. Neither do they bear any guilt for their refusal to do so. In Deshpande's own words, "More important than knowing what we are not is to know what we are, what is possible for us."[15] To the male insistence on clinging to these patriarchal instruments of coercion, these characters seem to be saying that a release from these restricted identities would help them to broaden the relational framework, providing not only more space for themselves, but also dignity to their relationship with men. As

Deshpande says, "When women can fulfil themselves ... and do not have to sacrifice themselves, it will obviate the need to play power games within home, to thrust ambitions on husbands and children, to work out frustration on them."[16]

Deshpande's works are complex amalgamations of multiple issues that contribute to a woman's place in society. *Roots and Shadows* studies the deep-seated gender and cultural mores which impinge upon a woman's identity in subtle ways to shackle her in the same constraints which she tries to break out of. *The Dark Holds No Terror* is analysed in terms of a woman's fight against guilt for daring to become an autonomous person, who places her identity above the gender roles prescribed for her. *That Long Silence* deals with a woman's decision to express herself instead of using strategies to mask her discontent. *The Binding Vine* portrays fight against a system, which regards a woman's "no" as an aberration to be punished with cruelty. It also deals with the necessity of liberating relationships from power struggles, to restore in them the vulnerability of true connection. *A Matter of Time* refers to a woman's decision to look for an identity outside the constructs provided by male presence. This is also shown as the beginning of the retrieval of her rightful place in family as well as society. *Small Remedies* deals with breaking through the fear of what lies on the other side, when a woman questions the exclusive rights of man over her. *Moving On* deals with the feasibility of survival outside socially constructed identities and the need for integrating this new independent identity into the framework of relationships. *In the Country of Deceit* also deals with the need to assess whether asserting one's individuality has its own drawbacks, particularly when it involves a devaluation of structured support systems. Thus, Deshpande analyses the discontent of her protagonists, which becomes their impetus to embark on the journey to self-discovery. It dwells upon their aspirations and their struggle to recover their voice. It helps them to recognize their humanness and their limitations. Finally, it gives them the clarity to demand a place which takes into cognizance their real identities, in context of the relationships and institutions in which they live.

Roots and Shadows, Deshpande's first novel, brings up the various issues which are to be dealt with minutely in the works which follow. Some of these are the factors responsible for a woman's progressively dwindling identity, the objectivity required to perceive it and the courage needed to initiate a reversal in it. With these, Deshpande sets into motion a process of analysis, elaborating on its various overlapping and contradictory facets. This novel is about Indu, who comes back to the family home which she had left at the age of eighteen, because of its claustrophobic restrictions. A motherless child, whose father has left her in the family home to pursue his interests, she has been raised by her widowed aunt who has blended herself into the gender mould, as have all the other women in the family. In a strange twist of circumstances, Indu is summoned back to the same home after many years, to be told that Akka the powerful matriarch of the family, with whom she had been in constant friction, has in an unprecedented reversal of norms, willed all the property to Indu rather than to the sons in the family.

As Indu passes through the myriad emotions of reconnecting to the family, she also becomes conscious of the disconnection she has been experiencing in her married life. She wonders why, in spite of having broken out of the mitigating rules of the small town, conservative life, she continues to feel claustrophobic in her relationship with Jayant. It is in her movement back to the cultural and ideological roots of her identity, that she discovers that breaking free from the mores which have travelled through centuries of conscious and unconscious internalization is more difficult than one thinks. It needs a brave leap into the unknown to be able to do so.

Indu realizes that the changes in her life which she has been so proud of, are just cosmetic in nature. They are more like pruning a tree, while the roots, deeply entrenched, hold within themselves the potential to renew that growth. If she had broken out of the need to please and be accepted in her family home, she had in another way, fallen into the same trap in her husband's home. It is only when she returns to the set-up she had once scorned for its redundant mores, that she realizes that she has carried them within herself all along. "Somewhere inside was a spider painstakingly completing its work."[17]

She realizes that her relationship with Jayant reflected her in the same light, in which she perceived the tradition bound, regressive women in her family. Just like them, she too had lost the ability to think of herself as an independent entity, complete as a person without the husband. If their fear of their inability to survive without their men is reflected in their superstitious rituals to ensure their husbands' longevity, the same is reflected in Indu's unthinking relinquishing of her independence for fitting into the niche created for her by Jayant. Indu discovers that whether the reason for doing so was a lack of options or an inability to proactively avail them, the impact remained the same. In either case it dented into a woman's sense of self.

Indu also discovers that beneath her sophisticated exterior, she was like all these women who had submerged their identities to the roles expected of them. She recognizes her own reflection in Mini's total submission to her role as a daughter, Kaki's submission to her role as a homemaker and Sunanda Atya, the miserable representation of the wife kowtowing to the wishes of her useless husband. In a way, Indu too is doing the same. She dresses, behaves, lives, to fit herself into the mode ratified by Jayant. She crystallizes the fact that it was he who determined their relative positioning in the relationship hierarchy. She had never tried to look for options beyond the position granted to her. She wonders "am I on my way to becoming an ideal woman? A woman who sheds her 'I', who loses her identity in her husband's" (49). This behaviour which she had justified to herself as an expression of love, now reveals itself as a manifestation of her fear of conflict. Perhaps she has been held hostage to her own desperation to prove her marriage a success, to prove to herself and others that her decision to marry Jayant was not wrong.

The most degrading aspect of this loss of self is reflected in the intellectual compromise she makes. A woman with strong views, to whom honesty to herself is of crucial importance, she nevertheless carries on with the kind of writing she despises because Jayant considers her work merely a means of furthering the life he has dreamed of. It is Naren, sharp-tongued and perceptive, who makes Indu look the truth in the eye, making it seem even more disgusting in contrast to his own intellectual integrity. Naren, well qualified, is persistent in his decision to work for satisfaction rather than remuneration. He has the strength to cope with the attitudinal fluctuations of those who accept or reject him in concurrence with his worldly success. His bohemian lifestyle is his way of emotionally distancing himself from those who judge him, according to his willingness to fit into the expected mould. In his caustic judgment of the kind of writing Indu is doing, he jolts her out of the somnolent submission which is denting her identity.

As Indu crystallizes the causes and results of engrained attitudes which take the shape of submission in different forms, she realizes that she would have to give a deliberate direction to her life. Should she become detached like Naren, who had isolated himself in his own solitary world? Or should she use her submission as a cunning tactic for survival in a relationship, where demand for a voice would lead to difficult realignments? None of these could provide the balance which she wishes to achieve because she realizes that the ennui she has been experiencing stems from her own failure to integrate her true self into her husband's perception. Her life with Jayant is important to her. So are the relational constructs it creates. What is required is a measure of autonomy within these. "Faith, love, devotion" she realizes, need not be "unbalanced, obsessive, unreasonable"(107). They should not become impediments in connecting to oneself. Hence, she would have to relocate herself in the paradigms which define her relationship, instead of relinquishing her ability to do so. Life was meaningful only in relation to the people one cares for, so it is important to "find freedom within this circle" (15).

She decides to initiate the process by resigning from her job without looking for Jayant's concurrence, to begin writing for her own satisfaction, to spend Akka's money the way she thinks is right. Indu knows that what she is embarking upon is a tough journey. She would be putting the very relationship she wants to retrieve, at stake. The future might look uncertain, but only out of that uncertainty could emerge acceptable alternatives. Indu finally emerges from the shadows of a cultural and personal past, which has tethered her to a consistently diminishing self. In the process, she acquires the ability to decide for herself rather than acquiescing to the image preordained for her.

The Dark Holds No Terror takes off from where *Roots and Shadows* ends. It deals with the road a woman has to traverse once she embarks on the forbidden journey to selfhood. The battles she has to fight are not always with others. More often she has to negotiate with herself. Saru battles the guilt which a woman faces for choosing to place her core self above the roles assigned to her. Her childhood is marked by repeated emphasis on the superiority of male role. So she decides early, to equip herself with power attributed to maleness, by abandoning the helpless feminine prototype. We see her single minded pursuit in her need to assert the 'I' which has been traumatized by the awareness that her identity as a girl made her less valuable than that of a dead son. She slogs for a medical college seat, walks over her mother's reluctance to send her to hostel, and chooses her father's monetary help for education rather than marriage. In college too, studies are the primary focus, always more important than the girlish crushes so important to others. Marriage is only a temporary lull in the ambition to forge ahead. On realizing that her husband cannot finance her higher studies, she decides to arrange for money herself. Thus she moves rapidly from registrarship to an MD, soon becoming a consultant with a consulting room of her own, thanks to the money and connections made available by Boozie, her flamboyant teacher.

In this pursuit of self-empowerment, Saru transgresses the Sita and Draupadi stereotypes of living within the husband's means and adjusting to the circumstances ordained by him. The implications are serious. Saru realizes that as long as she had lived happily, in the one room chawl with its stinking passages, she had been the ideal wife, entitled to the husband's love. However, as soon as she had recognized his disinterest in improving the situation, and decided to improve it herself, he had lost both magnanimity and equanimity. The conception of the kind of life she wants for herself and for her family, the wish to have a house of her own, "furnished with all the gee-gaws,"[18] evokes his oblique query about whether they could afford it. Instead of the expected remorse at her temerity for looking beyond her husband's means, she answers "we must" and goes about accumulating it on her own. So the colour coordinated furnishings, good school for children, etc., which would not be possible in a lecturer's pay, are paid through a doctor's earnings. In the process, the male prerogative to be in total control is challenged.

Deep-set gender orientations make Saru feel uncomfortable too, because she feels, "I was doing something which took away shreds of my feminity" (56). Perhaps she is not the only one feeling that, because in the loss of her feminity lies the discounted masculinity of her husband, whose lost confidence is apparent in the myriad underhand means of control he resorts to. The discontent and rancour in Manohar are manifested in his cruel schizoid behaviour and Saru's life is reduced to the split existence of a successful doctor in the day and the physically abused wife in the night. Saru is tempted, time and again, to give up the identity she has carved outside the constructs of domesticity, and to revert back to the role of a wife and a mother.

However, she knows that in catering to such a coerced concept of feminity she would be untrue to herself. Her ironic revision of the Sita and Draupadi myths makes her wonder if their devotion to their husbands had stemmed from some such survival strategy. She wonders wryly, if the system had always been cruel to women who dared to diminish male authority by rising to their full stature. Had they consciously abandoned their right to freedom "because that was the only way to survive" (137)? Saru can no longer sustain the romantic illusions surrounding man–woman relationship, as her sharp insight penetrates to the bottom of the power struggle. She reflects on the irony that not only is the system perpetually partial to the male but that the onus of keeping the scales tilted in favour of man also rests on the female. As a woman, you have to constantly pretend "that you are not as smart as you really are, not as competent as you are, not as rational as you are, and not as strong as you are" (137).

Freedom from these constraints is not easy because of the social consent they enjoy. Modern perceptions are related to the anger women must have felt at all times in history. Shakuntala, for instance, is advised by the ascetics to stay back in the king's harem as a slave, even though he refuses to recognize her as the woman who has conceived his child "because he was, after all, her husband" (138). Angered and humiliated, she wants to return to her former life and triggers the self-righteous reproach of the same ascetics, who call her a wanton for desiring independence over living a slave's life in deference to the husband's venerable position in society.

Retrospectively analysed, we discover that Saru's inability to act against the coercive system, in spite of her understanding of its unjust mores, is rooted in her own subordination to it, through generations of conditioning which formulates the female consciousness. This is true not only with respect to her reaction to her husband's cruelty, but also in many other aspects of her life. The impact of the burden of an enforced identity is reflected in Saru's disintegrated emotional response at her own overtures to move out of them. All she can muster up is a muted belligerence. Her anger against a long dead brother is one such ineffectual form of protest, which leads to her own alienation rather than any change in the system. She can never question the preference for this brother, who had insisted on burdening her with the disliked epithet "Saru tai" and the responsibility it entailed. She fails to give credence to the fact that she herself had been just a child when the accident had occurred. Dhruva's death and her mother's words "you did it, you did this, you killed him" (191), penetrate to the recesses of her heart, so that each night she dreams of him looking at her accusingly. What follows is an attempt to escape this guilt through false belligerence, "why should I blame myself, what did I have to do with his dying? He was a silly idiot ..." (181).

This defensiveness destroys her connection not only with her dead brother, but also her mother. She defies her in terms of choice of career and marriage, and rebels against any emotion which wishes for a reconciliation. This in turn induces more guilt for having abdicated her responsibility as the only surviving child, again seeking escape from guilt through more belligerences – "I have no happy memories of her. I don't want anything of her" (59). She thus negates all those emotions, which seek connection and emotional bonding and thus carries within her a lasting sense of deprivation. The same fight against guilt embitters her relationship with Manohar. The diminished status of her husband in contrast to her own professional success infuses her with guilt making her feel that she deserves the cruelty he inflicts on her by way of sexual abuse. The guilt is quickly mutated into antagonism, where she fiercely rejects the idea of her contribution to his failures. "It was his failure. I had nothing to do with it" (87).

Saru eventually realizes that she would have to step out of the self-limiting mental blocks imposed upon her by social and cultural mores. She would have to draw her own parameters, her own balancing between right and wrong. She knows that she would have "to blunder her way through this to some kind of a life, which would be right" (22). For this, she would first have to break through the guilt which accompanies every achievement outside the prescribed role. It is a guilt which is rooted in the very conditioning of a girl, who is taught to regard her life as worthless, except in terms of her responsibilities towards others. Saru needs to go back to those roots, liberate herself from their strangling hold and learn to negotiate for a rightful place. In this context, her journey to her father's house becomes a journey towards a decisive break with the guilt woven into her total being. It is the recovery of a realization that this guilt is society's means of self-propulsion to perpetuate the role, thus harming vital emotions and relationships.

Saru's sojourn to her father's house is in effect a journey into the emotional labyrinths of her childhood, to recover that self which had been lost in transition to a compromised adulthood. This entails a dual process. The first is the symbolic divestiture of the spurious fiction she has lived by and the second involves reclaiming herself as an agency, to make conscious choices. The first of these takes her gaze back to the ethos of masculine privilege represented by her long dead brother, Dhruva. His death had confirmed her superfluity, implied upon her the legacy of inferiority, and underclassed her through withheld maternal love. By coming back to the paternal home, this time in the absence of her mother and her complicity with the masculine ethos, Saru finally exorcises the ghosts of the past. The act of forgetting Dhruva's birthday, with its once iconic status, is symbolic of freeing herself of his privileged status.

The second part is achieved by taking herself back to the traditional role. She lives in the paternal house in her two sarees, preoccupied with the kitchen. The simultaneous assessment of the emptiness of this life in spite of the ostensible wholeness it projects, makes her realize that one could not adjust oneself to social roles which one has outgrown. Nostalgia for the old order which she has so far perceived as the lost haven diminishes as she recognizes that the secure wholeness it promised was itself illusory and fragile. The emptiness on the face of a recently widowed neighbour, and the self-deprecation of an elderly woman, who questions the necessity of her existence after her husband's death, makes Saru confront her choices.

As illusions strip away, Saru realizes that in order to survive the demands of the social roles, it is important to cater to other aspects of one's personality instead of denying their existence. She recognizes that even men with their more powerful social positions could lose hold on their core selves under pressure to live up to gender roles. Her father for instance retrieves his identity only after her mother's death and recovers his nurturing instincts, buried beneath the patriarchal facade. Madhav, his surrogate son realizes it much sooner and displays the streak of self-preservation, when he refuses to sacrifice his career for family obligations: "It's my life after all" (208), he says. These words penetrate to the recesses of Saru's heart and she realizes that "the guilty sister, the undutiful daughter, the unloving wife – she was all these … but if she was all of them, they were not all of her" (220). For her, it is like finding the "connecting link" (220). Saru feels that with this realization, she had washed away the ugly slough of some disease. As she looks into the mirror, she feels the same tenderness towards herself, which she would have felt towards some stranger coming out of an ordeal.

Recognition of the need to give her individuality its due place helps her to step out of the self-abnegating myth and clears the way for retrieval of confidence. She finds herself connecting to all lost relationships – to Dhruva in her metaphoric looking after Madhav through the night, as he burns in fever, and to her mother in finally seeing her as a woman struggling with her grief at the loss of a son, not a cruel woman mitigating another of her own sex. Once released from her guilt Saru ceases to be in the defensive mode. She is now comfortable with the person that she is and the way she has been moulded by the times she lives in. Regressing to the past patterns can no longer suffice for her. Clear and objective in her attitude, she feels equipped to open the channel of communication with Manohar, instead of turning her back on him. Inherent in the decision is the possibility of retrieval, if he agrees to provide the space he has denied her so far. If he still dithers on that, then also inherent in it is the option which her father has shown to her, "It's up to you isn't it" (217)?

If Saru learns to break through the guilt which a desire for personal empowerment induces in her, Jaya's fragmented interior monologue in *That Long Silence*, gives us a glimpse of the many psychological constraints which prevent women from connecting to their true selves. We are brought into close touch with events and emotions, which have shaped not only Jaya's personality, but also sub-stratums of awareness emerging from the debris of the myth which had enclosed it. Deshpande regards this as the most important of her works because she sees it as the story "of a woman trying to get at her real self through all the conflicting demands and roles of her life."[19]

Jaya realizes early in her marriage that in acquiescing to be part of an institutionalized relationship, based on gender roles as established by the patriarchal norms, she had given herself up, to the necessity of role playing. The hard-working, ambitious, independent and aggressive Mohan has sought the cultured and English-speaking Jaya in the belief that she would be a magical combination of a sophisticated exterior and traditional interior. This is coupled with Jaya's own social conditioning with its veiled threats, "wait till you get married", "wait until your husband comes", "wait till you go to your in-laws home,"[20] making that wait sound like "waiting fearfully for disaster, a catastrophe" (30). It ensures that Mohan's approval becomes paramount, as the approval of the one who holds the superior place in the hierarchy. She falls into the grid propelled by the force of the whole system.

Her role as a wife is so sharply defined by the expectations of the husband and his family that she realizes at a subconscious level that the freedom from guilt and consciousness of doing right could only come from acquiescing to the demand of that role. Hence Jaya, who had once loved Trollope and Austen, had dreamed of going to Oxford, whose father had said, "You are going to be different from others" (136), relinquishes that difference and spends years deciding menus for lunch and dinner, changing sheets and scrubbing the toilets, thus living out the approved role of a house-proud woman. The woman, who had once been amused at being mistaken for a worker's wife for her lack of self-consciousness, now creams her face and brushes her hair fifty times on either side to prevent her husband from falling out of love with her. The spirited Jaya ostensibly metamorphoses into a "smiling placid, motherly woman ... who lovingly nurtured her family, a woman who coped" (16), a wimp who needed to be protected from anything ranging from a cockroach to a mob.

The grid into which Jaya finds herself pushed, makes claims on her thoughts and feelings as well. She discovers that she had to be a person divorced from all emotions like anger and resentment which presaged discontent. She had to be totally content with her role as the devoted wife, the natural homemaker and the nurturing mother, or at least pretend to be so. Ugly emotions destroying the perfect placidity of the pre-planned picture were frowned upon. So Jaya the wilful girl who had never made a secret of her feelings, who had "For everything a question, for everything a retort" (27), now has "neither any questions nor any retorts" (27). She discovers through the distaste on her husband's face that she had to censor her feelings too, for "my emotion had made me ugly, as if I got bloated with them" (83). Anger, she realizes makes a woman unwomanly. Terrified of his disapproval, she also learns a plethora of responses which alone made her an approved woman.

This selective appropriation of her personality is best reflected when her need for expression as a writer is coerced into silence – one long silence, which effectively suppresses any dissenting emotions, which might disturb the order of the scene. The one attempt she makes at honest writing, elicits Mohan's anger at the possibility of Jaya's characters being equated to his family members. That decides that nothing controversial should ever be written again. Certain truths had to be kept out of sight. The "Sita column" which she writes, within the parameters of what her husband thinks correct, becomes the ironic symbol of a system, where free expression needs to be curtailed because it might come out with the unspeakable.

The question perpetually lurking between the lines is how much of Jaya has actually been converted to Suhasini, the ideal wife and mother? Does every woman eventually metamorphose into a Sita or does she only role play because she does not have an option? If it is so, then what is the residue which emerges out of the dichotomy between the two? Jaya finds that the person beneath the mask never changes. As she looks back at the years, through her diaries, she sees in them "an utter stranger, a person so alien to me that even the faintest understanding of the motives of her actions seems impossible. There was no clue there, nothing that gave me a chance to connect" (70). The years that had gone into creating that woman become redundant because under the first objective analysis, Jaya finds Suhasini, her coerced identity as a wife and mother, dwindling into nothingness.

As she dwindles, she leaves behind an account of the discontent latent in every aspect of her life. It manifests itself in the scum of hostility which she has often perceived over the perfectly presented facades. As she follows the dishonoured Mohan to the Dadar flat, it appears in the image of one bull yoked to another, which superimposes itself on the images of "Sita following her husband into exile, Savitri dogging death to reclaim her husband, Draupadi stoically sharing her husband's travails ..." (11). Jaya sees the irony implicit in the expectations men have from women and the forms which these actually take. She realizes that the truth was that bulls moved in the same direction only because, "To go in different directions would be painful; and which animal would voluntarily chose pain" (12)? She connects that discontent to the unspoken angst, of Mohan's mother hitting her face with her floured hands, of Vanita Mami locating meaning in her pots, pans and cats, of her cousin Kusum who jumps into the well where the springs have finally dried. What Mohan's coloured vision perceives as a woman's strength and toughness, Jaya sees as "a despair so great that it would not voice itself ... a struggle so bitter that silence was the only weapon. Silence and surrender" (36).

The potential for damage inherent in the negativity underlying this hopeless silence is metaphorically presented through the silent marchers, whose total silence does not dilute their simmering discontent, but in their very quietness lies the threat "to the design or the pattern" (54). That it could cause a similar destruction in her own life becomes clear to Jaya in two things. The first is the recognition of aggression in her own attitude towards Mohan, as soon as she sees him divested of the authority which claimed her subordination. Having borne the ignonimity of his malpractices and seen him bewildered and disoriented in the absence of his masculine props, she discovers that "the way we lived and what we were, was no talisman against the ugly terrible things we imagine" (6). And if the safety promised by this entire institution was a fake promise, then with what authority did the system demand a woman's subordination? Jaya says, "I have to be honest with myself. It was not he who had relinquished authority; it was I who no longer conceded any authority to him" (9). She realizes that this aggression was only the outer manifestation of the same subtle resistance she had offered, the guerrilla warfare she had waged for years.

The second thing which shakes her out of her stupor is her son Rahul's running away from the forced holiday with his father's friends. In this symbolic rebellion against pretensions inherent in relationships constructed for superficial benefits, Jaya can identify her own subconscious inclinations. The terror and hysteria which she experiences at the possibility of losing Rahul reflects her own latent desire to run away from the pretension of her marriage. She goes to the Churchgate flat; the symbol of all those ostensible trappings for which she had acquiesced to the pretension of her marriage, and finds to her surprise that nothing in that house reflected her. Even those trappings reflected her total annihilation in the relationship. Had she succumbed to the bait offered by Yajnvalkya to Maitreyee and believed that any aspiration beyond material life was "a crazy idea" (62)? The horror, with which she realizes that what she had taken as scum on the water in the dusty, neglected vase was actually a cluster of dead ants, becomes symbolic of the realization that hostility can become lethal and destroy relationships based on coerced proximity.

In the self-assessment which follows, Jaya realizes that it was not just the system that was lopsided, but her own strategies of survival, which helped in maintaining its imbalance. Jaya, who had once ridiculed the opinion that a husband is like a sheltering tree, later utilizes the same maxim to her own advantage. She remembers how she had stopped herself from laughing at her husband's superficial and pretentious behaviour because she did not want a "dwarfed husband" (169). She remembers too, that it was she who had deliberately pretended to be helpless and in need of protection, to make Mohan feel larger than life. Like this she made sure that she always had her hole to crawl back into. It was she who had made Mohan feel in total control by not letting him know of the subliminal life below the facade of perfection. It was so much easier to just stay silent about her abortion, her surreptitious writing, and her intellectual relationships with Kamat. Deshpande finds here the eerie echo of Draupadi's advice to Satyabhama, on the strategy to be a successful wife when she tells her "be silent about what you think."[21] Deshpande says, "to speak of a strategy is to acknowledge the possibility of discarding it, the possibility of rejecting that strategy."[22] In her decision to relinquish these deceptions lies Jaya's readiness to face the complications involved in integrating the truth into her relationship with Mohan.

Jaya also realizes that in order to resuscitate herself and her relationships, it was necessary to remove the mask from her anger and vocalize it, so that balance could be restored and hostility mitigated. Hence, she decides that whatever is the risk, she would speak and let the imbalance and hostility be visible. The weighing of loss and gain would have to be done from either side. When Mohan, angered by these overtures at change, leaves home and goes away, Jaya is scared and there is a strong desire to slip back into the earlier role, but she stops herself. In her courage lies a sense of responsibility. She remembers the last words in her father's diary, "I have given you knowledge. Now you make the choice" (192). Her identity as a child, hands in pockets, sure of the resources within herself, was still a part of her. She could no longer be the female character of Sanskrit drama, who could only talk in the baby lisp of Prakrit. She wants her voice to be heard and will insist that Mohan listens to it.

Implicit in this resolution is the hope that she would have more to offer to the relationship than just deceit and guile. The arduous path she chooses is the only way, not only to self-retrieval but also for retrieval of honesty in relationships. Mohan might not understand it right away, and could regard her adamant insistence on being heard as an affront to his masculinity. Yet there was the possibility of a reciprocal change in the future. Thinking of Mohan as she considers his telegram informing her of his return, she dwells, "we don't change overnight. It's possible that we don't change even over long periods of time. But we can always hope .... Life has always to be made possible" (193).

Jaya's success in finding her voice is complemented by Urmi in *The Binding Vine*, who insists on seeing reality from outside the conjecture that man's rights are inviolable and any shift from his needs a transgression. Implicit in it is her argument against the male demand for total surrender. Deshpande seems to be saying that total surrender is not imperative. A woman is entitled to her space and independence, and if this assertion elicits a coercive response, she needs to stand up to it, as her contribution to resistance against an imbalanced system. When Urmi's brother obliquely asks her why she needs to get involved in other people's business, she says, "What is my business? It always makes me think of snails – crawling away blindly, you know, enclosed in their shells. But snails get trampled over too, don't they?"[23] Her concern reminds one of her childhood insistence on correcting the misaligned wheels of her bicycle and riding it again in spite of her bleeding knees. Urmi's crusade to discover this alignment is reflected in her involvement with her mother-in-law Meera's angst-filled poetry and also her involvement with Kalpana, the young rape victim in coma.

Meera, as Urmi discovers through her poems and diaries, had been an intelligent woman, different from other in terms of having possessed intellectual faculties, which demanded a space denied by claustrophobic roles and relationships. Marriage and the entire system surrounding it, is bent upon converting her into the likeness of all other women. The small comfort, which the old system offers in return, is useless to the woman, who cannot contain the fire raging within. Marriage, in denying her the inner space becomes a nightmare. Her attempts at retaining her selfhood, convert her obsessed husband into a rapist, because he cannot bear the thought of being denied any part of her. Meera dies at the age of twenty-two, while giving birth to a son. She had desired a boy, perhaps because of what she went through as a woman. The pain of the life she has led and Urmi's own emotional response to it magnifies Meera's ironic reflection on the glorified relation between man and woman when she refers to the revered image of Laxmi-Narayan saying:

> But tell me, friend, did Laxmi too
> twist brocade tassels round her fingers
> and tremble, fearing the coming
> of the dark clouded, engulfing night? (66)

Years later, as Urmi reads the poems and feels the angst suppressed in Meera's heart, she knows she must do something to make this angst visible. She plans a book, which would be written in Kannada and published from Ranidurg, the place where Meera had lived and died. Social pressure against a woman's discontent being made visible comes in the form of Vanaa's anger, who is afraid of what her mother, who has taken Meera's place after her death, would have to go through, when it became public that her husband had been cruel to his first wife. Vanaa asks Urmi why she had to go into what had happened so long ago and Urmi replies, "they never had a chance. It's not fair; it's not fair at all. And we can't go on pushing it – what happened to them – under the carpet forever, because we are afraid of disgrace ... have I answered your question" (174)?

Running parallel to this exploration is Urmi's involvement with Kalpana, lying in coma in a hospital, having been brutally raped. Instead of seeking to expose the heinous crime, even the girl's own mother, Shakutai, tries to cover it up for fear of a defiled reputation, which would stand in way of a decent marriage for the girl and her younger sister. She goes to the extent of blaming Kalpana for being too wilful and too independent in her ways and thus inviting this fate for herself. Urmi's involvement with the case and her getting media attention focused on it annoys her own family and also angers Shakutai. The *morcha* outside the hospital and the TV coverage, unnerve Shakutai, because now the truth about her daughter is exposed to the whole world. This is exactly what Urmi is fighting against – the irrationality of the whole twisted logic, which claims that it was Kalpana who was disgraced by what had happened. Her fight is against everything which denies the truth – the opinion that "there can be no rape, because it can't be done, unless a woman is willing" (181). Her fight is also against the social assent to this system of denial, reflected in the police officer's attempt to portray the case as an accident, rather than a rape.

Given the impact of the social conditioning, it is not surprising that even Shakutai, the stronger among women, who has reared up her children independently rather than listening to the dictates of an inefficient husband, succumbs when social pressure threatens on a larger scale. More significant, however, is the shift in perspective and the realization that a struggle at an individual level is not enough. If the system on the whole is not questioned, it would inflict cruelty on others, among them your loved ones. Urmi, who has initiated this change by making Shaku a part of the concentric movement beginning from herself, understands the difficulties in the venture but also fails to see any alternative to it. She says, "the thought of all that lies ahead, oppresses me, but I can see no role that can take us back" (203). Shaku, having discovered that her daughter had been raped by her own uncle leading also to her sister's suicide, understands that "her daughter's tragedy, her sister's death, can no longer be shrouded in silence" (203).

This social conditioning which makes Meera and Shaku wary of an open expression of their pain and angst is interwoven into Urmi's psyche too, in spite of her persona as the liberated woman. Urmi's discontent stems from the parameters within which her relationship to her husband is constructed. However, she vents her anger in self-debilitating forms, instead of verbalizing it and negotiating for a better deal. In attempting to verbalize the discontent of others, Urmi is actually trying to step out of this conditioned pressure, which impels a woman to shroud her discontent in silence. She needs to verbalize the pain, which the underlying distance between her and her sailor husband Kishore causes to her. There is a part of him, to which he never gives her access. His place in her life, as an infrequent visitor, who maintains no emotional link between his random appearances, hurts her. He seems complete in himself without her, making Urmi feel vulnerable about revealing her own painful need for him. The anguish it causes to her is hidden under the armour of invincibility, which is actually a defence against that pain. It is the same armour, which prevents her from releasing pain after her daughter Anu's death. Her asthmatic attacks, her banging her head against the wall to will the wound to bleed, reflect her need to rescue herself from her own suppressed emotions. She discovers that her latent resentment has contributed to her own apprehensions at reaching out to Kishore. She had always stopped herself from expressing her need for him, for it had made her feel vulnerable, against his ostensible lack of need for her. If Meera had suffered from her husband's aggressive possessiveness, Urmi suffers because of her husband's assumption that she would give all of herself to their relationship while he continually displayed her dispensability to his wholeness. She knows that this latent discontent had to be brought out into the open for retrieving the proximity of the relationship, even if it left her exposed to the possibility of unreciprocated sentiments.

Urmi realizes that she would have to take off the armour in order to bridge the gap between Kishore and herself. The "blank wall, glass topped, the glass bits shining menacingly ..." (15), which she sees in her dream, separating her from Kishore, would have to be toppled, and she hopes she can find the courage to bear the vulnerability involved in doing so. Meera's words echo her feelings:

> Smiling and joyful, Karna tore off his amour.
> His body trailed blood.
> Will that courage be mine, when denuded?
> I stand naked and bare. (137)

She tells Vanaa "I'll tell him what I ... think and feel ... what will Kishore say? I must know the answer. It matters to me" (175). Urmi thus risks what lies beyond silence, because only through it can she reclaim her rightful place in the relationship. If it was still denied to her, then she would need to "think it over" (175). Thus, through her attempts to give voice to Meera and Kalpana, Urmi also discovers her own potential to negotiate. She discovers the possibility of vocalizing herself. She also finds the courage to attempt retrieval of love in spite of the hurt it might entail. Beyond that lies the last option of searching for alternatives.

If Saru, Jaya and Urmi have fought prolonged battles against their conditioned response of subordination to the stereotypes, Sumi in *A Matter of Time* dispenses with them by walking out of the system which puts woman in a supplicatory position. In Aru, her daughter, who symbolizes the continuation of her journey, we also discover the possibility of perpetuity through daughters.

"What is a woman, without a husband?"[24] Deshpande considers the implication of this belief in terms of the worthlessness it inculcates in a woman, making it impossible for her to measure her worth as an individual or to see her potential as a human being. It is in Kalyani's life that we see what a woman can be reduced to, in her desperate clinging on to her married status, even though her husband has not talked to her for thirty-five years. Images of Kalyani hitting herself in frustration, banging her head against the wall, crying and blaming her fate, mingle together to remind Sumi of the desolation which that relationship had imposed upon all of them. Yet this personal frustration is borne because social conditioning makes it subsidiary to the privilege of being recognized as a married woman. For Sumi, it is a strange set of rules. She wonders, "... is it enough to have a husband and never mind the fact that he has not looked at your face for years, never mind the fact that he has not spoken to you for decades? Does your wifehood make up for everything, for the deprivation of a man's love, for the feel of his body against yours, the warmth of this breath on your face" (167)?

For Sumi, this is not enough. Therefore, when her husband walks out of sixteen years of marriage, she neither turns hysterical, nor makes frantic appeals to him to return. She does not cater to "the questions and innuendos" (62), which seek to hold her responsible for his desertion. Social opinion that "Sumi took Gopal and her marriage too casually, she never cared as much as she should have" (17), fails to induce guilt in her. The loneliness, the feeling of humiliation, the fear of being left alone is all there, and Sumi does not deny this. But along with these is a sense of dignity, which refuses to let herself be converted into an object of pity. She regrets having left her job to follow her husband with the blind faith of a child and realizes that she is now left with a begging bowl in her hands. This initiates the process of recovering herself as a person with competencies. Learning to ride a scooter, managing to get a job, fending for her daughters, are all parts of this process of discovering the ability to survive. She refuses financial aid by her father and relatives and gradually finds her moorings in her own capabilities. The confidence which she discovers makes her feel, "that anxiety about money ... is almost a relief after the earlier inescapable haunting fears" (194).

In discovering her ability to survive, Sumi discovers herself as a person. Her passion for writing provides her with an agency of expression, through which her desires and aspirations take a concrete shape. When she goes to Gopal to tell him of her plan to move away, he realizes to his amazement that she had come to ask for her own freedom, rather than granting freedom to him. Only then, when she stands complete in herself, without him, does he realize that she too might have had her dreams of freedom when she lived the role of a wife and mother. The truth of that thought is reflected in Sumi's appeal to Aru, "be happy for me Aru. This is the first thing in my life, I think that I got for myself ... and now suddenly I want to do so many more things" (230–31).

Sumi's conscious movement away from the socially constructed role of dependency and the success she achieves in it, also brings forth the need of similar deliberation in other debilitating constructs, the most significant among these being the restitution of the rightful place in matters of inheritance. The process is difficult and requires women to step out of the conditioned response that they as females are not links in perpetuity, and hence not entitled to a share in the family assets. The social alterations required for this change are delineated through the lives and responses of four generations of women, culminating in the assumption of the rightful place by Sumi's daughter Aru.

Deshpande takes us back in time to Manorama, Vithalrao's beautiful wife resplendent in her silks and diamonds, who fails to produce a son and is afraid that her husband might marry again for a male heir. Manorama's inability to think of a daughter as an inheritor leads her to the cruelty of arranging a match between her young daughter and her reluctant brother, in the belief that retaining the property in the family would absolve her of the crime of not producing a son. The same vicarious guilt is displayed in the red carpet treatment accorded to her daughter Kalyani, when she gives birth to a boy and later in the cruelty meted out to her when she returns without that mentally retarded son, as a deserted wife. Kalyani, with her inbuilt acceptance of her subsidiary status as a girl, and later as the intruder who returns to her father's house with two daughters, never questions why her mother had willed the property to her husband Shripati and not to her. The internalization of her marginalized status determines Kalyani's attitude towards her own daughters, Sumi and Premi. They are forever silenced, putting such deep-seated isolations into their hearts that it becomes their personal place of exile.

When Sumi returns to her parent's house, initially she considers herself and her daughters intruders too. "We are interlopers, she thinks, my daughters and I. Just passing through. From where had this idea comes to her … from the walls of this house that seem to cry out that the very reason for their existence was a son?" (71–71). Sumi thinks, "I have no right to be here. For, whether in the stable in Bethlehem or Nunda's house on the banks of Yamuna in Gokul, the male child belongs" (71). We see Sumi and her daughters involved in make-shift arrangements as if they know that they must move out soon. Sumi's house-hunting, Aru's carefully rolling up her bedding each night, etc., are all indicative of the same.

It is Aru's perceptive gaze, sharpened against the injustice of the situation, which for the first time, raises questions about the system and its agendas. It is significant that Aru belongs to a family, which has never made the absence of a son an issue. Sumi and Gopal have thus given a sense of wholeness to their daughters which had been denied to both Kalyani and Sumi. Thus, Aru automatically begins to assume responsibilities, making Sumi reflect that she was trying to become the man of the family. We see this in her steadying hand as her mother learns to drive and her sharp reaction to anyone who tries to marginalize Sumi. Her decision to go and meet her father is not an act of self-pity, but a purposeful visit to put before him, in full clarity the humiliation and disgrace he has piled upon them. She goes to tell him that he had forfeited his right to suggest what was right and wrong for her.

It is this Aru, free from gender conditioning who breaks through her grandfather Shripati's reserve. She can relate to him as a person and her feelings are reciprocated. Shripati's pleasure at the thought that she would succeed him as the lawyer in the family, and his awareness of her ability to steer her mother and sisters through the stormy passage of change, translates into a gesture which breaks through a lifetime of ill-conceived convictions. Although not explicitly clarified, one can assume that the will bequeathing the property to Kalyani, in her capacity as the daughter of Manorama and Vithalrao rather than as Shripati's wife, is that substantial gift which Shripati insists that Aru should get on the eighteenth birthday. It also becomes an acknowledgement that a daughter's right to be a successor is as natural as that of a son.

Kalyani accepts the same, when she gifts Manorama's glittering diamonds to Aru on her eighteenth birthday. It is Kalyani's way of resituating a daughter's rightful place in emotional terms. She says, "For so many years I thought I had nothing ... my mother did not care for my children either. Daughters again, she said" (125). Kalyani tells Aru how she considered herself luckier than her mother because she had enjoyed her daughters as well as her granddaughters. "Aru's grave acceptance carries an understanding of what Kalyani is doing" (227). The coincidence that Aru shares her name with Kalyani's grandmother becomes symbolic. From one Arundhati to another, four generations later, the connection is indelible. The uncanny resemblance between Manorama, Sumi, and Aru also spells out the same genetic lineage, which is denied by the system. This is what needs to change and will. It is just a matter of time.

In *Small Remedies* we have one voice but many lives explored through that voice, so that Madhu's quest for identity merges with the exploration of what this quest entails for women in general. What emerges is the necessity of releasing one's choice from the threats of the system. For Madhu, the moment of reckoning comes, when she either reconciles to a marriage in which compassion and companionship wither away under the first threat to male ego, or insists upon alternatives.

Madhu has adjusted into the structured parameters of family life because she believes in the authenticity of the relationships it upholds. However, she finds that those relationships threaten to give way when confronted with male affront at being denied the sole proprietorship in the ensuing equation. Som makes many years of their married life irrelevant, by focusing on one act of adolescent sexual transgression. She is amazed by his anger, by his doubts about her sexual integrity after marriage, and his temerity in questioning her relationship with every other man, including Tony who has given her a brother's love.

Her anger goes beyond the question of chastity. In fact, it converges on the fact that her husband cannot see beyond her loss of virginity. He cannot understand that she is not confessing, but trying to share with him the despair centring on her father's impending death which had led to that encounter. She is trying to find solace through him, for the horror of the realization that her appeal for intimacy had eventually led to that man's guilt-ridden suicide. For her, Som's insensitivity is a betrayal to which she responds with total withdrawal. She decides, "I will no longer answer him, I will say nothing, I will deny nothing ...."[25] Implicit in it is anger at so many aspects of her personality being subordinated to the issue of virginity, the symbol of male proprietorship. The realization that for Som, his right over her body is more important than all else she has given to their relationship, devalues the concept of marriage.

In this context, their son's violent death, closely linked to their conflict, can be symbolically interpreted. A child is the concrete manifestation of trust between a man and a woman. In his violent death, we perceive the despair over the total loss of that faith. Madhu tries to come to terms with her loss away from home, having agreed to write the biography of an ageing musician, so that she can give herself time to clarify her thought processes. The shift away from her marital home is her statement against the system which refuses any flexibility and expects a defined perfection from a woman. Therefore, when Som writes to her, asking her to come back for their son's death anniversary, she knows that he is also referring to the "fact of their continuing life together" (323). In it lies his realization that a woman is more than a body, that a man needs to treat her as a companion, not a possession. Madhu's return to Som integrates in itself her ability to have her say in their relationship.

The same decision to make a conscious choice is reflected in the life of Savitri Bai Indorekar, the legendary singer, to write whose biography Madhu has gone to Bhawanipur. Bai's decision to move out of the precincts of married life with the help of a Muslim tabla player, in order to pursue her passion for music has given rise to many speculations. Madhu too struggles with many doubts which cross her mind, as she thinks of this reclusive woman who has forsaken not only marriage and respectability but also motherhood. She seems to have utilized Khan Sahib the tabla player who stood by her in hardships, but whom she never married. Her reputation as 'that' kind of a woman, who had pursued success and fame with cold-blooded ambition, is hard to break.

Madhu discovers eventually that for Bai, morality, as defined by society was not enough in making a choice. As the writer says, "what we wish for is a choice that saves us from unhappiness" (226). For Bai, the only way to escape that unhappiness was pursuit of music, if not within the place allotted to her, then outside it. Madhu discovers that she had moved from marriage, not to some instant fame or glory, but to years of poverty, hard work and ostracization, knowing fully well that even when success came, the price for her choice would have to be paid.

She pays that price in full awareness. That is why she never tries to retrieve a half-baked respectability by marrying Khan Sahib, or by telling the world that she had never resorted to the easy way of becoming some rich patron's mistress. Neither does she resort to gimmicks like singing religious songs. She does not scream to the world that it was not she who had forsaken her child, but the male system which had forsaken her right to motherhood by erasing her out of her daughter's life. The stark honesty which Madhu discovers beneath the many silent zones of her life, reflect Bai's awareness that choices cannot come without a struggle. For Bai, that struggle must have involved facing the many guilts towards those, whose lives her decision had affected, particularly that of her daughter. She lives with the awareness of the choice and its price, in her journey towards her destiny as a singer.

If Bai has moved beyond social constraints in pursuit of her personal passion, Leela, Madhu's aunt, has broken out of the convention of widowhood and reached out of her small room to look for justice for the weak. She breaks caste constraints, works for the rights of mill workers, becomes a corporator, and goes to jail during emergency. She is not afraid of what people would say when she, a widow, well beyond her middle age, decides to marry Joe. In the process, she is ostracized by her family, hated by her mother, pursued by goons and seen as an aberration by the many around her. Yet, Leela finds her compensations in the awareness of having followed her heart, and in finding relationships which revolve not around social obligations, but mutual respect and individual dignity. She has broken out of the mythic constraints much before others and discovered that what lies outside could be more rewarding than the suffocating existence inside.

Moving On further expands on Deshpande's analysis of the mythic identities and their redundancy in the present context. Significantly, the evaluation here comes not from a woman struggling to break through these myths, but from one who has already made the leap. Hence, the analysis is retrospective. Interestingly, while the retrospection endorses and validates the need to break form archaic models, it also assesses the ones created by the rebound. In the process, it calls for the balance, which aims at better relationships, not a self-centred individualized autonomy.

The elder of the two daughters, Jiji has been brought up by her father to take up the role of a provider. Her exuberant and tom-boyish ways are a contrast to the docile and restrained behaviour associated with a picture-perfect girl. She remembers herself as "running out without buttoning up my dress, my hair coming out of my plaits, the tying tape of my knickers trailing below my dress. My emotions were just as untidy and all over the place ...."[26] Her mother's disapproval of her unfeminine ways includes the hope that she would learn to behave in a more appropriate manner and fit well into the role of a wife and a mother. However, when Jiji finds herself widowed, without a means of livelihood, with two children to rear up, she decides to manage on her own, so that she never again ensconces herself in the false sense of security which the traditional role imposes on a woman. Her attitude is explicated in her response to the driving instructor who uses brakes on behalf of the trainee. She recognizes that "It gave the woman too an illusion of safety, which I thought was misleading; it was dangerous, in fact, to have this kind of dual control" (83). For herself, she demands that the driver keep away "how would I learn if I didn't have to cope with risks myself? ... He let me manage and I learnt to control the car" (84).

The same attitude filters to the every aspect of her life, confusing the men around, be it her father or Raja, the childhood friend, now persistently wooing her. If she wants to have a car, she gets it in spite of Raja's warning against squandering money. If she wishes to type, she fumbles her way into learning the computer. If the property sharks try coercing her into selling the house, she fights them off to save it for her daughter. The process of overcoming panic and fear is the one which makes her grow up from a girl eager to please, to one determined to make her own decisions. Jiji's life lacks the placidity of traditional female life. She also lacks the feminine helplessness and restraint which men find attractive. She is neither mild nor docile. However, she does have control over her life.

To validate Jiji's point of view, Deshpande juxtaposes her to other female characters who have lived their lives adapting to the image expected of them and shows how it dents into their personalities. One of them is Kamla, wife of Jiji's father's friend. Once a gentle, smiling, never dissenting woman, absorbed in her children, looking after her husband's comforts, she ends up as a shrill, overbearing woman, who at some point in her life "has given up coping" (92). Even more perturbing is the picture of Hemi her daughter. Nobody realizes that she is not a normal child, because as Jiji ironically reflects, "did they think that to be soft, docile, and silent was the right way for the girl to be" (93)? The fact that Hemi grows up into an angry, wilful, frightening and self-absorbed woman, becomes symbolic of what false role-delineation can do to an individual. In contrast, it seems that the boisterous unfeminine Jiji ends up as more balanced individual.

As a woman functioning from outside the strictures of the approved female rule, Jiji has to constantly assess herself against social disapproval and find her own parameters of right and wrong. When she chooses to live the life of a single, working mother, the impact of her prolonged absence from home, upon the family structure, is brought under the social scanner. Jiji remembers the guilt she had undergone, when her father had pointed out that her ram-shackled life would do no good to her children. When, as a young widow, she leaves her children with neighbours, and goes out to earn a living, there is this torturous uncertainty of right and wrong. Later in life, when she assesses her son Anand, and finds in him a sincere and genuine concern, grounded in right values, she feels justified for the stand she has taken. Comparing it to her own childhood, she realizes that "we had a stable enough life ... our father had enough time for us, our mother was always there when we returned from school ... look at what happened to us! So what difference does it make" (46–47)?

If *Moving On* deals with the myths imposed upon women through centuries of subordination to false ideals, it also assesses the ones created by the retaliatory reaction, making women look for an idealized independence. Among these is the question of female sexuality and the feasibility of fulfilling its demands as a matter of right, by dissociating it from the emotional quotient of relationships. Jiji is not ashamed of her physicality. She is unlike her mother who is ashamed and angry when her body responds because she considers it a transgression of the restraint and decorum, which a woman must possess. Jiji's marriage to Shyam in fact had involved complete connection and body had been the medium through which she had related to him. However, when her physical needs lead her into a purely sexual relationship with her tenant Raman, her defensive arguments are subjected to her own sense of right and wrong. The very furtiveness and guilt associated with it negates its worth, even as a mere "arrangement" as Jiji describes it. She is angry when Raja questions her and retaliates with accounts of men who had tried to take advantage of her. She even questions the practicality of the supposition that she should have lived the life of a chaste widow after losing her husband at the age of twenty-one. However, even Jiji eventually recognizes the dislocation inherent in such an arrangement and opts for a stable relationship.

Through Jiji's life, Deshpande also questions the pursuit of individualized autonomy as a goal for female liberation. She seems to be sceptical about the satisfaction which this break from social involvement could bring to a woman. Having adamantly escaped the emotional vulnerability involved in relational involvements, Jiji finally finds herself alone in the house after her father's death. She is now in possession of property, money and independence – all the ostensible requisites of autonomy. Yet, she finds herself facing "a blankness, that carries a sense of anarchy" (61). She realizes, "not to have anyone making demands on you, not to have to meet others' demands, makes for a lack of order in life. It is others' demands that shape our lives; our own are so confused, so chaotic, so many, that they create nothing but disorder … free from the necessity of having to do anything for others, I understood the exact meaning of those words" (61). Deshpande thus reiterates that isolated independence is no utopia. It is in relation to the others that autonomy becomes relevant. Jiji recognizes that her belligerence is nothing but a fearful defence against the vulnerability associated with emotional bonds. The hurt she has suffered in her relationship with her family and her husband has made her turn away from all human connection. However, she eventually realizes that if a system fails once, it is no reason to give up on it. What is required is the insistence upon demanding the rightful place within it. For that matter, the system could change too. It is Raja's father B.K., who puts things in perspective for her when he says, "Give him time. He will learn to accept as you are" (339). Jiji's implicit assent to Raja's proposal towards the end, her forgiveness for her sister and her parents, her retrieval of the trust she shared with Shyam, are all indications of the restoration of faith in relationships and institutions. It is this, which helps her to move on towards participation in life, which might never be conclusively perfect, but is the only way to live.

Another facet of the same issue is explored in Deshpande's latest novel, *In the Country of Deceit*. Devayani, living alone after the death of her parents finds herself involved in a relationship with Ashok Chinappa, the Superintendent of police, who although married and with a teenage daughter, is living alone during his short posting to Rajnur.

Through their relationship, Deshpande makes an assessment of the feasibility of substituting established and institutionalized relationships which have social sanction, with unstructured ones, which seem to offer greater possibility of exercising personal choices.

Devayani's relationship with Ashok is unfolded with a double perspective for the reader. Running parallel to it is her aunt's account of her experience in marriage, which weaves through the novel in a series of letters which she writes to Devayani. The contrast between the two is not painted in black and white. Each has its own highs and lows. Yet, through it emerges a clear perspective on what could provide a better option from the woman's point of view.

Devayani, in her relationship experiences resurgence in exploring the natural urges of the body. The sheer delight of being the immediate focus of a socially powerful, sensitive and intelligent man involves a high which relegates all other relationships to the background. Underlying it is defiance against the circumstances which have forced her existence into a staidness which offers no escape. However, although the relationship takes her life up to a crescendo, it also builds up a tautness which makes her high strung, furtive and wary about anything that might disturb the precarious balance. On the other hand, her aunt's reflections on her relationship with her husband accounts for another kind of experience. The fact that it is her second marriage, and that it has given her space for her individuality, is indicative of Deshpande's belief of how the notion of marriage itself needs to be recast. Beyond that, it reflects the emotional comfort of a relationship which grows and mutates with the changing phases of life, which has the awareness of imperfections integrated into itself and which does not have to carry the burden of furtiveness.

The contrast between the two relationships brings out an implicit endorsement of the latter. Deshpande obviously implies that what needs to be pursued by women is a feeling of personal comfort. To assume that it is more easily accessible outside the ambit of institutionalized relationships could be a fallacy. Perhaps an insistence upon space within those established institutions would beget both a sense of individuality and the collective experience of male–female bonding, which is a part of their identity as social beings.

Integrated into this revaluation is the story of Rani's life. A onetime heroine, she has already destroyed her first marriage for a man who eventually refuses to divorce his wife. In the process, she has also divorced her husband, depriving her daughter of the family which should have been her right. Her second marriage is also losing its bonding because in her desire to go back to acting she is once again making her children and husband the second priority. A road accident eventually ends her dreams of stardom forever. Perhaps Rani's life is a reflection of the fact that what lies on the other side and looks like the panacea one has been searching for, might really be an illusion which disconnects us with what might not be perfect but is concrete. In contrast, there is Savi's marriage which is integrated into her responsibilities as a wife, mother, sister and daughter-in-law, more balanced for each one of these, even if the last of them is observed more as a duty.

Deshpande also dwells on the validity or otherwise of a relationship which justifies itself as an expression of personal choice. Throughout her relationship with Ashok, Devayani finds innumerable ways of defending it to herself. Yet, the deviousness which it implies in other spheres of life, leads to a revaluation of her own justifications, which finally impels her to walk out of it, in spite of its seemingly vitalizing impact on her life. This involves the realization that personal liberty, sexual or otherwise, cannot be divorced from the impact it has on others. If it encroaches on the rights of others, as on the adolescent daughter of the man she loves, then there are ethical issues, which if left unaddressed could trap one into yet another kind of claustrophobia. Love might be a wonderful emotion but that does not absolve it of responsibility. Devayani concludes that "The word love can't change anything. It is not a detergent that can wash out the stains. Wrong remains wrong."[27]

Deshpande's fresh feminine perspective, thus advocates a resolute search for identity outside redundant constructs. Her characters rightfully look for a life, which endorses individual desire and equal partnership. This in itself dispenses away with the need for degrading deceptions, projected desires, guilt and anger, which have become a part of woman's life within the false identity imposed upon her. What makes these diverse yet converging concerns significant is the fact that they reflect a grounded common sense which refuses to be carried away by the novelty of theoretical assumptions. Deshpande's keen perception gleans through vital new perspectives and adopts the insights which she sees as imperative for pushing through the much needed change in the way women are perceived and how they perceive themselves. However, she deftly weaves these precepts into the warps and wefts of the social fabric, altering the patterns without renting the fabric itself. It goes to her credit that her far-sightedness amalgamates her surety of purpose with the reality of the larger context, and sees it as a step towards a more balanced system of relationships.

An important strain running through this search for identity is the parallel desire to exercise individuality from within relational structures. Jaya and Madhu are successful in making place for their true selves within their relationships. There are those who are not so lucky. Bai makes an attempt but the system falls short. Sumi keeps the channels open but does not degrade herself with pleas of retrieval. Urmi decides to give the relationship a chance at the risk of being hurt herself. Saru gives Manohar a chance to decide if he can adjust to her reality. Jiji shows that she can survive on her own terms and then goes back into the relational fold, realizing that independence does not necessarily oppose relationships. These women have moved on from the identities imposed on them, towards the real ones. They give themselves the privilege of option and therefore become capable of negotiating a more relevant place for themselves in the existing social order. They know that "it is time to seek a new image of Sita – one who does not have to return to Earth, but can resolutely claim it."[28]

How men respond to these constantly changing relational dynamics and their own precariously poised identities, is discussed in the chapters which follow. The responses analysed are neither simple nor static. The plethora of influences which work upon the displaced notion of the self, results in behavioural shifts which cannot be categorized in simplistic terms. Therefore the particular perspectives from which the role of the husband, the son and the father have been analysed, do not constitute mutually exclusive categories. Each of these portrayals is composed of overlapping strains. The attitudinal inertia, the willingness to share privilege and liability, the supportive stance are possibilities inherent in every male role. They form different stages in the continuum which marks the shift in the very conception of masculine identity.

Notes

1. Diana Meyers. *Gender in the Mirror: Cultural Imagery and Women's Agency.* <http://www.philosophy.uconn.edu/department/meyers/meyers.html.>
2. Shashi Deshpande. "Telling Our Own Stories." *Writing from the Margin and Other Essays.* New Delhi: Viking, 2003. p. 87.
3. *The Free Dictionary.* <http://www.thefreedictionary.com/>
4. Elaine Showalter. "Introduction". *The New Feminist Criticism: Essays on Women, Literature and Theory.* Ed. Showalter. 4th ed. London: Virago Press, 1993. p. 15.
5. MSN Encarta. < http://www.msn.com.>
6. Vijaya Ramaswami. "Researching Icons, Representing Indian Women." *Researching Indian Women.* Delhi: Manohar, 2003. p. 46.
7. Ibid.
8. Uma Chakravarti. "Whatever Happened to the Vedic Dasi: Orientalism, Nationalism, and a Script from the Past." *Recasting Women.* Ed. Kumkum Sangari and Sudesh Vaid. New Delhi: Kali for Women, 1989. p. 79.
9. Kumkum Sangari. *Politics of the Possible: Essays on Gender, History, Narratives, and Colonial English.* New Delhi: Tulika, 1999. p. 161.
10. Susan Gubar. "The Blank Page and Issues of Female Creativity." *The New Feminist Criticism: Essays on Women, Literature and Theory.* Ed. Elaine Showalter. 4th ed. London: Virago Press, 1993. p. 297.
11. Prabhati Mukherjee. "The Eternal Triumvirate." *Hindu Women: Normative Models.* London: Sangam Books Ltd., 1993. p. 50.
12. Ibid., p. 51.
13. Toril Moi. *Sexual/Textual Politics: Feminist Literary Theory.* London: Routledge, 2002. p. 64.
14. Shashi Deshpande. "Telling Our Own Stories." *Writing From the Margin and Other Essays.* New Delhi: Viking, 2003. p. 99.
15. Ibid., p. 100.
16. Shashi Deshpande. "Masks and Disguises." *Writing from the Margin and Other Essays.* New Delhi: Viking, 2003. p. 189.
17. Shashi Deshpande. *Roots and Shadows.* New Delhi: Orient Longman, 1983. p. 2. All other references to this novel are from this edition and page numbers are given in the text in parenthesis.

18. Shashi Deshpande. *The Dark Holds No Terror.* New Delhi: Vikas Publishing House, 1980. p. 92. All other references to this novel are from this edition and page numbers are given in the text in parenthesis.
19. Shashi Deshpande. "In First Person." *Writing from the Margin and Other Essays.* New Delhi: Viking, 2003. p. 16.
20. Shashi Deshpande. *That Long Silence.* UK: Virago Press Ltd., 1988. p. 30. All other references to this novel are from this edition and page numbers are given in the text in parenthesis.
21. Shashi Deshpande. "Masks and Disguises." *Writing from the Margin and Other Essays.* New Delhi: Viking, 2003. p. 189
22. Ibid., p. 182.
23. Shashi Deshpande. *The Binding Vine.* UK: Virago Press Ltd., 1993. p. 183. All other references to this novel are from this edition and page numbers are given in the text in parenthesis.
24. Shashi Deshpande. *A Matter of Time.* New Delhi: Penguin Books, 1996. p. 167. All other references to this novel are from this edition and page numbers are given in the text in parenthesis.
25. Shashi Deshpande. *Small Remedies.* New Delhi: Penguin Books, 2000. p. 256. All other references to this novel are from this edition and page numbers are given in the text in parenthesis.
26. Shashi Deshpande. *Moving On.* New Delhi: Penguin Books, 2004. p. 183. All other references to this novel are from this edition and page numbers are given in the text in parenthesis.
27. Shashi Deshpande. *In the Country of Deceit.* New Delhi: Penguin, 2008. p. 236.
28. Namita Gokhale. "Sita: A Personal Journey." *In Search of Sita: Revisiting Mythology.* New Delhi: Penguin Books, 2009. p. xvii.

4

The Moment of Inertia: Husband

A shift in gender roles demands a concomitant change in the attitudes, not only of those who initiate it, but also of those who feel its consequential effects. Only then can it integrate and blend into the social fabric without causing a rent. This becomes crucial in context of the male response in heterosexual relationships, where the slightest change in existing relational equations threatens the precarious masculine identity, and the entire system of male domination which rests upon it. Deshpande's women, invested with an insight which cuts through the surface, assess the anomalies and insecurities underlying the aggressive and domineering male aura. They see men trying to maintain a forced status quo amidst the socio-ideological changes impacting gender roles. As the consequent bitterness ruptures through the veneer of normalcy and threatens relationships, these women also see the futility of regressive compromises. The only way to retrieve relationships, they realize, is an insistence on recognition of their true identity and it's amalgamation into the social psyche, which must begin from men themselves. It is the strength arising out of this clarity of perception which propels men into new modes of thought, which hold in themselves the promise of perceiving the many benefits of balanced gender equations. They also corroborate with the author's broad vision, which sees female empowerment as a logical step towards a better male–female relationship.

Men in their position as husbands, as portrayed in Deshpande's works, emerge as products of their individual predilections in a complex interplay with their socially drawn roles and gender identities. Their position in the system and milieu which Deshpande writes of is peculiar. The unchallenged authority which culminates into the injunction that "a married woman should worship her husband before all,"[1] bestows upon the Indian husband, a position that has not been open to debate. Interestingly, a husband's position has been privileged, even within the male domain, to which the woman has been expected to subordinate herself. This is reinforced through religion and mythology. Parvati, Siva's consort is "suitably rewarded by fifty two ... places of pilgrimages,"[2] for choosing her husband over her father. Another Sanskrit text eulogizes the woman who places her husband's comfort over her child's life. Deshpande sees in the story, the confident male assertion that "... your duty to *me* comes first. Even the children come second."[3] Such power coupled with hold over economic benefits, placed in the hands of ordinary men, has led over the ages, to assumption of an invincibility of their superior position, irrespective of the validity of their claim to it. However, as this eulogized image is pitted against changing socio-economic conditions, the aura breaks, revealing average human emotions working under pressure to sustain the structures, which provided this privileged identity. The position of power in the gender hierarchy no longer appears invincible, except through the emotional props provided by women. In fact, even in providing those props, women make men dependent because the image of the man is magnified in inverse proportion to the woman's ability to diminish herself. No wonder that these men "react suspiciously to alterations in status arrangements,"[4] and try to maintain status quo through coercive control tactics. Underlying these designs of mastery is the neurosis inducing stress of maintaining the hierarchical difference, because the masculine identity evolving through it has allowed "esteem to become its hostage."[5] Any suggestion of a shift amounts to a demand that men relinquish their mythical status for a human one, that they lift control over the very source which sustains that image. This obviously amounts to a crisis for the male, for whom it is like being asked to aid in dismantling the normative which gives him his identity.

The female assessment however is evaluative not defiant. As Deshpande's women comprehend these anomalies, their attitudes shift from confusion to anger, at times even pity, and finally to a decisive demand for change. They see what men have put at stake in an attempt to maintain their superiority. Apart from inducing bitterness, they have put relationships at risk of deception, leaving no option for women but to create their own survival modes within patriarchal constructs of power. In their bid to wield power, they have risked the loss of emotional binding which might then be sought elsewhere. Besides, they have distorted their own psyche into patterns of domination, destroying the natural instinct for love and nurturance. In this respect, "The liberation of women is also the liberation of men. The tyranny of patriarchy has hurt men more, robbing them of their ability to be this messy thing called humanity."[6]

While Deshpande's protagonists analyse the destructive potential of inflexible male attitudes, they also insist on a change in them, not only for themselves but also for the retrieval of love and respect in their relationships. At the same time, there is a focus on the openness, honesty and companionship in those relationships where men display emotional and intellectual maturity, making place for the woman's individuality and getting in return genuine love, regard and even gratitude. Thus the female gaze does not seek male disempowerment or a dismantling of those social institutions, within which men and women construct relationships. Instead it looks for a new equilibrium in those institutions, and in the male–female interactive zones. It sustains in itself, respect for relationships, and trusts its own ability to validate them through redrawn alignments.

Perceived through the double feminine gaze of the writer and her female protagonists, men in Deshpande's works are portrayed as responding variously to the changes in female sensibility. Jayant in *Roots and Shadows* is so sure of his place as a husband that it never strikes him that his wife could have desires and wishes which originate in her as an individual. Manohar in *The Dark Holds No Terror* gets used to the benefits of having an earning wife but also suffers from a loss of confidence as the male prerogative of being the provider, with its concomitant privileges, gets eroded. Mohan in *That Long Silence* is insistent on maintaining a facade of sharply delineated gender roles, thus falsely hoping to bypass the undercurrents of change which threaten existing power equations. Both Manohar and Mohan create bitterness, driving their relationships to the brink, before showing signs of realization that they would need to locate changed positions in the new paradigms, for saving the relationships they have been trying to dominate. Gopal, in *A Matter of Time*, revels in the pleasures of marriage before deciding to move out of it, because he realizes that he is not cut out for the responsibilities involved. Yet his ego is deflated when Sumi, instead of panicking, utilizes the situation to carve her own freedom. Kishore, in *The Binding Vine* will need to answer Urmi why she requires to take the burden of loyalty upon herself, when there is no reciprocal expression of need from him. Within the story are two other facets of male retaliation to female overtures at self-hood, leading to an irretrievable loss in terms of emotional connections. Meera's husband and Kalpana's uncle represent unchecked male aggression in two separate social strata, one sanctioned by marriage, the other crude and blatant in its disregard for any sanction. Both are brought out in the open by Urmi, who realizes that the social pressure to sweep such issues under the carpet is itself a tool of male control. Som in *Small Remedies*, a loving husband, is nevertheless a product of social conditioning and cannot dissociate marriage from sole possession over body as a precursor to man's relationship with woman. It takes time for him to comprehend the greater importance of emotional bonds, particularly those of pain. This becomes a precursor to an impending change in attitude. Som's attitude is juxtaposed with that of Joe and Hari, who through their balanced, intelligent attitudes, cultivate respect and love in their respective relationships. *Moving On* shows a definite shift through retrospective male analysis, regarding what has been lost in the insistence on dominating relationships. Jiji's father dwells in his diaries, on the inadequacy of his own attitudes, and their contribution in alienating those whom he loves. It also depicts a changed male portrayal, where flexibility of approach leads to acceptance of the changing profile. *In the Country of Deceit,* Deshpande's latest novel explores various attitudes which are generated through the traditional mould. At the same time, it questions the availability of satisfactory options outside the institutionalized security of man–woman relationship.

Roots and Shadows, Deshpande's first novel is like a microcosm of the world she is to create in her following works. Here we find the female gaze assessing the male image, giving us glimpses into its unexplored zones. As Deshpande traces male attitudes through different generations, she points at the changes, but more significantly to the similarities couched in different forms. Indu, back in her family home after many years, discovers an objectivity which distance offers, to retrospect on her own marriage. Her reflections are interspersed with images of other men in the role of husbands, which the vast connections of the family offer. She realizes that if in spite of her education and exposure, her cultural orientation makes it difficult to escape her conditioned responses, it is no different for Jayant, her husband. He too is bound to the identity created for him by generations of cultural and gender conditioning.

Ostensibly suave and educated, Jayant remains the traditional male beneath his exterior polish, who takes it for granted that his wife should blend herself into his conception of her. Equipped with a confidence which comes to him through years of gender conditioning, he exercises his authority through a subtle manipulation of Indu's need to be "loved, desired, admired"[7], thereby moulding her to "... what he wants. What he would like. What would please him" (49). Jayant is sure of complete right over Indu's affairs, which include the kind of work she should take up and the social persona she should maintain. Any digressions into her own desires are met with a silent disapproval, enough to make Indu squirm with discomfort.

Back in her family home, Indu realizes that Jayant is only cosmetically different from her uncle, the small town, conservative male who takes it for granted that his wife should spend her life assisting him in shouldering family responsibilities, thus leaving her to years of cooking, cleaning and catering to the needs of a large extended family. It never occurs to him that she might be a person with desires of her own. Ironically, the moment kaki tries to question the responsibilities imposed upon her, her 'temerity' is attributed to womanly pettiness. In either case these men draw their authority at least partly from the acquiescing female attitude which is quick to suppress its own latent discontent, in order to avoid disapproval.

It is the same fear of disturbing the status quo which prevents Indu from asserting her sexuality as an inherent part of herself. She realizes early that initiation of proximity by her is disapproved by Jayant. On the surface it appears that Jayant does not like the transgression of the imperatives of coyness and docility, the hallmarks of a woman's gender identity. She says, "it shocks him to find passion in a woman" (83). Perhaps deeper in the subconscious is the fear that in doing so the woman is exercising agency, thus challenging the male's mastery over the situation. Lurking in the reader's consciousness is another husband who has forced himself on a mere child, leading her to pain, confusion and humiliation, creating in her a lifetime of anger. When we compare Jayant to Akka's husband, there are obvious differences. Jayant is not aggressive or brutal and in that we see the changes wrought by an exposure to a more civilized way of life. However, the need to master the situation is present in residual forms, even though it takes a different shape. He does succeed in what he considers a battle won, but does not recognize the discontent it induces in Indu.

Why these emotions need to be located and crystallized becomes evident in the dangers they pose to the very relationships they attempt to control. An irrepressible desire to connect to that aspect of herself which has been suppressed for so long, leads Indu into a deliberate and guilt-free physical intimacy with Naren, who recognizes not only the needs of her mind but also those of her body as integral part of her womanhood. Retrospectively, Indu realizes the need to integrate these suppressed parts of her personality into Jayant's perception of her. The process could be difficult, for it would erode the norm through which Jayant perceived himself as a man. His response to the shift in the expected modes of the gender behaviour is expressive of his fear of losing out on the advantages which masculinity and its attributes have ensured for him. She has already experienced the volatility of his response the only time she has had her way in resigning from her job. "He had been furious.

And bewildered. As if I had cheated on him" (13–14). Indu knows that she would have to encounter the same set of emotions each time she declared herself to him. She is ready for it, because she knows it is vital for the realignment of anachronistic paradigms which are inadequate in relation to her own understanding of herself. Jayant might take time to understand what was already clear to her, but their relationship could survive only if it was supported by the possibility of change.

In a way, Saru the protagonist of *The Dark Holds No Terror* is the obvious successor to Indu for she stands at that crucial juncture from where her relationship with her husband must take a decisive direction. Having attempted the guilt-ridden trapeze between her aspirations as an educated professional and the role expected of her by her husband, she finally gives up trying to cope. As she looks back, she can now analyse her husband's mutating attitudes in response to her own growth and success. Her anger at him is underlined by recognition of his pitiable attempts at hanging on to his receding authority, and the dwindling confidence, which manifests itself in cruelty. Saru's analysis of the male response is also underlined by a confession of her own contribution to this crumbling masculine identity and a wish that it could have been otherwise, with the system supporting and integrating her need for growth. In spite of her husband's coercive attempts, she finds it impossible to go back to the traditional female role with its deceptive subservience. If the relationship is to last, the male response would have to change, giving her a more dignified passage for her aspirations of enhancement.

In order to understand Saru's reaction to Manohar's response, it is crucial to understand that on account of her own peculiar background, Saru has grown up differently from other girls, who settle into traditional gender roles, with built-in coping mechanisms, for adjusting to unequal relationships. Saru is hurt by the devaluation arising from her secondary status as a daughter and angry at being told that lack of physical beauty made her a weak contender for male affection, which was the only objective of female life. This results in a personal struggle for autonomy, through which she seeks to alter her status of a liability. She uses professional and scholarly success in place of good looks to achieve a sense of worth.

Manu's success in sweeping Saru off her feet in spite of her independent streak rests on the powerful image endowed upon him by cultural patterns. In spite of her self-empowering efforts outside the gender constructs, the social conditioning which calls for female submission to the superior all-knowing male, takes over. Manu, the soul of the dramatic society, the budding writer, with his superior condescending attitude, his aura of being the master of the situation, the man who decides things, fits perfectly into the picture of the superior male, conditioned into her mental make-up. Saru cannot believe that he chooses her, the plump, pimply-faced, gawky girl, over the beautiful coquettish girls who fall all over him. Starry eyed, she puts her life in his hands, marrying him against her parents' wishes. It is only later that she realizes that this image of being the master of the situation, actually rested on her own denial of her ability to manage life. He could remain smugly ensconced in his larger than life image, only if she did not rise to her full stature.

Looking back, Saru discovers that the superior male integrated into her subconscious, is an image which needs constant sustenance, not just by its magnification but also by the constant diminishing of her own stature. This becomes increasingly difficult to sustain because Saru's better professional qualifications make her more successful than Manohar. She earns more than him, she is the one who picks up loans and raises their standard of living. She even writes his career for him by advising him to become a lecturer instead of a journalist. In doing so, Saru's continuing subordination to the conquering male image become nothing more than "a withering superfluity."[8] By utilizing her own potential optimally, Saru unknowingly diminishes Manu. The designer home, the expensive clothes, the five-star holidays, and even the money required to further her career, are managed by Saru. To make matters worse, her success owes itself to financial help by Boozie, her boss at work. She thus strikes at the root of the male provider image. It is much later that she recognizes that the same thing which made her inches taller, made him inches shorter. The broken image of socially accepted gender dimensions costs both of them in varied measures.

According to Doreen D'Cruz, "the endangered male, unable to accommodate the loss of his mythic validation through the metaphors of rescue and dominance, find it in the act of villainy."[9] Saru discovers how Manu had devised other ways to coerce her into subordination. One of these is infusing her with constant guilt. Her heart gives "painful, quivering little jumps"[10], for as she performs her professional duties, she is constantly aware of the fact that he is observing her absence from home and silently marking the hours in which her focus has shifted elsewhere. She has to constantly prove her penitence and contrition and find ways of appeasing him. As Jeremy Hawthorn says, "a gendered relation to the gaze is both the product of patriarchy (the power exercised by men over women) and also a way of reinforcing male dominance."[11]

She realizes, that under his cool, accommodating facade, she arouses in him, some basic fear about his adequacy as a man. This is manifested in sexual cruelty, which peaks each time he silently skips over references to Saru's role of something more than a homemaker. The recognition she gets as a doctor, finds her "shrinking from his love making" (42). A friend's wife taunts them about going for a holiday at Saru's expense, and this leads to "hurting hands, the savage teeth, and the monstrous assault" (112). His quiet acceptance of the fact that another man is financing his wife's rapid rise in career is followed by suffocating "long devouring kisses" (86). Saru recognizes, as least subconsciously, Manu's desperate attempts to retain his masculinity by forcibly claiming her body. That is why she also recognizes sexual failure as directly related to loss, in terms other than physical.

What Saru find amazing is, that even as he attempts to assert his identity through cruel, underhand means, Manu is pathetic and bewildered in parts, as he desperately tries to retrieve the magnified image, which Saru had once held up for him. As he silently accepts the news of Boozy's financial favours, his aggressive assertion, "that's enough. Come to me now" (86), is strangely accompanied by a pathetically appealing look. His voice just falls short of begging when he says "don't refuse me now" (86). The only time when Manu is the benign protective husband, Saru realizes, is when she appears emotionally vulnerable, seeks his permission or shows guilt in some form. Tired of physical abuse, which she knows originates from her professional success, she offers to quit working. That night she is disgusted at her own tone of appeasement. Manu, on the other hand again becomes "tender, teasing and infinitely protecting ..."(81). Crystallization comes later, when she says, that a woman "can nag, complain, henpeck, whine ..." (137) and get away with it all, for it leaves the man that much bigger and stronger. It is only when she refuses to camouflage her competence, rationality, and strength that she commits "a wrong which will never be forgiven" (137).

In fact, as Saru recognizes gradually, in spite of the reversal of gender roles and the cracks in gender identity, there remains in Manu an urgent need to carry on with the structural facade. He tries to regard all aberrations to the context as non-data, as though the familiarity of the pretence would let him hold on to his "design of mastery ...."[12] The emotional cruelty, the physical abuse that he directs at Saru is never mentioned otherwise. Tired of it, when Saru decides to go to her father's house, he is genuinely bewildered and wonders why she needs to go. When Saru offers to quit work, he says, "but why ... has something gone wrong somewhere" (80)? After a night of sexual savagery she finds the same face smiling at her in the morning, enquiring if she had slept well. Everything has to be a normalized, reassuring, closed retreat, whose balance no upheaval can upset. When he questions about why she looks tired on a holiday in Ooty, she knows that she is expected to give the diplomatically correct answer, never to actually share her troubles. The policing of identity demands not a production of question, but the reproduction of a foreknown answer. "The sole function of female identity is to ensure the validity of its pre-defined answers."[13]

While Manohar practices his coercive control techniques, thinking it would maintain his hold over the relationship, Saru begins to look for alternative means of gratification. Her frequent meetings with Padma, a college friend, clearly rest on his interest in her as a woman. Saru realizes later that she had deliberately initiated the furtive relationship because she had hoped, "... it would give me an escape route, something that would lead me out of my loveless trap" (132). She withdraws from it eventually, but implicit in her initial overture, is the fact that Manu's focus on power tactics has led to a loss in terms of satisfaction in interpersonal relationships.

Saru's journey to the father's home is a more concrete attempt at reclaiming herself as an agency, of her final breaking away from the ethos of masculine privilege. Surprisingly it works its way through her last attempt to reshape herself into the traditional mould. As she tries to slip into the role, which she had seen her mother performing, she crystallizes the power praxis which goes into it. Saru realizes that here women perpetuate the male role and accede its privileges, to find some residual space of their own. The stronger among them employ the same to edge out men from areas they appropriate for themselves as innocuous privileges of their deprived gender. Her mother had managed to dissociate her father totally from the kitchen and the puja room. However on retrospective analysis she realizes that such tactics were the result of a lack of better options. For a woman who could carve out her own security, devious tactics for measly compensations were a redundant option. Equipped with more dignified means of survival, Saru realizes that she cannot revert back to a pattern which entails constant diminishing of the self. Ironically, she is aware that the withdrawal of the supplicatory stance would strike at the root of her husband's identity, making him look like a "victim, grotesque in an enforced death"(44). Yet, it is impossible for her to exist in that moment of inertia, from where Manu refuses to move.

Manohar's attempts at re-establishing communication with Saru, reflects a man's need for his relationship with a woman, despite his high-handed attitude. Saru refuses to respond to his letters and is angered when he tries to use emotional blackmailing by bringing the children into the picture. It is clear that it is not possible to draw her back into old parameters once she has stepped out of them. In his act of coming to Saru's father's house to talk to her, is the implicit recognition of the need to redraw those parameters. If Saru agrees to meet him, it is only to open the avenues for an altered male response, which accepts her in her real dimensions. In agreeing to meet Manohar, rather than running away from him in the end, she keeps alive the scope of new alignments, which understand her need for an equal arrangement.

Jaya in *That Long Silence* is once again a woman integrating in herself, opposing influences, which make it impossible for her to exist in stasis, even if that is the only means of survival in her structured surroundings. The upper-middle class housewife, with all the comforts and amenities of a metropolitan city, suddenly finds herself back in a suburban flat, waiting for the furore over her husband's financial irregularities to fade out. As both Jaya and Mohan find themselves divested of their respective gender roles, cracks begin to surface. These cracks provide Jaya with a channel of vision that looks back at the facade of perfection covering their brittle relationship. Through retrospective crystallization she discovers a not wholly unsympathetic understanding of the anomalies of the male psyche. Hence, at one point when she tells Mohan that she knows him better than he knows himself, neither of them quite comprehend that she has actually penetrated to the skeletal essentials, over which layers of psychological and social demands have piled to create the individual that he is.

Jaya, who is initially only surprised by Mohan's seriousness in upholding the mantle of a responsible provider, traces the force of his purpose to a race against the ghosts of past. Mohan is chasing an image and she, as his wife, has to be "a mediator in his own specular relationship with himself."[14] Time and again, she finds a direct contrast between his childhood experiences and his carefully structured present. Hence, the irresponsible, cruel father of his childhood, who never bothered about the family's insecurities, leaving his mother to work as a cook, and himself on the mercy of others for his education, is replaced by another, who constantly needs to be assured of his worth in terms of the provider. He is driven to providing a good house, a gas connection, a fridge, first-class tickets for travelling, and the best schools for his children. The perfect house which Jaya needs to maintain is a compensation for the sloth in his Saptgiri parental house. His need to have powerful friends is his means of escaping the commonness of his own background. Jaya sees that he is chased by silent forces into a race for accumulating money, status, security, even at the cost of his integrity. So when he is exposed and blames his action on the necessity to provide for her, she is angered beyond measure. She knows that what he has done is part of constructing a self-image. The structured life he has erected around himself is a prop to validate the persona he has created for himself. The slightest crack in the veneer evokes uncontrollable anger. Here, there is no place for Jaya's own set of complexes and needs.

Jaya realizes that far from trying to understand her as she really was, Mohan had been preoccupied with making her undergo the changes dictated by him. The relationship cultivated by him is almost that of a colonizer and colonized. "At the basis of the entire construction is one common motive – the colonizer's need, which substitutes for logic, which shape and explain each of the traits he assigns to the colonized."[15] Here, the need is to trivialize her, for procuring a constant measure to prove his own superiority. So, Jaya finds herself changed from Jaya to Suhasini, "a wife, a smiling placid woman ... a woman who coped."[16] Her talent for writing is deftly converted into a safe 'hobby' which he 'allows' her to pursue within the parameters which he finds correct. Instead of writing about women with real problems, he encourages her to write about Sita, the society lady. Positive reinforcement from Mohan comes only for attributes which make him feel manly. Hence, Jaya's profile changes from that of a spirited young woman to one who was "scared of cockroaches, lizards, nervous about electrical gadgets, hopeless at technical matters, lazy about accounting ... nervous, incompetent, needing male help and support" (76). She now fits the slot of the house-proud woman, whose entire intellect goes into planning meals and changing sheets. He makes her worth centre so totally on this role which he allots to her, that if a button remains unstitched or a meal gets late, she cringes in guilt. She realizes in disgust, that when he praised "I almost wagged my tail like a dog has been petted by its master" (84).

However, the colonizer's identity is an unfulfilled identity. "The colonizer needs the colonized to postulate his superiority."[17] Jaya realizes that her responses all along have been elicited to this effect. Ironically, the more he uses her for such affirmations, the more vulnerable he becomes in terms of his dependence on her. All his questions to her are met with expected answers. So, when he asks her if he has ever been irresponsible, her quick answer is in negative. She feeds his ego, creasing out his insecurities, with dishonest placations and shows him a magnified image, letting authority seep into him. The extent of his dependence is exhausting for her, as she almost feels the burden of his wanting. At one point she compares him to a hydrocephalic boy, whose eyes are always frantically searching for his mother and who whimpers every time she moves away. She can feel his eyes and thoughts following her always.

The urge to assure himself of the completeness of his own world, of the continuity of his own structured experiences, makes Mohan either incapable or impervious to seeing Jaya as an individual, whose need for an identity is greater than what she is in relation to him. He prefers to cut off bits of her, which are not his wife. In the process, he makes himself vulnerable to a deceitful relationship, and leaves her open to emotional fragmentation. While Mohan is busy fitting her into a convenient slot, she is silently internalizing and understanding the factors which have gone into making her mother, mother-in-law, aunts and cousins the persons they are, their lives, silent, trivialized accounts of who cooks better and who controls the husband better, through devious, degrading means. Jaya's attraction for Kamat is the result of his recognition of her as the person beneath the persona. Thus, time and again, she turns to him for sharing her deepest desires. It is the emotional and psychological bonding between them, which at one time finds her on the verge of responding to him at a physical level too.

Structure depends upon stasis, and stasis as Jaya says, is an aberration. External circumstances place Mohan in a time bubble, devoid of props. New voices disturb the carefully silenced zones of his life. Even as Mohan tries to cover up the discontinuities in his experience, Jaya observes the psychological dislocation it causes to him. As he finds himself cooped up, in disgrace, in a house belonging to his wife, Jaya observes him steadily losing his sense of identity – the only one he has known so far. It is significant that Jaya's recognition of the coercion that has gone into reducing her to a 'role', and the cracks in that coercion, are played out in the Dadar flat, the repository of her unpublished failures. It was here that she had once tried to find a voice, but had never been able to lift off the restraint because of the caution invited by her career as a wife. Kamath's advice to throw away that restraint and her turning away from him in his death has been symbolic of her turning away from the potential for authentic narration.

In an ironic reversal of situation, Mohan is no longer the provider, the protector, around whom everybody must structure their needs. Without his files and the paraphernalia he looks lost. A barrage of accusations starts flowing, stunning her with their total lack of context. He digs out incidents from the past, picks up new events in the present, and tells her, "You're so unconcerned" (116), "I've never mattered to you ... how can I expect you to have feelings for me" (119). She realizes then, that the only context in which he has known her is that of a woman, who had married a man with a promising future. His obvious conclusion is that "you despise me because I've failed" (121). There are pathetic attempts to retrieve the situation by referring to past incidents like her being afraid of the striking workers, and his managing the situation, of many other occasions when he had been the protector and saviour.

Jaya's acute realization of the deceit underlying their relationship is strengthened at this emotional bartering. She realizes the potential for destruction in this role playing, for both the transcriber and the transcribed. Images clutter her consciousness. Mohan's precarious persona reminds her of the big sheltering tree which had died because over-watering had led to white ants eating it away. Jaya knows that she has nurtured his larger than life image with lies, because it served her purpose as well. It has kept Mohan safely tied to his superior image, and her well provided for. But in the process, she had reduced him to a pathetic creature, constantly dependent upon her placation for the sustenance of that image. The moment she refuses to provide the input, Mohan becomes like a child, from whose mouth the nipple has been snatched. While Mohan has remained smug in his orchestrated role playing, in which Jaya willingly or unwillingly has participated, their relationship has lost both companionship and compatibility. She realizes that her relationship with Mohan would not sustain, if she allowed the dishonesty and deception to continue.

Mohan's angry reaction at Jaya's decisive break, with both the role playing and the deceit it involves, indicates how difficult it is for a man to relinquish a role, which has ensured his ostensible position of power. Mohan goes away from home, leaving Jaya in anguish and emotional disarray. However she refuses to buckle down under pressure, or to acquiesce to the old pattern in their relationship. Therefore, when Mohan's telegram announces his impending return, we find in it an implicit assent to Jaya's insistence on change. It reflects his awareness of the necessity to re-negotiate a place for himself in the changing relational paradigms. This also presages a relationship which will be based on honesty and recognition of each other's needs, rather than constant role playing involving power struggles. What Jaya has initiated is an insistence on an authentically worded text, through which she would continue participating in her duties as Mohan's wife and her children's mother. She however would no longer speak in the baby lisp of Prakrit, vacating the central role for Mohan. Mohan would have to participate in the process of her integration into the restructured paradigms, giving her an equal status in their relationship. This she realizes is essential not only for retrieving her own dignity, but his as well.

Sumi in *A Matter of Time* analyses the precepts through which the male attitudes work, and discovers their roots in the socio-economic and cultural structures which combine to place the woman in a position of subordination, requiring her to assess her worth in terms of male approval. As a corollary she also studies the response to the change in female attitude, as she works her way through these socio-cultural constraints, towards an independent identity. Sumi's first exposure to male response comes from her observation of the relationship shared by her parents, Kalyani and Shripati. This is aptly captured in their wedding photograph where Kalyani's pose as a new bride, with a nervous appeal for affirmation is contrasted to Shripati's stern self-centred expression, which makes his identity complete, irrespective of the woman standing next to him. The very fact that Kalyani's mother has willed her property to her brother and then persuaded him to marry her daughter, decides the hierarchy in the relationship and gives the prerogative of assertion to the male. Shripati's response to the loss of their only son, for which he blames Kalyani, reeks of the same arrogance. He locks himself in the upper story room, breaking all connection with his wife with a finality which refuses to consider her frustration and grief. The arrogance which makes him sure that she would still continue to respond to his bell, hinges on the knowledge that her position as a married woman is her only claim to respectability in society. Sumi's memories of her mother's hysterical overtures to win him back, of her hitting herself in frustration and her father's unmoved attitude are embedded in her psyche, moulding her own future attitudes. Deep in her unconscious is the realization that the arrogance of the male response is directly proportional to the female susceptibility to it, in economic and emotional terms.

It is not surprising then that Sumi's attempts to break out of the masculine stronghold begin early. She breaks out of the paternal hold, while still unmarried, by going to Gopal's room in the middle of the night and asking him to marry her. Even her role as a wife and mother is marked by a refusal to live up to a role. Her laid back housekeeping, her unhurried attitude, her refusal to prove her maternal instincts (she at one time refuses to nurse her child) and her refusal to be infused with guilt for having borne three daughters, are ways of maintaining her individuality and means of breaking out of male authority. Thus, when Gopal walks out on her and her three young daughters, her response is not characterized by typical female submission to the strictures of the male order. It evokes anger which is coupled with the silent resolve of not letting herself become an object of pity as a deserted wife and mother of three daughters. Her repose and equanimity appear strange to others because there is "no maxim available to account for it."[18] It is precisely in negating the norm and in stepping out of the binary, that she acquires the clear questioning gaze which looks at the male attitude, stripping it of its aura of philosophic intellectualism.

Her gaze rests not only upon the man but the male system, which presumes the male assumption of a central role and then projects it as limiting to man's pursuit of higher goals. She is not impressed by the many explanations Gopal offers for his abdication of all responsibilities. His claim of a lack of trust in the permanence of relationships because of a breach of faith by his father is not substantial enough. Neither is she interested in his pseudo ramifications about the ultimate aloneness of human beings. His pursuit of an elusive quadrant, where he wants to seek an answer outside the present, does not absolve him in her eyes. Rather she questions the self-centredness of the male attitude which gives itself the option of walking out of a relationship which is built on a trust in his honesty and responsibility towards it. Her gaze is fixed on the fact that Gopal has dismantled the entire structure resting upon him. She says, "The 'why' that all of them are pursuing leaves me cold."[19] What angers her is the fact that Gopal has left her and her daughters with a begging bowl in their hands. "If Gopal's life is shaped by his being what he is, what about us ... we are here because of his actions" (27). She thinks of him in context of his favourite lines, "Like children at play/who build a mud house, and then/tiring of the game/destroy it and go away" (84). As Jasbir Jain say, this "puts a question mark on the four fold division of ashramas which gives the husband the choice of moving out of a householder's life."[20]

Sumi's anger is validated when she discovers that while she and the children undergo the trauma of being deprived of a familiar life, Gopal is living close by, never thinking of informing them of his whereabouts, and saving them the humiliation of their desertion becoming public knowledge. She perceives the same self-focused attitude in Gopal's inability to be touched by the plethora of emotions he has unleashed by his action. He cannot relate to Sumi's grief, to Charu's confusion, Aru's anger or Kalyani's pleas. All he can think of is his own intellectual need, even if its fulfilment rests upon the pain inflicted on others.

The same self-centredness is implicit in Gopal's assumption that his need to get away from the physical life would automatically coincide with an end to Sumi's physical desires as a woman. Sumi can see that while the male sexuality is naturalized, a woman's sexuality is suppressed in the sphere of relationships and symbolic values. Whether it is the rejected Kalyani, the widowed aunt, or the deserted Sumi, their sexual needs are non-data, because recognition of their sexuality would prove dangerous to the patriarchal system. Among other things, patriarchal arrangements encode "intense resentment of individual mobility through beauty or sexuality."[21] Therefore a woman needs to deny her physical and emotional needs if marriage fails to provide the same. There is never an attempt to analyse the coercion behind her mute assent. As Sangari says, "Could she guarantee ... chastity or asceticism without extra familial institutional structures to support?"[22] Even her daughters resent her seeming proximity to a male colleague. Sumi's interpretation of Surupanakha's open assertion of her sexuality and the anger evoked by it, aptly analyses the male response to a woman's sexuality, through the ages.

Looking at patriarchal modalities, from the vantage viewpoint of a woman untethered to relationships, Sumi discovers herself as an individual outside the phallo-centric structures. From here she can see that the patriarchal-conjugal fiefdoms, both male domains, force the woman to resort to cunning manoeuvring, if she has to survive. The story of the princess, who manipulates the father to marry the man of her choice, leads Sumi to wonder whether she would also find another weapon to retrieve the power, which that man would definitely assume, once he marries her. Could it be a weapon that would not destroy her as well? Sumi is angered at the degrading options open to women and decides to opt out of the system, to find more dignified means of sustenance, where power is in her own hands, not in another's.

Sumi also recognizes that the male insistence on being the sole focus in his relationship with a woman, is also a means of control through which the man curbs her ability to engage in multiple bonds. This neurosis inducing emotional limitation deprives a woman of emotional buffers. She recognizes the retrieval of this ability to connect to others, as a strategy of survival adopted by Kalyani so that towards the end, it is Shripati, the melancholic old man, who sits alone in his room, while Kalyani learns to weave a "complex network of relationships like a spider scuttling through point to point, drawing silken threads out of itself, weaving in the process a beautiful design" (184). The same multiplicity is manifest in the female's capacity for resurgence, which provides her with fresh beginnings in the cycles of growth and renewal, of which she is a participant. Sumi sees Kalyani's life evolving in her oneness with the cycle of seasons and festivals. Shripati on the other hand, is restricted to his room, ugly and incongruous like a stopper on further growth. Similarly, while Gopal finds every situation a dead end, and eventually reaches a point, from where there is nowhere to run to, Sumi stays where she is, and discovers that "nothing is over, things keep coming back over and over again" (219). Seema's menarche, while her own cycle is turning erratic, Aru's association with Hrishi, while her own relationship is conclusively ending, the beauty of life in spite of its ugliness, are all a part of that resurgence. The female gaze thus discovers its own power, its ability to adapt, evolve, invent and move on, once it breaks through the rules inscribed by the male order.

It is Gopal's reaction to the changed, more empowered Sumi, which clarifies the presumptions beneath the facade of his hermit like detachment from relationships. Sumi, empowered through her own small efforts, becomes increasingly independent. She learns to drive, picks up a job and eventually arranges for an independent set up in another city. Along with it she gets a sense of achievement, which infuses her with a new life. Emotional and financial independence, rejuvenate her. When she goes to Gopal the one last time to inform him of her future plans, she observes Gopal's deflated response to her revivification. She notices the puzzled look on his face, when she talks of his going in terms of his 'moving elsewhere' rather than in terms of 'leaving them'. She realizes that there is something subdued about him as he listens to her plans about future. His excitement, when he thinks that she is about to grant him his freedom, is deflated when he realizes that she has instead come to ask for hers. Even as he says, "I am glad for you" (223), Sumi knows that his tone, in spite of the emphatic words, is flat and dull. He looks chastened. She also realizes that there was nothing she could do for him, "not now anyways" (223).

If Sumi is angered at the duplicity of a system biased towards the male, her objectivity also locates male helplessness in a system which imposes constructs of masculinity, which are not always congruent with individual personalities. She realizes that the system constructs larger than life images, and imposes them upon men not suited to it, in the process, staking the security of all those who come to depend upon them. It is towards the end that Sumi, wiser and more mature, begins to see her father as a victim of patriarchy too. Underlying Shripati's arrogance, she realizes, is the anger at being coerced into a role of responsibility which leads him into a loveless marriage and destroys his professional ambitions. The life of a recluse, which he chooses to live, involves loneliness for him too. Perhaps the same holds true for Gopal as well. He, Sumi realizes, is not cut out for the role of responsibility which marriage brings. She has known all along that he always had it in him to leave her and the children. His inability to sustain relationships over the years, his whimsical resignation from the job which provides for his family, are indication of a man who cannot fit into the image of the provider. Yet, propelled by custom, he takes on the role and eventually fails at it, putting so many other lives into distress.

The changing identity of women elicits a change of response from men. The crises which Sumi faces and the strength of purpose with which she handles it, makes Shripati see the necessity of equipping the daughter in emotional as well as material terms. This realization also influences his attitude as a husband. He rectifies a lifelong mistake by willing the property, once belonging to Kalyani's parents, back to her. Gopal too returns to his daughters after Sumi's death in an accident, indicating a revised understanding of her stature, and a renewed need for connection to her. As he goes to Alaknanda to immerse her ashes, he hopes to retrieve a part of their relationship through memory. There is a trace of regret that the freedom which Sumi had desired had come to her in the form of death. In this regret lies the revised male perception which recognizes a woman's desires and her identity as separate from the image imposed upon her by society.

Madhu in *Small Remedies* is yet another link among Deshpande's protagonists who observe the varying male responses to the changing female ethos. If on one side, she looks at the inflexibility of those responses, on the other hand she discovers that alternatives do exist. The possibility of a parallel growth is seen as imperative for a shift to more satisfying paradigms.

Madhu has grown up in a set-up, which makes her responses different from traditional ones. Brought up motherless, by an unconventional father, who never imposes the usual restrictions upon his only daughter, she has not learnt to submerge her individuality to outside dictates. Her father dies when she is fifteen, leaving her in the custody of her unconventional aunt, Leela. Madhu fights her own battles (as with Paula), forges lifetime relationships (as with Joe and Tony). At the first opportunity, she takes up a job to gain financial independence and begins living on her own. Som meets this unconventional girl who lives alone, does not mind boys coming to her room, and even shares an occasional drink with them.

When she marries him, she presumes an equation which keeps into account her individual make up. Instead, she finds that marriage brings with it a unidimensional image which alone can sustain and validate the relationships associated with it. In one awkward twist, Som who has known her as a tough independent person, begins perceiving her as a waif-like delicate creature, a frightened, worried and fragile woman, who needs her husband's support and protection. When she startles him by saying that she wants physical intimacy as urgently as he does, the data is quickly slipped into incomprehension. Madhu soon recognizes that a family for Som is like a school primer, setting out relationships and goals. "This is baba. He is the father. He goes out to work. This is aai. She is the mother. She looks after the home and children."[23] Each one plays out the allotted role to perfection – so different from her own set of chaotic relationships. Madhu gets further sucked into this game of 'house, house' with the birth of her son Aditya. Every role now achieves validity because of the support systems it provides to him.

In this ordered male world, Madhu discovers, there is no place for stray emotions, which defile the image of the woman as constructed by man. Any aspect of her life outside these constructs, challenges his control over her. The crisis occurs when from the recesses of her unconscious, there emerges the memory of a sexual encounter at the age of fifteen. Madhu's first response is to tell Som about it, for she regards him as one with herself. She expects him to understand her panic at discovering that the man (her father's mistress's son), had committed suicide because of what happened between them. But, what follows rips apart Som and Madhu's relationship, reducing Som to a possessed man, who is sure that her silence conceals untold things. He begins questioning her relationship with her friends, her cousins and even Tony, whom she treats like a brother.

Madhu recognizes that for a man, ever more important than an intact hymen was the intact control over the woman's self. Man cannot accept that there is any part of a women's life, which is not revealed to him and stamped by him. Being a woman, she is not entitled to any privacy, which maintains her identity as a person other than her husband's wife. She says, "... for the first time I understand that I should have offered my entire life as starter to our matrimonial meal" (256). She knows she could have assuaged his grief and anger if she had presented the episode as a rape in which she was a victim not participant. But she cannot do so, because that is not how it was. A man, she discovers, before being a friend, a partner, a parent, remains a male assessing his right over his woman. While she tries to convey her horror implicit in that act of self-destruction, all Som can think of is the single act of sex – "how often it had happened, how long had it gone on" (262). In the days to follow, he changes from the genial, generous, affectionate man she had married to a distraught, possessed one, who turns savage in his love making and is bent upon ruining their relationship. Jasbir Jain sees this obsessive concern with ownership of body as the same instinct which propels men to claim land and property, thus making a "... travesty of the holistic idea of marriage as a companionship."[24] As memories flood in, in another time frame, Madhu draws a parallel between this ruin and the ruins of the Vijaynagar Empire. In either case the seeds of their destruction are inherent in the exploitation on which these institutions are based. Marriage like monarchy is destroyed by its power politics. Madhu dwells upon the futility of the collective amnesia which denies these power struggles that shape man–woman relationships.

It is Madhu's subsequent shift away from home and her interaction with people living through shifting stages of gendered parameters, which gives her a comparative perspective on man–woman relationship. Her interaction with Lata and Hari, with whom she lives in Bhawanipur, and her analysis of the particular identity which the male system has imposed upon Bai, acquaints her, both with the possibility of changed equations and their necessity for making relationships more fruitful for men and women. Her comparison of the different situations clarifies the uselessness of male control tactics, considering the cost they incur in terms of relational hostilities, and the rewards that could be gained by a change in perspective.

As she compares, the sense of fluidity in the Hari–Lata household, with her own rigidly structured life of 'Aai Baba Images', Madhu discovers that relationships exist more spontaneously in parameters which change along with the changing times. In Madhu's shift between the past and present, the two male responses, i.e., Som's and Hari's stand contrasted. Som has tried to fit Madhu into an image. Hari fits the image around Lata. Hari does not mind adjusting to Lata's life, sharing her ancestral home, and helping her in looking after her father and his business. The ease with which Hari can cook a meal, his ability to enjoy the passion with which Lata cleans her scooter, while the house remains undusted, reflects the movement out of gendered norms. Hari, while retaining his male role, accepts Lata's participation in their responsibilities, so that she works to support him through his project. Contrasted to this is Som's insistence on pursuing the provider image by accepting humiliating assistance by an old friend, but treating his wife's talent for writing as a hobby and not a profession. As opposed to Som's and Madhu's carefully constructed veneers, Hari and Lata, with their broken Kannad-English conversations, actually relate to each other. Madhu realizes that she is sharing the house "not with a married couple, but with a pair of lovers" (39). The openness of this house where no doors are ever closed is a contrast to the darkness of the other house where the curtains are always drawn.

While the ability to change marks Hari's attitude, Joe, Leela's husband, embodies the ability to dissociate relationships from a sense of possession. As Joe rightly puts it, love is an adult emotion. It requires respect for each other's identities and the construction of a relationship around that respect. Joe's attraction to Leela rests upon her grit and her capability to give herself to others. The rebel among six sisters, who studies after marriage, sustains her dead husband's family and finally involves herself with social issues, is anything but the eternal clinging female. Yet, Joe waits fifteen years before she says yes to his proposal. When she does, they connect to each other as persons – she in her 'ayah sarees', her Marathi outpourings and her love for chai-pao, and he, with his quotes from Bronte and elitist lifestyle. Madhu recognizes that the relationship between these two middle-aged people is like that of young lovers. Since Joe's love rests on the individual and not on the image, it does not require seeking Leela in the unidimensional role of a wife. She maintains her connection with Maruti chawl, the locus of her identity as an individual. Her financial independence and her room in Maruti chawl symbolize the alternatives that he accords to her, so that their relationship does not suffer from claustrophobia. When Joe eventually dies, Leela's quiet and dignified response, mourns the loss of cherished companionship. It is not marred by the panic of widowhood or fear of financial insecurity.

Interwoven into these comparisons lies Savitri Bai's story, which gives Madhu a glimpse into another world, which stands separated from other lives, just as her own life stands separated from that of Lata and Hari. Madhu sees Bai's life in context of the male world's inflexibility to accommodate facets of a woman, which oppose her assigned role. Her passion for music cannot be integrated into her identity of a married Brahmin woman. Her husband is portrayed as a silent voice, which will not or cannot break through the male ethos to accommodate his wife's individuality into the system. The best she can get there is a pathetic music teacher or opportunity to listen to music concerts from the women's quarters, "... the world of food, cooking, festivals, rituals, pregnancies ..." (219). The same male obsession with the 'role' comes in way when she approaches Pundit Kushinath Buwa from within the precincts of married life. He too feels that music is no profession for a respectably married woman.

Ironically, when she forgoes this respectable married identity, by going away with Ghulam Saheb, she is accepted into the exclusive domain of male initiation by the same guru. The system, which is instrumental in the course she chooses, presupposes that she has chosen less respectable means of male support for furthering her career. Even Chandru, the 'modern' man, who continues having affairs after his marriage, asks Madhu not to write of his father having being Bai's physician because then people would put two and two together. It is a different matter that Bai has never taken the easy way out. She has not even married Ghulam Saheb to give respectability to their relationship. The temerity of a woman who refuses to put up facades in deference to male parameters obviously evokes a reaction, slotting her a woman of easy virtue.

The silent zones of Bai's life represent those aspects of male aggression which punish a woman for her transgression of the limits constructed around male interests. They impose a heavy penalty for her refusal to suppress her difference fiom the prescribed role. The most touching of these is the "erasing of her from her daughter's life" (283), symbolized in her daughter's marriage card, where the mother's name does not figure. There is something pathetic in Bai's attempts to portray her life as complete as she understands the price she has had to pay. Implicit in this pathos seems the authorial wish for a system, which could integrate female individuality in relationships and social structures. When Madhu leaves Bhawanipur, she carries with her tapes and documents pertaining to Bai's life. It becomes symbolic of an effort at understanding the past. This understanding has to become the instrument of change – as long as there is memory, there is always the possibility of retrieval. Som's letter, asking her to come home, and her decision to do so, presupposes the retrieval of their relationship through more flexible contexts.

Urmi in *The Binding Vine* is Madhu's companion in this revision of identities. An educated, independent woman, she lives with her mother and children while her sailor husband is an occasional visitor to the house. The crisis occurs when her young daughter dies leaving her numb. She is unable to experience the grief, and hence be released from it. The inability to let down her armour against grief leads her to an analysis of her own attitudes, and traces it among other things, to her wariness of the vulnerability of emotional dependence, particularly in her relationship to her husband.

Urmi's penetrative gaze has seen through the pattern of male responses in her parents' relationship, early in life. Her father's silent assertion of control is manifested, in his word being the last on all matters. Inni, moulded in the traditional image, can only be an instrument for the implementation of his desires, never the one to emphasize her own. As it is revealed later, she cannot even have her way, when for perceived negligence she is separated from her daughter, who is sent away by her husband to live with his parents. Inni, as Urmi remembers, could be subjected to her father's disapproval whenever she transgressed. She remembers her father's utilization of anger and silence as weapons against which Inni had no defence. At such times Urmi could see "her constant pre-occupation with his feelings, her groping towards him, her hurt when he rejected these overtures."[25] Inni's only form of appeal, was redrawing the feminine role, and crawling back into the comfort of male protection.

The attitude entrenched in childhood gets magnified when Urmi grows up and enters into adult heterosexual relationship. She sees male insistence on woman's dependency, in economic and emotional terms, as means of coercive control. It is a tool for keeping the woman in a position of vulnerable subordination. Urmi is quick to grasp that the sense of vulnerability, and the threats associated with it, would increase manifold in a relationship, in which her own predilection for it grew out of her social conditioning. She knows that she has succumbed to it by falling in love with Kishore, precisely because he had taken things in his hands and broken through her vulnerability after her grandfather's death. Her armour now is her insistence on a spartan living within her own means, and refusing to use the money sent by her husband. Male response comes in the form of Kishore's terming it the 'kept woman' syndrome where the male might withdraw at any time and therefore necessitate strategies of survival by the woman. For Urmi, it is a question of maintaining her selfhood.

Kishore stays away for months at a stretch returning home for short periods, only to leave again, without investing those meetings with any tangible emotional assurance. Urmi deals in silence, with her physical needs and the emotional deprivation which comes from living alone and dealing with the requirements of two small children. Her gravitation towards the young bachelor doctor causes concern to her mother and sister-in-law. But Urmi finds in this relationship, a focus on her as a person, her desires and thought processes. Beneath her competent facade is a woman who wants companionship and openly expressed love, which her husband considers trivial. Not wanting to show her vulnerability, she maintains a strong exterior. Yet it makes her susceptible to other emotional props.

The totalitarian control which Urmi wants to avoid at all costs is also evident in the attitude of Harish towards Vanaa, Urmi's childhood friend and now her sister-in-law. It does not escape her notice that Harish can construct modes of control out of every day practices. The order and perfection he expects is like a demon pursuing Vanaa. The rooms have to be cleaned, the children bathed in time, the *poories* rolled out perfectly. Even if Harish is not around the routine set by him has to be meticulously followed as if has some kind of remote control over her. The contradiction is that the vulnerability on which Harish plays, also gives him the option of leaving all the responsibilities on Vanaa. She is to be blamed if anything goes wrong, she is the one to slog workman like, and also the one who has to cope with everything. The instrument of control is so subtle, that Vanaa is not even aware of it. When Urmi tells her not to crawl before Harish, her surprised answer is, "I don't crawl, and I do what I want" (80). However, Harish knows what he is doing. Vanaa's nervous running around, her attempts at making him feel important, are not laughed off. They are expected and endorsed. Urmi observes he has no humour in such matters. For Urmi, this is too big a price to be paid for the comfort zone of an allotted role.

If Urmi's attitude remains incomprehensible to others, she finds its corroborative echoes in the poetry of Meera, her mother-in-law. The poems depict male insistence upon total possession, and what it can do to women like Meera and Urmi. The male world brushes aside Meera's attempts at self-expression as non-data, as is evident in a contemporary poet's advice to her to go home and produce children. The same negation of identity manifests itself in marriage which changes her name and then her whole being, till she finds herself resembling her mother, who could do nothing and was eventually reduced to being nothing. Urmi traces Meera's attempt at retaining the self amidst the system which uproots, segregates, and expects a woman to feel contented with the morsels provided to feed her soul and spirit. The force against which she is pitted is the entire structure, represented by her husband who rapes her night after night in an obsessive pursuit of the self which she denies to him.

The analysis of the male reaction to a woman who refuses to submit is also analysed in terms of its manifestation in the lower strata of society. The impulse remains the same but the response gets reflected in all its crudity, because of the lack of superficial social veneers. There is Shakutai, for whose raped daughter Urmi is putting up a fight. Married to a man who neither works himself, nor lets her work, she finds herself living the life of wretched dependence, where she faces the constant humiliation of financial constraints. All she gets for her submission to his ego-bound insistence on her dependence, is shelter in a condescending relative's home and her husband's demand for his conjugal rights, even if the only place available is a public passage. When Shaku refuses to live this wretched life and decides to work and educate her children, retribution is quick and comes in the form of the other woman who is allowed to usurp her place as the wife.

The male threat of withdrawing security if a woman attempts to find an identity outside his domain, can crush the weaker among them, as is portrayed in the character of Shaku's sister, Sulu. However, the irony inherent in the woman's subordination to such coercive modes of domination is its impact upon her self-worth. Sulu, the fearful, trembling, waif like sister, scrubs and cleans till her home and vessels shine, but is still afraid that her husband might desert her because of her lucoderma and her inability to produce a child. The degradation that a woman can suffer, by man's exploitation of these fears, is portrayed in Sulu's complicity in catering to her husband's base desire to marry her niece. The incentive is the promise that he would allow her to live on, in his home. In the end, when she realizes that he has raped Kalpana, she commits suicide. Shakutai echoes Urmi's belief that "nobody should live like that ... so full of fears. What kind of life is it" (195)? The arrogance of the male attitude is also reflected in Sulu's husband's attitude towards Kalpana, Shakutai's sprightly confident daughter, who refuses her uncle's lecherous advances and ends up facing the inhumanity which the need to control can lead a man to. Unable to bear her decision to marry a boy of her own choice, he rapes her so brutally that she ends up in coma, in a hospital.

Shaku's decision to register a police case against her absconding brother-in-law, in spite of the social stigma attached to her daughter's rape, is symbolic of a fight against the male-dominated society which uses convoluted psychological pressures to elicit a coerced silence in response to its control tactics. It reflects the changing perspectives, where the sister's death or daughter's rape can no longer be shrouded in secrecy. It is only in breaking through, the seemingly invincible male domain, that life can move on. Urmi's silent support to Shaku's decision is heavy with the realization that the terrain is a difficult one. What lies ahead burdens Urmi, but for her and her likes, there is no alternative but to trudge on resolutely, insisting upon an acknowledgement of their selfhood in the male world. Significantly, Shaku's initiative coincides with Urmi's own decision to voice her discontent to her husband. She realizes the need to bring out issues into the open, instead of simply bearing them, or turning defensive against them. The power struggle inherent in the male propensity for control and the female struggle to escape, leads to a terrible waste of the emotions of love and binding. It requires a mutual decision from both to reach a balance, from where relationships retrieve these essential components and relinquish the underlying power struggle.

Moving On is different from the other novels because the perspective belongs to a woman, who has already done away with the necessity of subordinating herself to social roles. In the process of dealing with a broken marriage, betrayal, widowhood and struggle to survive as a single woman in man's world, Jiji has moved on from being a young girl eager to please, to a mature woman who lives by her own rules. Her gaze travels retrospectively, assessing male attitudes and their import on relationships. Since the novel is structured around Jiji's reading of her father's diaries after his death, the female gaze very often gains depth from male introspection, as emerging from her father's writings. In a definite advance from the earlier novels, this interaction of visions involves not only a woman's objective analysis, but also a revision of male attitude which promises a different approach, if given another chance.

It is primarily Jiji's analysis of her parent's relationship which brings the male attitude under scrutiny. The revaluation of the fairy-tale image of her father and mother, which had all the elements of a stock romance to a child's eyes, reveals the subtle power wielding by the father and the undercurrent of resistance by the mother, which explains the eventual disintegration of their relationship. Jiji realizes that her father's claims of giving his wife the central place within home are countered by the unspoken assertion that it is his decision which would ultimately prevail. Mai had been a hub only in theoretical terms. Looking back from an adult perspective, Jiji recognizes that her father "gave in only when it was something that didn't matter to him. When it came to things he cared for, yes he had his way."[26] Even more significant was the fact that "... he never openly stated his wishes, so you never knew he had got what he wanted. It sort of slid from your hand to his" (29). Whether it is small matters like having the picture of the skeleton in the house which Mai eventually has to get used to, or the ritualistic Sunday visits to B.K.'s house when she would have liked to go for a movie or something else, are examples of the same assertion of authority. There are other things too. The annual visit to Baba's sister's home in Bangalore is undertaken despite Vasu's discomfort. Neither can she do anything when Baba decides to break off with her brother Laxman. Jiji says, "Now that I've opened the records, the list of battles she lost seems endless, I could go on and on" (30). The arrogance implicit in the attitude becomes clearer to Jiji because she sees that there is a conscious and deliberate dismissal of her mother's silence, boredom and displeasure. Sadly the male need to assert supremacy gains ascendancy over genuine love. Jiji rightly wonders, "was he really so unaware of these things as he seemed to be? Or was it just a huge pretext" (30). She also realizes that her mother had understood the mechanics of power, and her innermost desires had surfaced in stories, where woman were not only respected and loved but were also "in positions of power ..." (123).

The novel also reflects male refusal to see a woman beyond the role he wishes her to be in. As Jiji thinks back, she realizes that her father had always projected her mother as someone to be protected. Jiji's childhood memories are permeated with images of Mai's head on Baba's shoulder, Baba's hand around Mai's waist, Baba's treatment of her as something fragile. She also remembers how Mai had always seemed stiff and distant as she played along because she had no option. She understands that it must have been difficult for a woman for whom her individuality mattered. Jiji recognizes that "what she valued most was freedom, freedom to be by herself, freedom to be on her own" (125). However, images of her keeping account of her earnings as a writer and her radiance when she takes out the family for a treat with her own money, are accompanied by dismissal by Baba as one dismisses a child's excitement. All it elicits from him is an indulgent teasing that he would leave his job and become a house husband because she could run the house with the money she earned.

The adult Jiji realizes how her father had very matter of factly proclaimed himself and his career as more important than her mother's work. In fact Vasu's substantial literary output, which had made her a recognized name in media, even leading to one of her stories being filmed, is always treated as secondary and inconsequential. Thus, while Baba's profession is a loud fact in their lives, Mai's work is never visible. "It was a kind of secret business, an activity she did in private, something, no one in the family ever spoke of" (121). Jiji remembers how it had been taken for granted that Mai would remove her papers from the study table and shift to the dining table when her father returned home. While his papers and journals lay strewn all over the house, her work was always kept out of sight. In fact her father had never ever read anything written by her because he had considered her writing trivial and flimsy compared to his own work. He never sees it as the reflection of her deepest feelings. Much later, Jiji wonders if her mother's revulsion at the physicality of her relationship with her father had been part of her resistance to being treated like a body alone, when her intellect was as much a part of herself. It is only much later that he realizes that in brushing aside her first attempt to involve him in her inner world, he had created a permanent distance. He says, "I failed to understand that this for her was as intimate a moment as when she let me see her body" (197).

As Jiji delves into these issues, she also questions the male assumption that a woman's subliminal discontent would not affect relationships in the long run. Jiji can see that silent anger, like termite had eaten away into what her parents had shared with each other. This is reflected in the change in Vasu's writings. The effacing woman of her initial story *Annapurna*, who submerges herself into the demands of the system, for her final reward – the husband's praise, gives way to *Mansi*, where the protagonist refuses to live with her husband in spite of all external luxuries that he offers, till he finally meets her on an equal footing. Finally there is *Black Out*, where she abandons the saccharine-sweetness of romance and family life and picks up "the spiked burr of lust, cruelty and hatred ..." (127). The woman here turns the man's privilege of decision-making upon him, so that he is beaten up by the crowd, while she switches off the lights, undresses, sensuously touches her bruised body and goes off to sleep. The change reflected in these stories also gets manifested in the distance between Baba and Mai, later in life, proclaimed by separate rooms with their single ascetic beds.

As Jiji goes through her father's diaries she discovers that eventually he too recognizes his own contribution to this disintegration. There is regret in his tone, when he writes, "I had to accept, I know nothing of her real life" (56). It is his realization of his deliberate diminishing of her potential, which makes him cringe like a coward, when later he is asked to speak on her contribution as a feminist writer. He also recognizes that over the years, Vasu had distanced herself from him. "I wanted to hold her close and comfort her, I wanted to take away that pinched look and bring back the composed, in-control-of herself Vasu. But I could not help, for she would not admit her hurt to me" (198). In fact he wonders if this lack of communication between them had made her bring her own death, for lack of a buffer with which to shield herself from the tragedies of her life.

This confessional male voice holds in itself the promise of an altered approach, for it recognizes the loss entailed by the power play in relational terms.

In the Country of Deceit does not have the husband's role as pivotal to its plot but the backdrop displays vestiges of the relational structures dealt with in earlier novels. Deshpande for instance, reconstructs Devayani's father as a husband through her reminisces and through what his sister Sindhu remembers of him. A nondescript man, he typifies the belief that as the provider of the family it is below his dignity to use his wife's money, even though he has to incur debt for their daughter's wedding. It is easy to see that he is a man caught in the expectations of a gender role which he is unable to live up to. Not only is he unable to meet the financial needs of the family but is also a failure in all ambitious ventures that he begins so that his meagre finances shrink further. A lifetime of futile effort to execute the dynamic male role eventually leads to a depression-induced suicide. Although Devayani's mother insists on remembering him as her knight in shining armour, Devayani knows that his unhappiness had filtered through to her life as well. Much as she grieves for him, the family is better off after his death and she less disjointed by constant awareness of his inability to reach anywhere.

In contrast we have the portrayal of men who instead of pursuing an image, prefer to be themselves and emerge as balanced individuals who make better companions as husbands. Keshav for instance has married Sindhu a widow against family opposition. They are two completely different persons and yet because their relationship is not cluttered with demands on the other, they share an easy camaraderie which becomes the foundation of a strong bond between the two. He respects her individuality and her space. The fact that she has done her PhD after the birth of her second child, has pursued a teaching career, has delivered her responsibility towards her parental family in being a surrogate mother to her brother's children – all speak of the autonomy within the institution of marriage which he never encroaches upon. Sindhu's letters to Devayani reflect the easy relationship she shares with her husband. Their companionship filters to the most intimate aspects of their relationship, making it a cherished and mutually satisfying one.

With this novel, Deshpande also ventures into analysing hitherto untouched aspects of male response, outside the structured institution of marriage. Devayani's relationship with Ashok becomes the medium through which Deshpande seems to be reminding us that institutionalized relationships are integrated with responsibilities which are as deeply engrained in the male psyche as their gender identities. Ashok Chinappa makes it clear that although he desperately wants to enter into a relationship with Devayani, he as a married man with a teenage daughter can promise her nothing in return. There is no doubt that what both of them share thereafter, is a period of intense joy emanating from two people giving of themselves unconditionally. There is love, companionship and gentleness too. On the surface, there seems to be a measure of freedom for the woman which marriage curtails. However, Deshpande's gaze is riveted to aspects which insist on placing this fairy-tale romance in a wider context, to question its workability for the woman in the long run.

Talking of relationships, Devayani's aunt, Sindhu says, "*Collective experience has value, individual experience has none.*"[27] In the hurry to dismantle the validity of institutionalized structures like marriage, one could be trying to validate the strength of individual choice and spontaneity of emotion which is unfettered by the structure of that institution. But in doing so, important aspects are overlooked. Relationships involve responsibilities, which in turn demand commitment. Institutions integrate these into the social psyche and despite their many constraints, provide a better chance of carrying them through the sometimes mundane stretches of a lifetime. Deshpande seems to be suggesting that it becomes easier for the man to relinquish this sense of commitment outside the defined parameters of marriage. How far this arrangement would suit a woman is a matter of contention. On the other hand, the constraints which men affect within marriage might be difficult, but do show a propensity for change even though at a slow pace. Perhaps what is needed is a restructuring of the relationships and not their rejection.

Beneath Ashok's profession of love lies a self-centredness which becomes increasingly evident in the course of their relationship. He keeps alive his connection with his wife and daughter but chooses to ignore the truth that his relationship with Devayani is alienating her from all those who care for her. Both of them know that it is an arrangement which cannot last forever. Yet while he maintains his buffers, she becomes increasingly vulnerable. The insecurities which raise their head are different in nature. The ostensible freedom from the constraints of a married life gradually mutates into a claustrophobic awareness of being involved in a relationship which is making the emotional space available to her increasingly constricted. His professions of undying love are not enough to make her blind to the fact that "He had his life, his work, his wife, his daughter. All I had was guilt" (152). With his options open, Ashok eventually choses his career and marriage over their relationship. Ironically, even then he wishes to carry on with the furtive relationship and it is left to Devayani to say no to the deceit inherent in this precarious relational alignment.

The preceding portrayal of male response, largely in man's position as a husband, depicts the many stages of denial and resistance with which men respond to the demands of changing gender equations. It is significant that Deshpande's objectivity never allows the anger of her female protagonists, to wipe out her own understanding of the reasons behind that response. Men are almost never portrayed as villains. In fact many of them have various redeeming qualities. Yet fear of a shift from their privileged position, coupled with their own inability to live up to larger than life roles, often translates into unreasonable behaviour. It is only through an understanding of this dislocation, that one can identify the persons beneath the persona. This is a sentiment echoed by other contemporary writers. Arshia Sattar condenses the issue in relation to her understanding of Ramayana, the mythical fountainhead of the relational images embedded in our social psyche. She says, "I find myself more and more involved with Rama and am convinced that a more complete understanding ... has to be through an inclusion rather than rejection of Rama and his questionable behaviour."[28] It is only through an understanding of man's reactions and his fear of change that alternatives acceptable to him can be construed. The process is indispensable because hope for a sustained alteration in social response is rooted here. If the changing profile of women is to be integrated into institutions of marriage and family, the male thought processes will have to be understood and veered towards an acceptance of that profile. Deshpande time and again stresses that in the process, men too might find themselves richer through returns like a stable locus in the new relational equations and honesty in relationships.

Notes

1. Prabhati Mukherjee. "The Theory of Ideal Womanhood." *Hindu Women: Normative Models*. London: Sangam Books Ltd., 1993. p. 13.
2. Prabhati Mukherjee. "The Eternal Triumvirate." *Hindu Women: Normative Models*. London: Sangam Books Ltd., 1993. p. 50.
3. Shashi Deshpande. "Telling Our Own Stories." *Writing from the Margin and Other Essays*. New Delhi: Penguin Books India, 2003. p. 89.
4. Sandra Lipsitz Bem. "Masculinity and Feminity Exist Only in the Mind of the Perceiver." *Masculinity/Feminity: Basic Perspectives*. Ed. June

Machover Reinisch, Leonard A. Rosenblum, Stephanie A. Sanders. New York: Oxford University Press, 1987. p. 305.

5. Patrick C. Lee. "Introduction". *Sex Differences: Cultural and Developmental Dimensions.* By Patrick C. Lee and Robert Susan Steward. New York: Urizen Books, 1976. p. 21.
6. Eva Ensler. "Girl Power". Quoted by Chitra Subramaniam. <http://woman. In today.in/story.jsp.sid=6913> November 2009.
7. Shashi Deshpande. *Roots and Shadows.* New Delhi: Orient Longman, 1983. p. 49.
8. Doreen D' Cruz. "Feminism in the Postcolonial Context: Shashi Deshpande's Fiction." http"//www.Murdoch.edu/Reading Room/Lit Serv/SPAN/Postcolonial Fiction.p.2/14.
9. Ibid.
10. Shashi Deshpande. *The Dark Holds No Terror.* New Delhi: Vikas Publishing House, 1980. p. 78. All other references to this novel are from this edition and page numbers are given in the text in parenthesis.
11. Jeremy Hawthorn. "Theories of the Gaze." *Literary Theory and Criticism.* Ed. Patricia Waugh. New York: Oxford University Press, 2007. p. 513.
12. Soshana Felman. "Women and Madness." *Feminisms: An Anthology of Literary Theory and Criticism.* Ed. Robyn R. Warhol and Diane Price Herndl. New Brunswich, New Jersey: Rutgers University Press. p. 18.
13. Ibid., p. 16.
14. Ibid., p. 18.
15. Serap Turkman. "Identity in Colonial Land: A Critical Overview of Postcolonial Studies." *Alternatives: Turkish Journal of International Relations.* Vol. 2, No. 3 and 4, Fall and Winter (2003). p. 189.
16. Shashi Deshpande. *That Long Silence.* UK: Virago Press Ltd., 1988. p. 16. All other references to this novel are from this edition and page numbers are given in the text in parenthesis.
17. Serap Turkman. "Identity in Colonial Land: A Critical Overview of Postcolonial Studies." *Alternatives: Turkish Journal of International Relations.*Vol. 2, No. 3 and 4, Fall and Winter (2003). p. 189.
18. Nancy Miller. "Plots and Plausibilities in Women's Fiction." *The New Feminist Criticism: Essays on Women, Literature and Theory.* Ed. Elaine Showalter. 4th ed. London: Virago Press, 1993. p. 340.
19. Shashi Deshpande. *A Matter of Time.* New Delhi: Penguin Books Ltd., 1996. p. 27. All other references to this novel are from this edition and page numbers are given in the text in parenthesis.

20. Jasbir Jain. "A Husband is a Sheltering Tree." *Gendered Realities, Human Spaces: The Writing of Shashi Deshpande.* Jaipur: Rawat Publications, 2003. p. 111.
21. Kumkum Sangari. *Politics of the Possible: Essays on Gender, History, Narratives, Colonial English.* New Delhi: Tulika, 1999. p. 369.
22. Ibid.
23. Shashi Deshpande. *Small Remedies.* New Delhi: Penguin Books, 2000. p.103. All other references to this novel are from this edition and page numbers are given in the text in parenthesis.
24. Jasbir Jain. "A Husband is a Sheltering tree." *Gendered Realities, Human Spaces: The Writing of Shashi Deshpande.* Jaipur: Rawat Publications, 2003. pp. 119-20.
25. Shashi Deshpande. *The Binding Vine.* UK: Virago Press Ltd., 1993. p. 81. All other references to this novel are from this edition and page numbers are given in the text in parenthesis.
26. Shashi Deshpande. *Moving On.* New Delhi: Penguin Books, 2004. pp. 28–29. All other references to this novel are from this edition and page numbers are given in the text in parenthesis.
27. Shashi Deshpande. *In the Country of Deceit.* New Delhi: Penguin Books, 2008. p. 41. All other references to this novel are from this edition and page numbers are given in the text in parenthesis.
28. Arshia Sattar. "Sita: A Personal Journey." *In Search of Sita Revisiting Mythology.* Quoted by Namita Gokhale. Ed. Malashri Lal and Namita Gokhale. New Delhi: Penguin, 2009. p. xvii.

5

The Burden of Privilege: Son

Among the many insistent and repeated motifs in Deshpande's work is that of the son. In focusing on the feminist aspects of her work, one undermines the importance of the issues explicated by this motif, thereby relegating it to the background and treating it as a backdrop. However, a closer look at the writer's preoccupation with it makes one realize, that she is actually touching upon one of the crucial aspects of male response, and exploring in it the potential for viable relational options in gender equations. For this, she analyses the sons in context of the system of privilege, responsibility and liability within which the cultural imperatives place them. She then traces the various responses, which the system generates in them, and uses them to assert the need to find alternatives. She also creates contexts, where the son motif becomes dominant by the very absence of sons. Out of these contexts too, she brings alive the possibility and inevitability of changing gender roles, which would lead to an equitable distribution of privilege and responsibility among the son and the daughter.

In order to place Deshpande's concerns into perspective, we first need to dwell upon the euologization of the son in Indian culture. The birth of a son is celebrated with an intensity of emotion which goes beyond the joy of a new life taking shape. It is the precursor of the many perceived positives, which arise out of the future roles assigned to the son. The report on "Son Preference and Daughter Neglect in India" by the International Centre for Research on Women says, "Parents expect sons – but not daughters – to provide financial and emotional care, especially in their old age; sons add to family wealth and property while daughters drain it through dowries; sons continue the family lineage while daughters are married away to another household; sons perform important religious roles; and sons defend or exercise the family's power while daughters have to be defended and protected, creating a perceived burden on the household."[1]

The sharp opposition of roles assigned to a boy and a girl, leads to the perception of the former as an asset and the latter as a liability. This in turn translates into complete adoration of one and severe devaluation of the other. One needs to delve into the socio-historical factors, instrumental in creating this imbalance through the division of privileges and responsibilities for the two. Like in many other social dictates, the defining reason is economic in nature. When the dominant Aryan race finally began to settle down, substituting their nomadic existence with that of land ownership, production and distribution of wealth came to depend on landed property. Prabhati Mukherjee in her book, *Hindu Women, Normative Models* says, "... the issue of inheritance became more important because of land, the fragmentation of which was not desirable through daughter's inheritance .... Since the dominant form of family was patriarchal, the transmission of property through male heirs helped its concentration within the family and further strengthened patriarchalism."[2]

Prabhati Mukherjee observes that "whenever there has been a felt need in society to perpetuate an institution, religion has always worked as a specious reason."[3] The Brahmins, themselves the owners of sizable property, aligned with the Vaishyas and the Kshatriyas, investing their political and economic clout with a spiritual sanction, which exerted a strong influence on society. Like this, "the inheritance of property was given a religious content in the form of funeral and post-funeral rites to be performed for the person, whose property was to be inherited. Anyone privileged to inherit the property must perform these rites. That justified the claim of a male heir for inheritance, instead of daughters, who were debarred from all religious rights. An innate son was eminently suited to fulfil all these obligations and he enjoyed an added advantage – his birth alone liberated his father from hell."[4]

"The inheritance of personal property by a male heir ... had a key role to play in the transformation of woman's status in society, requiring re-adjustment of customs and institutions" says Mukherjee, as "their husband's property and its inheritance ... would be linked to their own security in life."[5] Sons became imperative and a woman's status in society began to depend upon her ability to produce male heirs. If the woman could not produce a son, she feared being deserted by her husband for another woman. Alternatives like 'niyoga', i.e., conception of a male child, through a man other than the husband, gained social sanction. In short, the entire system was geared to the importance of procuring the male child, who became the instrument of holding property to some, and the indirect means of future security for others.

In order to prepare the son for this future role of responsibility, he was encouraged to cultivate masculine traits like aggression, independence and will to succeed. Irrespective of his capability or inclination he was provided a role model, which beneath its ostensible recognition of his masculine abilities, carried the subtle threat of disapproval and ridicule, if he failed to live up to it. Along with it, control tactics took the form of emotional appeals to the son's sense of duty, and an insistence upon a hold on every aspect of his life. Any inclination to pursue interests or ambitions outside the ambit of duty towards family, were frowned upon and thwarted. Within the family, the male child was given more privileges in recognition of his impending role of responsibility. These privileges, in fact, became instrumental in the devaluation of the daughter, who found herself relegated to the secondary position, even if she was more competent than the son. Her sense of deprivation at being excluded from the hallowed precincts of financial and emotional privileges, hammered in her status of a liability. The system, in denying these privileges, forfeited the right to consider her as an alternative security. The daughter denied the many props which equipped the son for his role, also internalized her inability to change the status quo.

While feminist studies have often explored the emotional and psychological profile of the daughter who "stands on the edge of the patriarchal estate,"[6] it does not adequately explore the son's response to being constrained *within* that estate. It is important to do so, because if the claustrophobia inherent in the system of privilege and responsibility, within which the son operates, is explicated upon, the impetus towards change will be invested with double the force. The daughters' fight for a more equitable status will carry within itself the potential for the son's emancipation as well. Thus, we need the son's perspective on whether he considers the privileges given to him, an instrument of control. Does he resent his pre-ordained roles, when they come into conflict with his individual desires? Is he always equipped to take up the responsibilities entrusted to him? Can he always live up to the impossible demands of masculinity, which holds his self-esteem to ransom? Is he in fact deprived of the possibility of opting out, by the threat of social ridicule and disapproval? Would he like the privileges as well as the responsibilities to be shared? Would he possibly emerge as a genuinely caring son and brother, instead of one who is merely role playing, if he was given the space to nurture his individual differences?

Kay Deaux, in her essay "Psychological Constructions of Masculinity and Feminity" says, "... traditional conception of masculinity and feminity have over simplified that which is not simple, have uni-dimensionalized that which is multi-dimensional."[7] In the process, it has linked ego identities to the roles imposed on individuals, compelling them to identify with roles which they might not be suited to. Sandra Lipsitz Bem talks of "the artificial constraints of gender on the individual's unique blend of temperament and behaviour,"[8] which interfere with his actual needs as a person. Attribution of distinct emotional temperaments, aiding social agendas, denies both males and females the right to experience the full range of their emotional requirements. "As long as the child is faced by two selectively distinct patterns of personality, each attracting him by its unique features, and is yet required by social pressure to accept one and reject the other, a healthy integration of personality may often be difficult to achieve."[9]

This brings us to the feasibility of a revision of the existing gender constructs. Such a revision is not only possible, but also important in the changing social contexts, where both women and men are questioning their preordained roles. M. Strathern says, "Myths about masculinity and feminity endure and change, as language endures and changes, because of their usefulness as symbols in society at large."[10] It is relevant to understand, rather than resist the trend, and rectify through a process of social change, the practices which are debilitating to both women and men. As Sandra Lipsitz Bem says, "Children could be far less likely to become gender schematic and hence sex-typed, if the culture were to temper its insistence on the functional importance of the gender dichotomy."[11] In doing so, it would also divest itself of the need to invest social constructions with "the sense of stability and permanence to that, which is inherently flexible."[12]

Deshpande's works touch upon these issues and the attitudinal inertia which permeates our cultural context, to suffocate all those who come within its folds. For this, she uses the absent son motif, which works like a double-edged instrument, simultaneously cutting through our world of unidimensional perceptions, and making way for new perspectives. Thus, on one hand, we have sons who choose to abandon their families and abdicate their responsibilities, bringing into focus the restrictive and claustrophobic dimension of the system of privilege and responsibility. On the other hand, we have sons who are absent by birth, who are dim-witted, who die. By their very absence or their uselessness, they provide contexts through which the feasibility of alternatives emerges. It is here that through a system of convoluted change, daughters finally emerge in tentative roles of responsibility. The simultaneous and consequential access to privileges, once reserved for the male heir, invest them with the potential to gradually shed the image of liability, which has so far precluded them from being considered as future security. It is in the underlying suggestion of shared responsibilities and privileges, that we see the potential of relational autonomy for both the daughter and the son.

Through this double-edged approach Deshpande seems to be suggesting the possibility of a new, more balanced equation where both privilege and responsibility could be shared by progeny of either sex. It would not only bring more dignity to a daughter's status but also reduce the claustrophobia inherent in the system, which perpetually tries to constraint and control the son to ensure that he can be encashed as future security. It is significant that while Deshpande's earlier novels portray the frustration which sons encounter in their restrictive gender roles and the devious means through which they try to escape them, the later novels show how balanced equations can liberate them from the liabilities which underline the ostensible privileges. We also discover that the sons who emerge as the most genuine care givers are those who have not been coerced into the role, but have willingly assumed it as per their capability, without letting that role encroach upon their personal fulfilment.

An overview of the novels being studied shows a persistent portrayal of the above-mentioned motifs. Indu in *Roots and Shadows* finds herself entrusted with privileges as well as responsibilities which traditionally go to the sons of the family. The fact that the change bears through Akka, who at one time had resisted Indu's attempts at individuation, shows the potential for change in the most resistant social set-ups. Dhruva, the timid younger brother in *The Dark Holds No Terror*, in no way measures up to his sister. Yet, he is the one chosen as the preferred child. Dhruva dies early but leaves behind an anger, which permeates Saru's life so completely that it does not allow seeing herself as an alternative to the dead brother. Dinkar and Ravi in *That Long Silence* choose to abdicate their responsibilitics through devious means – Dinkar, because he wants to live an unfettered life and Ravi, because he is incapable of handling responsibilities. Jaya's anger at being left to shoulder the responsibilities, for which the brothers have enjoyed the privileged status, is tempered with an understanding that this is the only way out of her secondary status as a daughter. *A Matter of Time* deals with the dim-witted brother, who gets lost in the crowd and yet leaves a shadow, which is sufficient to devaluate his two sisters. It is Sumi's movement out of this devaluation, which culminates in her daughters being accepted in the role of responsibility, thus reflecting a definite change in opinion. *The Binding Vine* carries the theme further by depicting refreshingly different relationships, where

Amrut and Urmi are invested with equal privileges as well as responsibilities. While Urmi shoulders the responsibilities, at times finding them exhausting, Amrut emerges as a balanced individual, whose genuine sense of care is not marred by attempts at perfecting the masculine role. *Small Remedies* is a study in contrast through a detailed analysis of a mother's obsession with her son and the portrayal of another son, who grows to his full potential, when he is free of this obsessive control. Aditya, who dies young, nevertheless experiences the constraints of being born a son. Tony, on the other hand, evolves into an almost complete human being, intellectually and emotionally. *Moving On* deals with Jiji who has grown up without debilitating feminine constraints, having been encouraged by her father to take up the provider's role. It also reflects how this helps her in maintaining control over her life, though her independence needs to be tempered with a restored faith in relationships. It also deals with Raja, who breaks out of the claustrophobic familial constraints to rebuild relationships on his own terms. Devayani, the protagonist of *In the Country of Deceit* also accepts the privilege of inheriting the parental assets and at the same time has to adjust her life according to the responsibilities which come with it.

Indu's family home in *Roots and Shadows* reflects the many shades of a culture in transition and its impact on the people who belong to it. To see the place of men in the role of sons and consequently brothers, one needs to trace the structure itself. Indu's grandfather has four sons and two daughters. The eldest of the sons, Anant assumes the responsibilities traditionally assigned to a son. He is the only one among the brothers who stays on in the family home, presiding over its births, deaths and marriages, shouldering the responsibilities of a widowed sister and a married one who nevertheless keeps coming back because her husband has no work. An infant niece is left by a younger brother, who too is brought up in the family home. There is old uncle, an ageing relative and Vithal, the young Brahmin boy, who are additional members living on the peripheries of the household.

While the support structure which a set-up like this provides to the family as well as the community is evident, the toll it takes on its permanent inhabitants is not so adequately voiced. It is heard in the voice of Anant Kaka's wife, who in one of her rare moments of self-revelation asks Indu if anyone had ever wondered what she had wanted. She vocalizes her resentment at the fact that the other brothers had conveniently established nuclear set-ups and returned to the family home only by way of formality, making token contributions which amounted to nothing. Madhav and Vinayak are insulated, somewhat self-oriented, lacking the ability to absorb and give which Anant does. But their lives also have an individual character which gives their spouses and children a measure of freedom which Anant's family does not have. Anant's wife's dreams of a small house, shiny steel utensils, a gas connection are dreams of freedom from the drudgery of the responsibilities which others have escaped and to which her life has been endlessly tied down. Perhaps, if he had not been burdened with the liabilities which come to him in the form of responsibilities, Anant too could have focused more on his sons and they might have turned out better than the nondescript specimen they are.

The third generation living in the family home comprises of Anant Kaka's children, three sons and a daughter. Anant Kaka's expectations from his sons are adapting to the reality of the changing priorities of the next generation who have begun to resent the liabilities which come to them as part of the legacy to sons. Kaka is in a hurry to marry off his daughter Mini, because as he asks Indu, "When I am gone, do you see her brothers looking after her?"[13] Even among them, Sharad the youngest, with his smart ways is already gearing up to move away from home to work in the proposed hotel which is to come up in place of the family home.

If the brothers' role is depicted with perceptivity, it is the daughters of the house, sisters who are expected to relinquish all rights and in return be spared the liabilities, who make us focus on the cause and effect syndrome which perpetuates anachronistic traditions. The story revolves around Akka, whose presence looms large, even though the novel begins with her death. Her strong, almost tyrannical hold over her brother's family, to which she had returned a widow, seems unusual by traditional standards. The past reveals itself, entwined in the plethora of responses, generated by Akka's will in favour of Indu, the rebellious daughter, rather than the sons of the family. We discover that Akka's ability to wield authority had been closely linked to her hold over economic power, which had come to her in the form of her dead husband's wealth. She is back in her brother's home, now equipped with the means to make a difference to the lives of others. Her potential for commanding and deciding which now takes centre stage, perhaps has been a part of her make up all along. However, a woman divested of the tools of power is easy to suppress. Once she retrieves these, Akka becomes the unopposed matriarch of the family.

It is significant that in the next generation, there is another daughter who returns to her brother's house, in a similar state of widowhood, but without Akka's money power. Narmada Atya is absorbed into the family too, but at a very different rung in the hierarchy. She has to efface her identity completely, and become that unseen, unheard presence, which caters to everybody's needs without ever mentioning her own. It is Atya, who bathes the babies, makes endless cups of tea, gets up before the others in the morning and takes upon herself the endless responsibilities in lieu of being given a place in the home, which ironically has been as much her's as her brothers'. Sunanda, the other sister is married and has a husband. But because her husband is perpetually out on work, she is back for prolonged periods, looked upon as an unwelcome visitor by the brother's wife and children. Even her anger at being denied the silver promised to her by her dead mother is manifested only through innuendoes. Her need to come back to the brother's home as a residual claimant prevents her from staking her claim directly. If deceit and guile become second nature to her, we need to trace it to the fact that she has not been provided with any means to survive with dignity and confidence. In the absence of both education and property, all she can do is to adopt the methods of the weak to placate her lecherous husband on one hand, and the brothers on the other.

To this very home belongs Indu, educated and well off, now more empowered by the monetary power bequeathed to her by the matriarch, who had once opposed her streak of independence. Indu's intellectual abilities and her confident assertion of her right to decide had always been resented by her male cousins and she wonders how much more they would dislike her when they discovered what Akka had done. She is invited into the hall, once the domain of the male members, to decide on what is to be done with Akka's money: "you're the most important person. We're waiting for your decision" (97). The power paradigm changes. Each one wants to draw her attention to their individual needs – a son's education, a daughter's wedding, a home to be renovated, a business to be started. The reversal in role brings its share of resentment. There is an underlying hostility which ranges from sarcastic mockery to barely controlled anger. But it is evident that these are not going to affect the larger changes already in making.

The transition is not without difficulties for Indu either. She too resents the responsibilities which Akka's inheritance brings. The expectations which others begin to have, impinge on her insulated existence. The claims and counter-claims burden her. However, it also brings to her a sense of responsibility and belonging which she had relinquished long back. She learns to be judicious and decisive even if it hurts the people she loves, in the process. She learns that personal preferences need to be subordinated in fulfilling responsibilities. She discovers that to be in charge also means to shoulder the burdens which others might not want to. Indu takes Narmada Atya to live with her after arranging Mini's wedding and finalizing the deal for selling the family home.

It is significant that with these privileges Indu also finds a voice to declare herself a person in other spheres of life, particularly in relation to her husband Jayant. The fact that she has a role and an identity greater than a wife gives her the ability to take decisions outside the ambit in which that single role places her. She finds herself equipped to turn down Jayant's insinuation that she could keep Akka's money for herself, instead of spending it on the family. It also brings with it a sense of responsibility towards her family which makes her dismiss her husband's assumption that she should limit herself to him and their home only. In fact the reinitiation of her integration with a larger network of relationship retrieves her from the almost neurotic obsession with him alone. This in turn invests her with an objectivity which restores balance in her life.

If Roots and Shadows deals with the possibility of impacting a daughter's positioning within relational constructs, through her integration into privileges as well as responsibilities, *The Dark Holds No Terror* questions the irrationality of forcing the son into the same role at the cost of alienating the daughter. It depicts how the system works to put the son into a mould, seeking and building up traits, which gear him for the dominant masculine role – whether it is congruent to his personality or not. Ironically, the system is represented by the mother, who herself is a victim of gender disparity, but cannot perceive an alternative to it. Saru's mother is one of the two daughters, who along with their mother have been abandoned by their father. She has grown up in her maternal grandfather's house, where "their obviously had been the burden of being unwanted, of being a dependent."[14] Now a mother herself, she selectively sees her son as the prospective security, which her own mother had lacked. Instead of equipping her daughter against the degradation she had once suffered, she sees Saru only as a responsibility she had herself been treated as. She neither expects any returns from her, nor feels the need to invest in her. The focus rests on the son, who is to bear the burden of all her expectations, as well as deprivations.

What this does to a boy is sensitively portrayed in Dhruva's short life. The precarious identity of the timid child, who needs to cling to the elder sister for his sense of security, comes across in the refrain that runs through the novel, "Saru Tai, wait for me, I'm coming" (190). Yet attempts to fit him into the responsible male mould begin early, with the underlying emphasis that if he doesn't fit there, he would be an object of ridicule. The mother insists that the timid child should sleep alone in a separate room, making Saru reflect caustically, "Perhaps she had imagined herself to be Jija Bai, the heroic mother, who moulded the brave son Shivaji" (84). The son, knowing instinctively even at this young age, the necessity to play along, waits for the mother to sleep, before crawling into the sister's bed, willing to do anything, "as long as he could get away from being alone in the dark" (84). The sister using ridicule as a tool, threatens to tell the mother that he is scared and elicits the pathetic appeal, "No don't tell Sarutai. Don't tell. I won't say anything to Ai.

I'll keep quiet. I'll do anything you say" (85). The victimization of the son through such psychological practices is analysed by Saru, when she talks of "something in the male which is whittled down and ultimately destroyed by female domination. Dhruva had been dominated by two females making him a creature full of terrors ..." (85).

Dhruva does not live long enough for us to see what kind of a man he would have grown up into. However, the possibilities are explored through two contrasting depictions, that of Sudhir, Saru's childhood neighbour and Madhav, Saru's father's surrogate son. Sudhir, almost Saru's age, and belonging to the same cultural context, is placed in the role of unshared responsibility and the price he pays for the privileges once heaped upon him. Saru, back in her father's house in search of a solution to her own trauma in the gender hierarchy, discovers Sudhir exhausted with his ostensibly privileged role in the same hierarchy. When Saru asks him about his old mother, his response reveals more than just her condition: "she has diabetes and she is supposed to diet. When we remind her of it, she gets furious. She tells everyone, we're ... Prema is trying to starve her. It's difficult. I don't know how to manage her. Old people are a problem" (75). His anger at his mother's unending expectations is evident when he says, "Ai grumbles all the time. She is never satisfied whatever we do. She is always nagging at Prema. Well ... he sighed heavily thinking of his grief" (75). The mother obviously wants to exercise her right to be the central presence in her son's life, in return for the investment she has made in him. For the son, it is his relationship with his wife, which now constitutes the 'we' and he resents the burden which the mother places over that bond.

On the other hand there is Madhav, who decides to resist the loop which his mother threatens to throw over him, even from a distance. She wants him to forego his own ambitions and assume the role of the eldest sibling. Madhav on the other hand, prefers to forge relationships where care and concern for each other is not converted into a tedious chore. The curious air of ease which surrounds his relationship with Saru's father, the companionship evident in their games of carom together, and the mutual nurturance they offer to each other in small things like cooking and cleaning, makes Saru think "it's a partnership, wordless, uncomplaining, and perfect. A tacit understanding, as all good partnerships should be" (35). This relationship does not work on the principle of ownership. Neither does it rest upon that obsessive control, which destroys concern for those on the peripheries. Madhav's refusal to cater to his mother's demand, that he sacrifice his career for family responsibilities, here in the form of pursuing a recalcitrant younger brother who has run away from home, is indicative of the growing need among sons for personal space. Madhav's refusal to lose a year by missing his exams, to go in search of the brother, sounds hard and callous. Yet, there is a self-preserving tendency evident in his decision when he says, "I can't spoil my life" (208).

Saru realizes that the relationship shared by her father and Madhav, represents a reconstitution of the system, which not only releases the son from the emotional manipulations and psychological constraints, but also in a manner, liberates the father from the apprehensions related to future expectations from the son. His concern for Madhav is not hinged to the benefits it accrues, but on a need to share and sustain. "Baba and the boy Madhav, the son of a priest seemed to have dismissed gods and pujas from their lives with an ease she wondered at. Perhaps, the thought struck her; Baba doesn't need gods because he has no stake in future" (148). Saru wonders why the same disinterested love cannot be sought in relationship with one's biological children: "Can one ever possess another human being? The act of birth can be crucially deceiving, making you imagine you have some claim on the human you bring into this world" (164).

Saru's perception of the burden placed on the son through artificial magnification of his potential amalgamates with her anger at the simultaneous demolition of the girl's potential in order to facilitate the process. Her reaction to the process of discriminatory relational treatment is crucial, because it doubly reinforces the need for change. Saru, the confident elder sibling, who wields natural power over the timid younger brother, is eventually subjected to a process of systematic diminishing through the small practices integrated into everyday life. Among these is her banishment from the puja room during her periods and the necessity to sleep separately like a pariah, for a biological function which is an affirmation of her regenerative role as a female. Similarly, while Dhruva is encouraged to be independent and brave, Saru is told not to go out alone. While his worth is projected in the reality of his future presence in the parents' life, she is assessed only for her potential as a future bride. While he is naturally entitled to the privileges of the family, expenses incurred on Saru need to be related to her future female role. Thus, the mother does not mind spending on gold earrings and bangles for her, but will not hear of money spent on her education. She does her best to thwart her husband's inclination to send Saru to study medicine saying, "but she is a girl" (144). The impossibility of seeing Saru as a potential care giver is evident when she says, "doctor or no doctor, you still have to get her married … can you do both? Make yourself a pauper, and will she look after you in your old age? … let her do her B.Sc., you can get her married in two years and our responsibility will be over" (144). Saru's anger at the working of the system is placed parallel to Dhruva's discomfiture with the role imposed on him, to Sudhir's exhaustion with the responsibilities which that role entails, and the rebellion it initiates in Madhav. Collectively, the situation calls for a revaluation of the system which seems to burden all those placed within its precincts.

Saru's reaction to this system is the first step towards this revaluation, and is obviously fraught with the difficulties and faulty digressions which accompany first attempts. If her devaluation occurs in relation to the male child, Saru decides to appropriate those attributes which make him the preferred progeny. The most important of these is acquiring economic independence through education. Her mother's question "what gives her the right to choose" (144), itself becomes the motive for making that choice. Saru's question to herself "Is that all I am? A responsibility" (144), makes her take the proactive decision to change that status. The difference in the attitude reflects how identities change in relation to changing times, making way for altered equations even if the process is a traumatizing one. We see Saru's reaction manifest in her refusal to seek recognition through her physical attributes, in her focus on empowering herself by becoming a professional and by marrying a person of another cast, against the wishes of her mother. Deprived of the privileges of a son, Saru feels disinherited not just from the dilapidated property, but also from the nurturance and affection which should have been her right as a child of the house. The angst which the mother's attitude instils in her pursues her through adult life, reducing her to a hurt, thwarted child, especially after Dhruva's accidental death for which the mother wrongly blames her. Her hysterical allegations "you killed him. Why didn't you die? Why are you alive when he is dead" (191)? fill her with an anger which never subsides. She refuses to go back to the maternal house as long as mother is alive.

However, placed in context of the development of the theme in Deshpande's work at large, one finds that Saru's anger is the petulant anger of a hurt child. Her's is not an adult emotion, which diverts itself into the constructive channel of change. Rather it manifests itself in one long series of reactions, which leave bitterness in their train. It is much later that she realizes, that she has unwittingly become an affirmation of her mother's belief, that daughters cannot be a source of future security. It is only after she gets the news of her death, that she realizes that she had never attempted to replace Dhruva in terms of taking up the responsibilities earmarked for him. "When Dhruva died, there was only me. And if there were any burdens on me, I threw them off and she died alone" (31). On coming to know that her mother had died suffering from pain, in the city where she herself practiced as a doctor, the anger is replaced by a feeling of regret. Her guilt surfaces when she wonders "who lit the pyre? She had no sons to do that for her" (21). Placed in context of the various reactions from the sons, Saru's anger and the subsequent guilt hold the potential for becoming a precursor to changed equations. It has in it, the seeds of a revised option. Instead of crushing the son under the burden of the privileges, and the expectations that those privileges entail, nurturance could be made available to both the son and the daughter – perhaps it could also become the precursor to a willing sense of responsibility in both.

That Long Silence carries the theme forward by depicting yet another situation, where the sons wriggle out of the responsibilities imposed on them, preferring to relinquish the privileges for a life led on their own terms. Where they do stay back in the encoded system, the price paid is enormous. It is their reaction to the system which also validates the daughter's quest for a more dignified status in the scheme of things. It also contributes to the gradual acceptance of a broader perspective within the system, where a daughter is seen as capable of undertaking responsibility, albeit out of sheer necessity.

Jaya's Ajji's house represents the microcosm of the social set-up, where sons are given that definite privileged place, which earmarks the necessity of their role in future responsibilities. Hence, the outer room with its privileged access is reserved for the sons, while the women operate from the inner zones. Ajji's room, a symbol of the system, shows its ostensible deference to the males of the house, indicated by the chair placed in the otherwise bare room. It is also reflected in Ajji's contemptuous anger at the daughter-in-law who fails to show preferential concern for her hydrocephalic son, irrespective of the ironic connotations of his future uselessness. It is after all a home where the family tree is to be sketched with sons and their sons.

Ironically, it is this male dominated home which shows total lack of compassion for the son, if his focus shifts from the family to individualized concerns. Jaya's father, the youngest son of the family, fails to make the smooth transition from the status of the privileged son to that of the responsible one, which his two elder brothers do. His nationalist inclinations and Gandhian leanings threaten to destroy the mother's investment in him as her future security. Hence in spite of the two other sons to fall back upon, Ajji prevents him from joining the Gandhi Ashram and pulls him back into the pre-designated role with a ruthlessness, which he cannot stand up to. The surface story of the mother's love for her favourite son becoming instrumental in bringing him back into the family fold is underlined by the control tactics which thwart his ambitions and evoke reaction. His anger is reflected in his decision to marry a girl whom the mother does not approve of, and in his walking out of the family home to establish a separate set-up. However, the process of change is not an easy one. The predicament of a son, born and reared into a system which makes him feel guilty for stepping out of the designated role, is reflected in Jaya's father's vacillation. His daily journey to his mother's home is accompanied by his childish need to perpetually reassert his identity, through small things like demanding the prohibited onion with his meals. Jaya's perceptive analysis of the situation sums up the strain caused by the system as she thinks of "Appa cycling three miles into town to see Ajji and three miles back home to Ai ... up and down the undulating roads, his heart pumping furiously ...."[15]

The parallel dynamics of Jaya's other Ajji's house reflects even more glaringly, how the system of privilege and responsibility can destroy the sons, while ostensibly placing them in the privileged position. There is Chandu mama, her mother's brother, who has been turned by his mother "from a lively ambitious young man, who wanted to do his FRCS, into a dull, small town doctor, married to a woman he had no feelings for, and filling his life with shoddy affairs with all kinds of women ..." (83). Then there is Makrand mama, the other son, who prefers to forgo the privilege for pursuing his dreams of becoming an actor. As Jaya retrospects, "it's a pity he never knew how much they admired him and sympathized with him behind the facade of hostility" (43). For Ajji, he remains an outcast whom she never forgives till the end of her life. Introspecting on the reaction of the sons to the system, here represented by the mother, Jaya correctly perceives that they had spent "their lives reacting against them; lives that had turned out to be, ultimately, a battlefields of dead hopes and ambitions" (82).

In this microcosm of the other Ajji's home, the daughters' status is exemplified through Jaya's mother who is never considered a source of future security, and is therefore never a part of the game of claims and controls. She is not thought of, when the mother wills the family property to the son, whom she has succeeded in retaining by stamping out his ambitions and desires. The daughter's unspoken hope for a minor share in the mother's jewellery, involves pathetic attempts to insinuate her own daughter into her affections, as a means of acquiring it. The situation speaks of a system which leaves women with underhand, degrading options which beget measly returns, like the string of pearls and the bracelet, which the mother eventually leaves for her. The only place allotted to her in her maiden home, when she returns there as a widow, is that of a liability. Once again her place in the family depends upon underhand attempts at controlling the brother by dominating his wife. Jaya's mother thus inherits her mother's role, in this case the focus of the tactics being shifted to the brother, since her sons seem to have slipped out of her hold.

It is in the attitudes of Jaya's two brothers, Dinkar and Ravi, that the sons' latent discontentment at being coerced into roles of responsibility, their inability to express it openly and the devious means by which they escape it, get reflected more clearly. Appa's death puts Dinkar the eldest son, into a position where he is constantly burdened with reminders of his responsibility towards his mother and sister. His suffocation at being pinned down into this position becomes apparent much later, when Jaya reflects on how he had manoeuvred her into marrying the first eligible boy. "Dada had wanted me off his hands; he had wanted to be free of responsibility for an unmarried younger sister, so that he could go ahead with his own plans" (93). The same desire to escape responsibility, with all the privileges that went with it is reflected in "the way he kept Ai at a distance after Appa's death, when she had shown signs of leaning on him" (105). Jaya remembers, "He had kept me at arm's length too, so that I had turned to Mohan" (105). Ai insists on giving the Dadar flat to him, but Jaya remembers, that for his own devious reasons he had always disassociated himself from that too. His impending visit to the United States, meant to be temporary, is preceded by his clearing this flat of all his personal belongings with a finality which makes it clear that he has no intentions of returning. He never does, thus escaping responsibilities, by willingly relinquishing the privileges meant to lure him to them.

Ravi, unlike Dinkar does not even qualify for the responsibility which the system expects him to assume. In Jaya's words he is "a man who lived by drifting on the edge of dishonesty" (110). His lack of commitment to everything in life is reflected in his inability to stick to any one work, his unsuccessful attempts to utilize his father-in-law's clout and money, and his messed up relationship with his wife. With the ability to wriggle out as the mainstay of his competence skills, he hardly seems equipped for the role expected of him. Jaya cannot help noticing with an ironic twinge, that in spite of insisting on paying the restaurant bill after having asked her out, he leaves it for her to pay. In the same strain, the purpose of his invitation turns out to be a pre-deliberated manoeuvre, to extricate himself out of his mother's expectations, and place Jaya in that role. Thus, concern for Ai is effectively entwined with insinuations that Jaya is better equipped to look after her. He makes his case stronger by informing his sister, of how hurt the mother was by her lack of concern for her. It takes Jaya a while to recognize the unscrupulous tactics which the brother has employed, to elicit the required response from her. She eventually realizes that "both Dada and Ravi had escaped" pinning her down "to the position of responsibility" (104).

What is significant in the whole sequence of the son's attempts to escape responsibility is the daughter's parallel inclination to participate in it. The changing social situation which provides her with the acumen to assess the established norms, also angers her at her own position within them. It gradually and tentatively sublimates into a desire for change which translates into an assumption of roles which so far have been outside the purview of a daughter's role. Jaya, introduced to the possibility of financial independence by her father, has always loathed the idea of being treated as a liability. She had been furious when she had come to know that her mother had sought her brother's help for financing her studies and her wedding after her father's death. Perhaps her insistence upon taking responsibility for Kusum, Vanita mami's depressed niece, later in life is an attempt to pay back for what she has considered charity. Her decision comes as a surprise to everyone, including her mother, brother and husband. Yet, she doggedly insists upon it. Ironically, here too, it is Kusum's prosperous brother Dalip, who willingly leaves her with Jaya for treatment. His own responsibility is more conveniently fulfilled by placing a fresh garland on his dead mother's photo each day. Jaya takes responsibility for getting the doctor's appointments for Vinita mami, who is suffering from cancer. In this case, she also fills the place of the son who has never been born to her childless aunt.

While Jaya willingly takes up these responsibilities, the forced assumption of the duties earmarked for her brothers, is accompanied by anger at the duplicity of the system, which piles all privileges on those who now conveniently abdicate the assigned roles. Her indignation at her mother's sudden interest in her as the possible alternative to the sons, arises out of the collective sense of deprivation which she has suffered as a daughter. She is disgusted with her mother's "smarming" (106) attitude. Jaya says, "I didn't know whether to be angry with her or to pity her for childish outbursts ... it seemed to me such a waste, all that emotions I no longer needed, no longer wanted, poured on me. When I had passionately wanted her love, she had ignored me and concentrated on her sons" (106). The flat which she had given to dada in a blatant display of preference and the pearls which she had given to Ravi's wife instead of her, are discriminations etched deeply into her psyche. When she finds herself facing the tricky dilemma of who would support the ageing mother, she has every right to extricate herself based on the inequitable distribution of privileges. Yet, she does not turn her back to the question, "why can't it be you" (104)? Perhaps in answering this question in the affirmative, lies the possibility of stepping out of the position of liability into one of responsibility, thereby releasing herself from anger and her brothers from guilt.

To round off the argument, towards the end of the novel Deshpande introduces Neelima, daughter of Mukta, Jaya's neighbour in the Dadar flat. Her irreverence for the social misgivings to her female identity runs parallel to Jaya's final tumultuous break with her secondary status as a woman. The very circumstances of Neelima's birth have been indicative of a break with stereotypical situations. Her father has died before her birth. Everyone comforts her mother with the assurance that she would give birth to a son who would "bring her both solace and support" (62). "Instead there is Neelima, proud of her birth" (62). As if to drive the point home, Deshpande shows the younger son of the family, escaping the overload of responsibilities at home by deciding to go abroad. In a sharp reversal of situation, the grandmother who had mourned the birth of Neelima is left with Mukta in the role of the bread-winner and Neelima as the logical heir. The absence of the son, either by chance or by choice, thus places the daughter in a context where she would find herself assuming responsibilities as the natural option.

A Matter of Time is a departure from the earlier novels, deals with situations where sons become all pervasive by their very absence, leaving a trail of varying reposes among three generations of women. This finally culminates in a conscious and willing assumption of responsibility by the daughter, with a reciprocal change of attitude in those who represent the social system. The process is a difficult one, and takes its toll on those who become the unwitting participants in the regenerative change. Perhaps Deshpande wishes to reassert the inevitability of that change, and shows how resisting it only makes the change more painful.

In order to locate the origins of the system which places such a huge premium on sons that it deprives itself of feasible alternatives, we are taken back in time, to the life of Manorama. Sumi's grandmother has no son, and considers her daughter the living emblem of her inability to produce one. Her obsession with the lack of a son is hinged to her fear that her husband might listen to insinuating relatives, who suggest a second marriage for producing an heir. Manorama's paranoia and all that it entails, stems from the fact that the "main crutch, that most women depended on, was denied to her. All that she had was a daughter, Kalyani, who would get married and become part of another family."[16] The daughter is never considered a potential care giver; hence Manorama sees no logic in investing her with the privileges reserved for a son. Her use is sought only in marriage, and the possibility of her producing a male heir. Hence, she deprives Kalyani of education and cruelly thwarts a tender and innocent romance to ward off the possibility of her marriage to an outsider. She eventually gets her married to an uncle much older to her in years, so that the property and the potential heir could stay within the family. An ironic depiction of her distorted priorities comes in the form of the red carpet treatment provided to this devalued daughter, when she gives birth to a son, who eventually turns out to be dim-witted. The irony gets sharper when he gets lost at a railway station. Kalyani is now deserted by her husband and finds herself back in her parents' house, bereft of her only claim to respectability. She has nothing to sustain herself, having already been deprived of education, and through it of financial independence. Her devalued status as a daughter is only further intensified, in her return as a liability with two young daughters. The hatred evident in the mother's attitude is devoid of an understanding of her own contribution to her daughter's position.

It is ironic that the lost son, who becomes the reason for Kalyani's wretched situation, first in her parent's house, and subsequently in relationship to her husband, is dim-witted and a lifelong liability in more ways than one. Yet he is perceived as that lost asset, which places the daughters in devalued contexts. For deeply entrenched in the collective conscious, endorsed by religion and philosophy, is the belief that it is the son who provides perpetuity, the son who frees a man of all his burdens. The *Brahd-aranyaka* says: "Whatever wrong has been done by him, his son frees him from it all; therefore he is called a son" (91). Kalyani, a product of this cultural orientation and social conditioning is therefore guilt-ridden for being born a daughter, and then of giving birth to daughters. She thus succumbs to the system and accepts the devaluation thrust upon her. Hence, Premi and Sumi grow up with their mother's hand clasped over their mouths, denied the right to question that system, or to assert their personhood in relation to it.

It is Sumi and Premi, placed on the threshold with opposing forces acting on them, who present the possibilities inherent in changing times. The tradition-bound conservative approach is now challenged by possibilities of empowerment, which question the necessity of accepting the devaluation imposed on a daughter. Premi, the younger sister, represents the continuation of the old system, which ostensibly works well for some, when everything seems to fall in place. Under her father's absolute authority, Premi qualifies as a doctor, is married into a respectable family, and gives birth to a son, thus finding herself comfortably ensconced into the system. However, a glimpse into the inner world that constitutes Premi, portrays the sense of deprivation and alienation, which the same system has instilled in her. Memories of a frustrated mother, who considers her responsible for the loss of her son, the hand clasped over her mouth, the nudges and pinches inflicted on her as though to efface her presence from the house, are part of the desolation she carries in her heart. The fact that her father has never talked to her till she is eight years of age, is a deprivation she carries into her adulthood.

Sumi, the older daughter, presents those adverse circumstances, which do not find readymade solutions in the system as it exists. It is out of these, it seems, that alternatives can finally emerge to make place for the daughter, who refuses to feel ashamed of being born a female. Back in the same house and in the same circumstances as her mother, Sumi does not display the same attitude. In spite of having been deserted by her husband and left to fend for her three daughters, living in her father's house with a secondary status is never an option for her. She refuses to accept monetary help from relatives. She does not degrade herself through hysterical lamentations and maintains a dignified demeanour, silently assessing the avenues to an independent life for herself and her daughters. She refuses to contemplate on the refugee status in the house, whose very walls seem to cry out that the reason of their existence was a son. Thus begin her attempts at looking for a job, learning how to drive a scooter and searching for an accommodation where she can give her daughters the dignity, which this house had denied to her mother, herself and her sister.

It is in her refusal to be seen as a liability, that we see the beginning of her empowerment. If it makes her father recognize her as an equal, it also gives Sumi the confidence to reconsider her subsidiary status as a daughter. For the first time she thinks of herself as the rightful successor to her father's property, something which her mother Kalyani had never been able to do. Parallel to the movement of her own empowerment, is Sumi's growing sense of responsibility towards her parents. She acquiesces to Shripati's appeal to stay with them instead of moving out to live an independent life, not because she wants to live off them, but because they need her in their old age. Even when she decides to move to another city, she knows that her two daughters, Aru and Charu would be there to look after her parents.

If Sumi's changed perspective comes as a reaction to her own devaluation, her daughter Aru's radical difference emerges from the confidence of being valued for what she is. In her we see the natural progression from her belief in her own potential, to her acceptance by others as that support, which is otherwise sought only in a son. We see the eighteen year old Aru's natural assumption of the supportive role towards her mother and her siblings, as she tries to become the man of the house, in the absence of the father. In Aru's questioning gaze and open declaration of hostility against the system, we also see Sumi's hesitant assent. Sumi decides, in spite of her apprehensions, that the black mask of protest on Aru's face, as she canvasses with a women's group, is better than Kalyani's hand clasped over her own mouth, preventing any voice of dissent.

Kalyani's eventual acceptance of Aru as the possible successor is aided by her daughter's changed attitude, as well as her own realization of the pain that accrues from subscribing to fossilized opinions. Her break from the system which has ruined her own life is symbolically portrayed, as she gives Aru the family jewels, a motif repeatedly used in other works to depict a daughter's deprivation in terms of family privileges. Kalyani makes an independent decision to bequeath her mother's diamonds to Aru. Aru accepts them as one would accept a privilege preceding responsibility. Sumi's sudden death along with Shripati, catapults her into that position of responsibility sooner than either of them have envisaged. We find Aru taking it upon herself to make the funeral arrangements as she stands by her grandmother with the firm assurance, "I am your daughter, I'm your son, I'm here with you" (233). Kalyani too, finally finds the courage to endorse the necessity of treating a daughter as an asset and trusting her potential to undertake the responsibilities for which only a son is considered capable. Her own retrieved position as a daughter is achieved in Shripati's reconsideration of her as the rightful claimant to her father's property.

Shripati himself comes across as a victim of his obligations to a mother-surrogate, which has led him into a loveless marriage, and the misery it has entailed for so many human lives. Perhaps, in his act of returning the property to Kalyani in her capacity as the daughter of Vithalrao and Manorama, we see his discontent with the system which has wasted his own life, along with that of others. It is the same realization which prompts him to tell Sumi, "let your girls learn to stand on their feet. Don't worry too much about getting them married" (168). In the larger context, it is this changed opinion, which will finally salvage both men and women from the constraints imposed upon them. One cannot help thinking of the symbolic depiction in the beginning of the novel of "bougainvillea clinging to the akash mallige, cutting deep grooves into its trunk, as if intent on strangulating it" (4). Placing this in context to Shripati's last conversation with Sumi, one sees an underlying significance. He says he had named her Sumitra, which translates into good friend. This is followed by his revelation that he disliked the name Premlata, which translates into the clinging love vine. Do we see here, an unspoken wish, for the woman as a partner, rather than a dependent, who suffocates through her dependence?

As if to stress the fact with emphatic persistence, Deshpande introduces the character of Yamuna Bai, whose only relation to the story is that Manorama had once studied in the school started by her. However, it is Yamuna Bai's dream which is central to the theme of the novel. Deshpande says, "She had a dream in which girls would not have to live with nothing more in their lives than the slavery of endless drudgery and child bearing ... education was the tool with which she would work for the realization of her dream" (185). The daughter of a rich family, widowed and back in her parent's house, Yamuna Bai has the option of living a comfortable life, with brothers willing to shoulder her responsibility. She prefers to utilize their help for setting up a school for young girls to help them become financially independent. Aru, the fourth generation representative, wiser through her knowledge of the many setbacks which women in her family have suffered, is brought a full circle, when she finds herself in the same village, where Manorama, her great grandmother had once failed to utilize the opportunity provided by Yamuna Bai. For Aru, it is like finally reaching the cat in the centre of the jig-saw puzzle. The solution lies in women's empowerment through education. This would liberate not just daughters but also the sons, as responsibilities and privileges could then be equitably distributed.

The changed perspective, which emerges out of the difficult processes of personal experience, finally seems to bear fruit in the next novel *The Binding Vine*. Urmi, the protagonist and her brother Amrut come from the upper-middle class background, where the influence of modern thought filters quickly, with education facilitating the process. The result is a uniform attitude towards the son and the daughter, and its influence on their respective lives. Equitable distribution of privilege and responsibility, one realizes, might prove liberating for the son, making him more humane and balanced. For the daughter, the privileges bring additional responsibilities, which could prove difficult to shoulder, but are necessary to carry the process forward.

In order to study the background which goes into these changed equations, it is important to study the role of the mother, who in all of Deshpande's works, emerges as the bearer of patriarchal values. It is significant that Inni, the mother figure still wishes to mould her children to the traditional role patterns. However, her overtures are overshadowed by a strong father figure, who aids in re-establishing the role models. The mother thus dwindles into insignificance as the children move on to new roles. Quite contrary to her hope that her daughter would vault into a "pearls and chiffon"[17] existence through marriage, Urmi marries into a middle-class family, pursues her career and prefers to live within her own earnings, rather than becoming dependent on her husband's money. Inni is irritated at Urmi's lack of interest in dressing up, her refusal to indulge in small luxuries, and her disdain at the feminine role which she herself has perfected. In fact, Urmi does not even fit into the mould of the helpless devastated daughter, who needs to cling to her mother while coping with her young daughter's death. Urmi has discovered her own potential as an individual in her father's belief in her capabilities. Being considered her brother's equal in being assigned the family privileges, as well as the responsibilities associated with them, she has discarded the helpless feminine role. Inni does not realize but it is precisely this, which also gives her the capability and confidence to take over her mother's responsibility, even after being married into another home.

If Urmi seems less feminine but more empowered through the changed equations, Amrut appears more human though less congruent with the masculine image. It is significant that when the son is not exclusively burdened with the parents' future hopes, and where his worth is not perpetually measured in terms of his potential as their security, he emerges as a more balanced person. Amrut knows his limitations and refuses to create a facade which exceeds his capacity. When the perfectionist father wants excellence from both his children, it is Urmi who wishes to prove 'I can'. Amrut on the other hand, declares his unwillingness to compete. He declares, "He expects too much of us ... at least of me" (52). In fact, the father before dying, sees the daughter as the more responsible of his children, and tells her, "I am leaving you all my burdens" (95). Amrut finds no affront in this. In fact when it comes to dealing with legal matters pertaining to the property, of which they are equal recipients he tells her, "Why don't you deal with it Urmi? Why don't you go there .... Anything you decide is fine by me" (95).

Later, when he comes to see Urmi, after her young daughter's death, he is fully aware that Urmi's strength as an individual is much greater than the support he can offer to her. He tells her, "damn it didi, I am scared of you. People seeing us always think that I'm the tough guy and you're my delicate sister; they little know it's the other way round" (22). Among them, there is no pretence that he as a brother needs to take on the protective role. He tells her, "I've never stood up to you, don't expect me to begin now. It's too late for me to shake off the big sister influence" (26). Yet Amrut comes across, as a more caring son and brother, than those portrayed in other contexts. His concern for Urmi is genuine in its own small measures. His attempt to draw her out of depression through his silly jokes is not devious in nature. Since his own future dreams are in no way thwarted by his responsibility towards his sister, his concern for her is not coloured with the need to escape.

Amrut's attitude towards his mother is significant too, because it reflects the altered opinion of the son who looks beyond the constructs designed by the social system. Since the sister shares responsibility in looking after the widowed mother, Amrut too is willing to do his bit, once he is settled down. Inni nurtures hopes of crossing over to a higher status in life through Amrut, who has already cleared the coveted IAS exam. Her search for a suitable Marathi daughter-in-law is underlined with her wish to insinuate herself into the son's future prosperity. However, his affection for his mother notwithstanding, Amrut intends to forge his own future relationships and deal with them as he considers right. Thus, we have the self-willed, South Indian Radha tucked away in Delhi. The balanced approach in his relationship with his sister is already filtering into his future relationships, which are being nurtured with recognition of the importance of respect and equality.

Amrut's attitude is contrasted to the relationship which Bhaskar the doctor who evinces interest in Inni in spite of her married status, shares with his mother. While the love and concern for the mother are common in both the relationships, it is the response to the element of control which sets them apart. Amrut cares for his mother, but does not let this became a license for her interference in his life. Bhaskar, on the other hand, recognizes his mother's attempt at controlling him and yet allows it because she feels that he is performing his duty as a son, by giving in to her possessiveness. He sees nothing wrong in her pre-occupation with searching for a "sweet, homely, fair, convent educated ..." (160) girl for him. She constantly reasserts her place in his life, and re-establishes her claim over him, by insisting on becoming the central component in every sphere of her son's life. The potentially disastrous effect of this obsessive hold on his future relationships, makes Urmi wonder, "How can she burden him with this" (159)? The contrast serves to round off, how changed attitudes are imperative towards cultivating more balanced relationships, releasing sons from the burden of claustrophobic control.

In *Small Remedies* the anger of the earlier novels is replaced with a distanced, ironic perspective, as though the author is looking back at the needlessness of discriminative tendencies, which have led to difficulties for both sons and daughters. Meanwhile, the protagonists move on and find success, acceptance, and emotional integrity, which make them better and happier individuals. It gives a sensitive portrayal of a mother's obsession with her son, her retrospective journey through the emotional labyrinth and her understanding of the need to be liberated of it. Contrasted to it is the depiction of another son, who grows up without this obsessive control and emerges as a complete human being, in full control of his diverse potentials, and his vast capacity for genuine concern for people and relationships.

The first of these is reflected in the portrayal of Leela, Madhu's clear-headed and strong-willed aunt, whose life reflects the possibility of breaking through the inertia of the social order. Leela the firebrand activist, who forges independent relationships, is one of the six daughters who are considered nothing more than a responsibility in a home which perpetually mourns the lack of a son. Their success or failure is measured only in terms of what they would make of themselves through marriage. The one daughter, who breaks through this system of evaluation, to achieve success in the external male world, is considered an outcast. As Leela herself retrospects, "I became a figure little girls were threatened with, when they were disobedient or troublesome."[18] Leela is the black sheep of the family. She is not only a widow who is remarried, but infinitely worse, remarried to a Christian. "These were the things the family spoke of. Leela's other activities did not matter to them, none of her achievements registered. Her years of teaching, her role in the trade unions, her work among the factory workers – these were blanked out, they did not exist" (46).

And yet, this is the same family, which goes through the pain of disintegrated relationships, infidelity and pain on account of the illegitimate son, who is born out of a liaison between Leela's father and a widow half his age. Leela's mother hides the truth from her daughters till late in life, perhaps because she finds it difficult to concede the hurt. The uselessness of the whole issue emerges in the fact, that the son cuts himself off from the family completely, to lead a wild and dissipated life, finally committing suicide. The irony inherent in the social concept of responsibility and liability, and its impact upon the lives of people is obvious. Leela on the other hand not only achieves success, but also forges genuine emotional bonds with people, who cherish her for what she stands for. Her marriage to Joe is founded upon a respect which invests both of them with dignity. It recognizes her need for her space and independence and yet incorporates a companionship, which transcends restrictive social models. Her relationship with Tony, her step son displays a similar integrity. In Hari, the young balanced and liberated man, we see an admiration for Leela, which symbolizes the acceptance of the changed female role by the new generation.

If Leela's life elicits revised opinions from others, Madhu's retrospective analysis of her relationship with her now dead son, involves a revision of her own tendency to control. It brings her face to face with the many underlying strains, in what she had once considered the unadulterated emotion of maternal love. Grieving over eighteen year old Adit's death, she realizes that her obsession with him had dented her own dignity, as well as his. She now sees all the joy centring on him, as an exaggerated reaction which reflects an imbalance of emotions. By the time she stops panicking for his safety as a baby, she begins to turn into a hypochondriac, imagining every little problem to be a terminal illness of which she would die, leaving Adit alone. Her frantic search for the right person to take Adit's responsibility in case of her death is almost macabre. At the same time, she delights in the power Adit's dependence on her gives to her. "She loves the feeling of being the central pole of a whirling universe for this small human being" (183). She revels in the absolute certainty that "this mother's love ... is never wrong, it can do no wrong" (184).

That is why she is hurt when Adit begins to enjoy the company of others as he grows up. Her reluctance to accept that "he has a world I can't follow him into" (136), is accompanied by furtive attempts to wriggle her way into his relationship with his friends, his teachers, his cousins, etc. Yet Adit recedes from her. His door is closed to her and his voice, when he speaks to her, is the one he reserves for strangers. It is only much later, after his death that she goes into his room and discovers that he had nothing to hide. She realizes, "It was his own self he had been guarding from me, from my possessive, grasping hold" (188). It is then that Madhu discovers that in looking at herself as a loving mother, she had selectively bypassed that possessive, frantic, frightened part of herself, which dreaded the prospect of losing the son. She acknowledges, "I have to go a long way before I will know that Som's father was right, that it's this word, carrying the load of meanings – confusion, ignorance, illusion, and pain – which is the right word and not love. *Putra moha*" (188). The process of coming to terms with Adit's death involves Madhu's reconciliation with all these facts. It is only then that she can liberate him as well. Her understanding reflects the importance of allowing sons to evolve as human beings, unfettered by the obsessive control which the system exercises on them.

In contrast to this control and the reactions it elicits, is the investigation into the possible response of the son, released from this system of claustrophobic concern. Would he cease to accept his responsibilities? Would he no longer be the security for which the system keeps him in suffocating constraints? The answers to these questions are explored in the relationship Tony shares with the people in his life. Tony, Joe's son and Leela's step son, grows up in unusual circumstances. His mother dies young, ending the possibility of maternal hold. For Joe, his father, relationships have nothing to do with control. Leela, his step mother believes in personal liberty for herself and for others. Hence, Tony grows up making mistakes, learning from them and evolving into a person who is just himself, and not one being fitted into any social role. If at all Joe is angry with him, it is out of sheer exasperation at his wild ways. His shift from arts to economics, from journalism to advertising, drives the otherwise balanced father into calling him a loafer and a waster. Thus we have Tony, whose personal life is independent of any control. Yet, he eventually finds his way to unprecedented success in the field of advertising, through his own methods of hit and trial, through "bewildering transformations, various metamorphoses" (203).

More significantly, Tony grows up into an adult for whom family bonds become the most important thing in life. If he is steady and steadfast in his emotional attachment to his wife, he is also a caring brother, not only to his real sister Paula, but also to Madhu, his step mother's niece. None of his emotions emerge through obligatory constraints. Madhu says, "what's between us is real ... he was Paula's brother. He still is, always there for her, as he is for me" (56). When we compare Tony's distress at his inability to assuage Madhu's grief after Adit's death, we cannot help comparing it to the devious facade of brotherly concern in other contexts. His affection for Leela is equally spontaneous. After Joe's death, he automatically assumes responsibility for her, although, she neither expects nor demands it. Madhu thinks of him as "the protean man" who is "in his personal relationships unflinching, loyal and steadfast. Constant to the people in his life. Above all, to four women: Leela, Paula, Rekha, and I. Son, brother, and husband" (203).

Thus, *Small Remedies* juxtaposes different facets of the issues at hand. Madhu's retrospective analysis of her obsessive focus on her son and an honest acknowledgement of what it does to both of them, affirms Deshpande's persistent emphasis on the need to release the sons from that control. The simultaneous depiction of Leela and Tony, who break through the stereotypes, and emerge as balanced individuals, in tune with their organismic and social selves, validates the argument to its logical conclusion.

Moving On is the story of Jiji, once again a daughter in a home without a son. Like always, this brings up issues concerning sons and daughters and how sheer necessity changes existing equations. To delve into the process Deshpande provides an overview through her glance across several generations. There is reference to Jiji's grandfather, the privileged son of an affluent Brahmin family, who chooses to forgo the privileges to live his own life, opting for the Gandhian way of life, and marrying a harijan girl. For all practical purposes, his family gives up on him. Then, there is his son, Jiji's father, who grows up in a tolerant atmosphere, with his sister Gayatri who is more of a companion than a mother figure, and a father who is not an interfering parent. He too marries the girl of his choice. A liberal hands-on father, he participates in the rearing up of his two daughters and never feels the lack of a son. In fact, he sees in them the potential of achieving all that a boy can. He dreams of making Jiji a doctor and moulds her in the image of a provider and a protector rather that someone who needs to be looked after. It is this confidence, given to her in the initial stages of her life, which gives Jiji the courage to single handedly rear two children after her husband's death. The absence of a son automatically places the daughter in a role of responsibility. After years of keeping away from her parents, Jiji returns to look after her terminally ill father. The father welcomes her presence. He understands that it is important for children to look after their parents, because this reconnects and also releases them from the negativities, which seep into filial relationships. Jiji's being a daughter is not seen as an obstacle to this process of care and connection. In fact he considers it her duty to be by her side when he dies.

Baba wills his property to his granddaughter Sachi, instead of grandson Anand. While it leaves even Jiji surprised, she decides to stand up against a social order, which considers property with a female heir as a soft target, easy to usurp. Jiji decides to fight the property sharks and their coercive tactics to scare her away. She intends retaining it for Sachi, even if she has to kill someone for it. With this, Deshpande moves to a different phase, where a woman's right to property becomes tangible, not only in legal, but also in social parlance. Interestingly, Sachi wishes to sell the house and divide the money equally among Jiji, Anand and herself. She will not forfeit her right, but neither will she usurp anybody else's.

The novel also deals with Raja, Jiji's childhood friend. The only son, with a younger sister, who is mentally retarded, and a mother, who is constantly nagging about the need to get her married, he finds the atmosphere at home claustrophobic. It is not surprising then that he has "escaped home early, leaving as soon as he had graduated on the pretext of wanting to work with a firm of architects in Bangalore, to get away."[19] He finds an excuse to leave and further asserts his individuality by marrying against his parent's wishes. The sense of responsibility ingrained in him as the boy of the family, keeps taking him back to the parents, but each time he comes back disillusioned. He asks himself, "I wonder why I go" and knows he does so only because "it's a duty he cannot get out from, however little pleasure he gets out of it" (91). Significantly, he prefers to be a surrogate son to Jiji's father, where emotional bonds do not degenerate into control tactics. Jiji's father can sense the rancour which Raja's father holds against him, but cannot explain that the rift was of their making and not his. While Raja's relationship with his mother is marred by his aversion to her cloying display of care, his relationship with the father improves, as he eventually begins to treat him like an individual, rather than an object of utility.

In the Country of Deceit, Deshpande's latest novel, does not deal with these issues as the central concern. Nevertheless the background forms a part of our understanding of what goes into the mental make up of the characters portrayed. Devayani's father's life which is a series of failures ending in suicide, prompts one to probe what might have gone into the tragic end. An understanding of his situation comes through his sister's reflections on the pressure with which he had dealt early in life. "As the eldest son of an irresponsible father he'd taken on the burden of his younger siblings' education, of his sisters' marriages."[20] Laden with too many responsibilities he had started working as a clerk, compromising heavily with his dream of an intellectual life. His personal life too, had been relegated to being the last priority. His marriage had to wait till he had fulfilled all family commitments. Much later, his sister analyses his depression in terms of his increasing inability to cope with pressures. She says, "he was tired of family responsibilities" (60). Faced with continuing problems in terms of losses in business and pressure to pay off debts, he finally finds recourse in ending his life on the railway track. Sindhu rightly assesses that a consistently diminishing threshold had made him increasingly vulnerable, till "Suddenly he threw it all" (60).

Why a son needs to shoulder all responsibilities, at times more than what he can handle, is a matter of concern in many of the earlier novels as well. The possibility of the daughter's ability to contribute has been constantly stressed by bringing in situations where a brother's absence brings her into the role of responsibility by default, thereby revealing her potential to take up the same role as a son, provided she gets the same privileges. Devayani's mother has grown up in a house without a son. Having been born into the ideological limitations of a culture which lays premium on the presence of a son, she has suffered her share of neglect at the hands of an ill-tempered mother, more so on account of her epilepsy which makes it difficult to marry her off. Yet in the absence of a brother, she and her sister eventually inherit their father's property, and the responsibilities which accompany it. She gets a bigger share which comes to her as her father's attempt to assuage his guilt for having neglected her illness, which he realizes he would not have done had she been a son. Devayani's mother bears greater responsibilities too and faces the same problems which are generally a son's share, in looking after ageing parents, in this case a thankless and foul-mouthed mother.

Devayani herself belongs to a home with two daughters, where the absence of a son has never cropped up as a major issue. Both she and her sister have been educated well, one being an architect and the other a lawyer. Devayani takes over the affairs of the family in the normal course after her father's demise. She looks after property matters, manages her sister's marriage and nurses her terminally ill mother. She also lives on in the family home with its dark, claustrophobic history of failure and disillusionment. But perhaps it is the personhood which her situation confers upon her, even though it comes shrouded in the sombre colours of responsibility and loneliness, which gives her the potential to restructure her life. Savi and Devayani eventually have the family home razed. The open space on which their new home is to be built is like a clean slate which gives these two daughters the ability and potential to redraw the future.

The change in mindset which the new position of independence brings to a woman is reflected in Devayani's attitude. She is not unduly perturbed at Savi's mother-in-law calling her a '*bechari*', because she is still unmarried at the age of twenty seven. As a woman who is equipped with education as well as financial security her worldview differs. She is in no hurry to marry the first man selected by her concerned relatives. It is true that need for human connection does not get mitigated by these changing situations. Devayani goes through the trauma of living through the breakup of a relationship, which perhaps has its beginning in her loneliness. Yet in tiding over it, she does not see marriage as the only solution. That would come at its own time. Meanwhile, she picks up the threads and begins to restructure her life by accepting the offer to join as a partner in a law office.

Deshpande recognizes that there are no clear and perfect courses to follow in the complex criss-cross of socio-cultural change. Gains and losses occur in relative terms. What she does emphasize upon is the need to correct the imbalance inherent in the system which classifies daughters and sons in roles which are suffocating for both. A change in the structure, she emphasizes, will bring its own share of difficulties. However that would be an acceptable price to pay for the selfhood and dignity at stake. The son, showered with privileges finds himself caught in a web of obligations, which he resents because it thwarts his impulse towards an independent life. The daughter, deprived in myriad ways is angry at the same system, which perceives her only as a responsibility and denies her the means to change that status. Through the use of the absent son motif, Deshpande tries to shake us out of the archaic mindset and makes us look at the feasibility of alternatives.

As her characters stand contrasted to those in generations preceding them, they show a distinct change in approach. The undercurrent of resentment among sons, gives way to an acknowledgement of their need for individuation beyond the role ascribed to them. This acknowledgement in turn comes as an impetus for a revision of opinion, which tentatively begins to include the daughters into the ambit of privilege. Their movement towards empowerment finally begins to be seen as an alternative, rather than a threat to the disintegrating system. The desolate vacuum created in the absence of a son begins to be filled up by the daughter. Significantly, the process of change is endorsed by both, since it emancipates the son in direct proportion to the quantum in which it empowers the daughter. Acceptance is slow to come, as is evident in the resistance which takes generations to give way. Yet the process continues, because it is only in acknowledging the dismissed aspects of each sex, that social roles can be redistributed in a balanced way.

Notes

1. Rohini Pande and Anju Malhotra. "Son Preference and Daughter Neglect in India: What Happens to Living Girls." < http://www.icrw.org/docs/ 2006_son-preference.pdf.>
2. Prabhati Mukherjee. "Rejoinder." *Hindu Women: Normative Models.* London: Sangam Books Ltd., 1993. p. 107.
3. ibid., p. 108.
4. Prabhati Mukherjee. "Who Needed This Ideal?" *Hindu Women, Normative Models.* London: Sangam Books Ltd., 1993. p. 96.

5. Prabhati Mukherjee. "Son's Inheritance, Realizing the Ideal." *Hindu Women: Normative Models*. London: Sangam Books Ltd., 1993. p. 83.
6. Sandra M. Gilbert. "What Do Feminist Critics Want? A Postcard from the Volcano." *The New Feminist Criticism: Essays on Women, Literature and Theory*. Ed. Elaine Showalter. London: Virago Press Ltd., 1986. p. 34.
7. Kay Deaux. "Psychological Constructions of Masculinity and Feminity." *Masculinity/Feminity: Basic Perspectives*. Ed. June Machover Reinisch, Leonard A. Rosenblum, Stephanie A. Sanders. New York: Oxford University Press, 1987. p. 301.
8. Sandra Lipsitz Bem. "Masculinity and Feminity Exist Only in the Mind of the Perceiver." *Masculinity/Feminity: Basic Perspectives*. Ibid., p. 311.
9. Lewis Termen, Catharine Cox Miles. "Sex and Personality: Studies in Masculinity and Feminity." *Sex Differences: Cultural and Developmental Dimensions*. Ed. Patrick Lee and Robert Susan Steward. New York: Urizen Books, 1976. p. 386.
10. M. Strathern. "Psychological Constructions of Masculinity and Feminity." *Masculinity/Feminity: Basic Perspectives*. Ibid., Quoted by Kay Deaux. p. 293.
11. Sandra Lipsitz Bem. "Masculinity and Feminity Exist Only in the Mind of the Perceiver." *Masculinity Feminity, Basic Perspectives*. p. 310.
12. Kay Deaux. "Psychological Constructions of Masculinity and Feminity." *Masculinity Feminity, Basic Perspectives*. p. 310.
13. Shashi Deshpande. *Roots and Shadows*. New Delhi: Orient Longman, 1983. p. 50. All other references to this novel are from this edition and page numbers are given in the text in parenthesis.
14. Shashi Deshpande. *The Dark Holds No Terror*. New Delhi: Vikas Publishing House, 1980. p. 17. All other references to this novel are from this edition and page numbers are given in the text in parenthesis.
15. Shashi Deshpande. *That Long Silence*. UK: Virago Press Ltd., 1988. p. 136. All other references to this novel are from this edition and page numbers are given in the text in parenthesis.
16. Shashi Deshpande. *A Matter of Time*. New Delhi: Penguin Books Ltd., 1996. p. 128. All other references to this novel are from this edition and page numbers are given in the text in parenthesis.
17. Shashi Deshpande. *The Binding Vine*. UK: Virago Press Ltd., 1993. p. 124. All other references to this novel are from this edition and page numbers are given in the text in parenthesis.

18. Shashi Deshpande. *Small Remedies*. New Delhi: Penguin Books, 2000. p. 45. All other references to this novel are from this edition and page numbers are given in the text in parenthesis.
19. Shashi Deshpande. *Moving On*. New Delhi: Penguin Books. 2004. p. 91. All other references to this novel are from this edition and page numbers are given in the text in parenthesis.
20. Shashi Deshpande. *In the Country of Deceit*. New Delhi: Penguin. 2008. p. 60. All other references to this novel are from this edition and page numbers are given in the text in parenthesis.

6

The Potential for Support: Father

If selfhood and autonomy are "developed in context of social situations,"[1] then the question of female empowerment necessarily calls for an investigation into the support it might get from those in positions of power within the system. For this, we need to take into account male roles other than the husband to "enable an expansion of the idea of men as partners."[2] Here man in the father's role emerges as the most likely source of support, primarily because he is less constrained by ego concerns, than he is as a husband. The daughter's empowerment does not challenge his authority directly. This, coupled with his knowledge of the coercive practices of a system, of which he himself has been a participant, impels him to equip his daughter against it. Control over material power and the privilege to be the decision maker, make his efforts towards empowering the daughter effective and wide-ranging. The following discussion attempts to study Deshpande's works in context of the centrality of the father's role in altering the status of the daughter. The imminent stress on its ideological contribution to the changing profile of her female protagonists seems to echo her opinion that in seeking male support for women's empowerment we should be "less dismissive of fatherhood."[3]

Fathers and daughters in Deshpande's works are not presented in smooth symbiotic relationships where the father understands the daughter's needs and helps her to achieve her goals. In contrast, we have complicated relational situations which present the myriad possibilities of what they might entail. Here we do not deal with a unitary definable identity called a 'father'. Neither is there any mechanical operation, to which we can subordinate an analysis of the various influences, which act upon a man who also happens to be a father. The father himself is a product of his circumstances, his culture, of the unique traits which he is born with and of his place in the socio-historical time zone where he finds himself. Hence, his role in his daughter's life may differ according to the various influences working upon him.

This is what explains the vast range of father figures in Deshpande's fiction. There are timid fathers, fathers who are harbingers of change, fathers who desert and abdicate responsibility, fathers who live on the periphery of domestic scene and fathers who give their daughters the right to speech. We have the uninterested and unresponsive absolute patriarch and also the father involved in family life. There are fathers who find themselves marginalized by wives reluctant to lose their hold upon the domestic fiefdom. Still others are made ineffectual by women, who as agents of patriarchy, prevent them from bequeathing benefits denied to a girl in the closed patriarchal society. Deshpande's father figures are depicted as real human beings, who in spite of their positional power, may be reluctant, or stand thwarted by the many undercurrents that run beneath the social surface. We also see in many of them a quaint hybridity, evolving out of an uncanny mixture of tradition and modernity. While they become agential in providing their daughters with an awareness of life beyond ascribed gender roles, in contradictory terms they also expect them to subordinate this awareness to the traditional roles.

Before embarking on a study of the father's role in Shashi Deshpande's works, it is important to emphasize the relevance of the study in light of the same influence on the author herself. Shashi Deshpande's father, a Sahitya Academy awardee, was an eminent Sanskrit scholar, a social iconoclast and an acknowledged intellectual, known for his contribution to literature and social thought. In order to bring to light the immense influence he wielded upon his daughter, one needs to make a parallel reading of two essays by

Shashi Deshpande. These are, "A Man of Integrity" in which she talks of her father and "In First Person", where she gives an intimate account of her own intellectual life, which comes across as heavily influenced by her father's thinking. "A Man of Integrity" tells us about the father, who encouraged intellectual development in his two daughters, and who "did not think of marriage as the only goal ..."[4] for them. She talks of his wish to equip them for economic independence through education. He never stopped them from doing anything, by the logic that they were girls. When we compare these views to what Deshpande writes in "In First Person", we find unambiguous echoes reflected in her own life. Even when she was married, with two children and well-settled, she still felt "a huge emptiness ... a constant nagging thought ... is this it? Is it all I am going to do in my life?"[5] She says that it was through this, "conflict between the female self and the intellectual self, that self-expression began."[6] It is significant that she attributes this intellectual self to a home where it was given due importance. Considering the deep impact, which her father has had on her life, it is not surprising that she keenly recognizes the potential of a father's contribution, particularly in ideological contexts, which impacts the daughter's expectations of herself. Running parallel to it is the assertion that if this support is not forthcoming, it would entail a reductive impact, impairing the daughter's movement towards autonomy.

A look through her novels shows the significance which Deshpande attaches to the father's role. We have a tradition breaker as Indu's father in *Roots and Shadows* who supports his daughter's decision to step out of the binding traditional structures and in the process helps her in becoming the person who finds assent from the most rigid upholders of that very tradition. There is Saru's timid father in *The Dark Holds No Terror,* who through his own growth as a character helps to bestow clarity to his troubled daughter, thus helping her in finding a direction for herself. Jaya's father in *That Long Silence* aids his daughter in perceiving a role outside gender constructs which eventually helps her to achieve an autonomous selfhood. Shripati in *A Matter of Time* is the cold patriarch, who eventually breaks through his own isolation, to aid his daughter through the crisis he had once inflicted on his wife. Giving multiple dimensions to this role are parallels and contrasts provided through two other father–daughter relationships, in two separate time zones. Kalyani's relationship with her father Vithalrao represents the past while Aru's relationship with Gopal represents the future trends. Urmi's father, in *The Binding Vine*, drives his daughter into becoming a superwoman through over expectation, so that she needs to find her own parameters for relinquishing his hold over her. Madhu's father in *Small Remedies* through his own attitude towards his daughter sets standards of mutual consideration, which she demands in her future relationships. The contrast to a strong and stable father figure, and its positive impact on the daughter, is delineated through the denial that permeates the life of Munni, in context to her relationship with the weak and unassertive father Ghulam Sahib. Jiji's father in *Moving On* becomes agential not only in giving her an orientation which breaks through the stereotype, but also in amalgamating it with her identity as a social being. *In the Country of Deceit* on the other hand, gives the picture of the deep-rooted insecurity which a weak and ineffectual father can instil in his children.

The father's role in *Roots and Shadows* is not exactly in sync with the father figure portrayed in later novels. Yet, there are similarities in terms of Govind's break from tradition in giving Indu an orientation which is different from the one provided to girls in the cultural situation they both belong to. Govind, one of the four sons, has angered his family by marrying a girl they do not approve of. Indu remembers her parents as having "overcome the then insurmountable barriers of caste and lived a tragically short but intensely happy life together."[7] Govind leaves Indu with his family, after his wife's early death, knowing that she would be looked after and leaves to pursue a career in freelance photography. He makes periodic appearances, but for all practical purposes, contributes nothing substantial to his daughter's upbringing. Indu dwells on this without any rancour, because she has had a measure of support in the adaptability of the joint family where she grows up.

However, there is an ideological support which Jayant offers to his daughter and which becomes her means of escape, when the same set-up begins to become restrictive, impinging on her growth as an individual. As Indu grows up, she feels hedged in by the domineering Akka, who's set of do's and don'ts make her feel claustrophobic. She resents Akka's insistence on constructing her as a lesser human being because of her sex, and wishes to move out of the home, which refuses to acknowledge her potential for a more substantial role. Significantly, it is to her father she turns for help. With his approval of her decision and the support which obviously must have been required in breaking through the defined roles, Indu succeeds in moving to a hostel to pursue her studies and to eventually carve out a career for herself. He also supports Indu in her choice of marriage to a boy of another caste, once again in defiance of the family, for he respects her right to think and decide. His presence at the civil marriage "full of happiness for me, because I was happy" (40) is what gives her the courage to take on the world.

How this support evolves into a shaping influence, is apparent in the contrast between Indu's confidence, her self-assuredness and her cousin Mini's quiet acceptance of whatever comes as her share within the precincts of archaic traditions. Mini's father, caught in a time stasis, has failed to connect to a way of thinking outside the orientations entrenched in the old family home. He has considered his duty towards his daughter only in terms of searching for a bridegroom, which becomes a particularly serious business because she has a problem with her horoscope. He eventually seals her fate by arranging her marriage in a home where all escape routes are firmly blocked.

What needs to be noticed is that the very mindset which had opposed the way Indu had shaped her life and approved the groove in which Mini had been shaped, eventually recognizes the benefits of the former over the latter. Akka, who at one time had staunchly opposed Indu's foray into independence, ultimately recognizes the result of that very independence as the identifying trait of the person, who could be the next head of the family. Mini's life, on the other hand, would be a continuation of her mother's, entailing endless drudgery with no concomitant return in terms of a say in the family. Considering the vast difference which support from a powerful quarter from within the dominant male world could make, a father's support thus emerges as a powerful tool in the daughter's literal as well as metaphorical movement across the gender chasm.

Deshpande's next novel *The Dark Holds No Terror* is the story of Saru's struggle to escape the schizophrenic behaviour of her husband, who stands diminished against her success as a doctor. At another level, it is also the story of her need to break through the many guilts, which induce an inert passivity, thus preventing her from active self-actualization. The paralysing effect of these guilts is reflected in her words "... there can never be any forgiveness. My brother died because I heedlessly turned my back upon him. My mother died alone because I deserted her. My husband is a failure because I destroyed his manhood."[8] The fact that the novel opens with Saru standing at the door of her father's house, thinking of the *Sudama–Krishna* metaphor, illustrates her hope of getting something from the father's house by way of reprieve from these burdens. It is reflective of the daughter's willingness to believe in the father's capacity to offer support. This in itself reflects the importance of the father–daughter relationship in the total narrative.

Saru's father, ostensibly the head of a middle class Hindu family, is actually an example of the many men, who are given this status at the cost of an entire area of life, which is kept outside their purview. Kumkum Sangari says, "patriarchies are ... imbedded in ... contractual and consensual element ...."[9] The most important of these are the ideological ensembles, such as the woman's unstated demand, that in return for accepting a subordinate position, she should be given total control over a subsidiary portion of family life. Thus, Saru's mother totally effaces herself from certain areas, relegates herself to the puja room, gives her husband the preferred status and clearly distinguishes his role as a provider from that of hers as the homemaker. At the same time, she also ensures that the home is her domain and he has little say in matters pertaining to the running of the house, or rearing of the children, particularly the daughter. The respective position of the parents, where home was concerned, is perceived by Saru as one where, "Baba didn't matter, because she so emphatically did" (105). Saru's father never seems to be able to stand up to his wife, even when he disagrees with her. Neither can he sympathize with his daughter, even when he sees the mother misusing her control over her. Saru recollects that after Dhruva's death, for which the mother had blamed her, her father had tried to console her but had not known how to offer the concern. He could never stop his wife from blaming Saru for Dhruva's death.

It seems a contradiction in terms that it is to this father, whom she time and again refers to as 'ineffectual', 'feeble-hearted', 'pusillanimous', that she turns to say "help me Baba, I am in trouble. Tell me what to do" (42). Perhaps underlying her condescension is the awareness that despite his apparent weakness he possesses a latent authority, which he had once exercised to rescue Saru from the anachronistic role which her mother had wanted to impose on her. The only plan which Saru's mother has for her is limited to marriage. The only way she can relate to her is in the female role. In fact she regards it as an unpardonable self-centredness, when the daughter wants the father to finance her education to pursue a career in medicine. However, against the mother's stiff opposition, her father helps Saru. To the mother's aggressive attempt, "I say, no, she can't go. Am I nobody here" (144)? The father's question to Saru is, "What's the last date for sending in your application" (144)? Retrospectively seen, this becomes doubly symbolic for Saru. A weak man, asserting himself in order to rescue both himself and his daughter from the gender constraints, seems to offer a parallel to her own weakness, and what she needs to do in response to the same constraints affecting her life within marriage. In this one declaration of himself as a person, she sees potential for herself to do the same. At the same time, in turning to her father for a solution to problems emanating from imbalanced equations, she is posing a question to the socially designated repository of power, for an answer to the many contradictions inherent in the system itself.

Saru's return to the father's house after her mother's death also becomes significant because of the contrast she sees between the father she once knew and his new identity, outside the bartering inherent in the power structures erected by gender imbalances. Saru thinks of her father as someone who had always been disinterested in his life, "a negative man incapable of strong feelings" (30), who had failed to show concern even when required. However, she now discovers a different person, connected to his emotional self and confident of his personhood. Saru recognizes the pure affection with which he treats Madhav, the young boy, who lives with him. Her jealousy soon gives way to surprise when she finds him treating her with the same care. His bringing milk for her, cooking food, heating water for her bath are all extensions of his newly acquired nurturing role. For the first time, he talks to her and enquires about her family with genuine interest. The curious air of ease which surrounds him and the spontaneity with which he accepts Saru back into the home, from where her mother had ousted her, are reflective of his individuation. It is not only his spontaneity which strikes Saru as new, but also his seeming declaration of himself as an individual. Talking to Saru about Dhruva's death and her anger at being blamed for it by her mother, he tells her "I never blamed you" (193). With the stress upon the 'I' he disassociates himself from his wife's behaviour, which he had either ignored or explained, but never opposed.

The same selfhood is reflected in his breaking down the gender barrier erected by his wife in his relationship to his daughter. On finding an undercurrent of tension in Saru's relationship with her husband, this time he does not turn his back and surprises her by saying, "What is it Saru? Why don't you tell me what it is" (198)? Considering the sexual implications of her troubled relationship with her husband, Saru is hesitant. She has grown up under her mother's directions to keep a distance from her father. This enforced distancing engendered through the social mores, by which a closed society functions, has permeated to her emotional relationship with her father. She says, "You're my father and I'm your daughter, but still … you are a man and I am woman. Can we talk of such things" (199)? Although it takes effort, still the father's response is, "go on", "why not … why not … go on, tell me" (199). By stepping out of gender definitions, Saru's father establishes his supportive role in his daughter's life. Doreen D' Cruz rightly says, "released from the master narratives, which dispose them to play roles, derived from the social constructions, imposed upon their sexed bodies, their birth order, or by progenitor both father and daughter feel reconnected."[10] It is significant that in stepping out of the gender constructs himself and in aiding his daughter to do same, Saru's father connects to her as a person and encourages her to verbalize her anger and pain. In encouraging her to give her side of story, he helps her to overcome the mental subordination to socially structured hierarchies. Doreen

D' Cruz says, "... the erstwhile silent corporeal text speaks, dissolving the gendered opposition between the writer and the text. In this way, he releases her from the gendered female identity which can only be inscribed upon."[11]

However, the father's role is not restricted to providing the daughter with speech. It also tempers that speech with maturity and balance of opinion. Hence, the speech is converted into an instrument of communication. He urges her to voice her feelings, to tell her husband of the impossibility of carrying on the relationship on the current terms, to provide him with an option before giving up on the relationship. "Give him a chance Saru .... Talk to him. Let him know from you what's wrong. Tell him all that you told me" (216). Yet, his appeal to her is not regressive in the sense of being devoid of options. To Saru's question, anticipating the denouement of a horror story, his reply is, "And then? It's up to you isn't it" (217)? What Saru for a moment thinks is withdrawal, is actually the father's assertion of his belief in her adulthood. He also releases her from her many guilts by emphasizing that her life was hers alone and the emotional baggage she carried was deadwood which had to be dispensed away with. His question "Are you not sufficient for yourself" (217), serves as the impetus she requires to find a life "which would seem right for her" (220). Thus, the father helps the daughter come out of her self-imposed negation, aids her in facing the crisis in her life and confers upon her the autonomy of choice.

That Long Silence too deals with a similar supportive role, which however has the desired impact long after the father's death. It sensitively portrays the deep ideological influence which manifests itself in spite of the social constraints, to connect the daughter to her true self. Before delving into the ways in which Jaya's father has influenced her life, we need to analyse the rebellious streak which leads to his own fight against oppressive traditions. It is this attitude which he bequeaths to Jaya, because it needs no didactics for belief to transfer from parent to child. Vasu breaks through the possessive hold of his widowed mother in more ways than one. He marries a Maharashtrian girl instead of a 'good Kannad girl' as she desires. He also moves away from the family home in the central part of the town with its tall rounded walls and smelly back alleys to settle on the fringes of the town with its clean little ribbon of a tarred road. The symbolic contrast reflects his preference for the new to the old.

This bent towards modernity is reflected in his choice of name for his daughter Jaya, which means 'goddess of victory'. It reflects a change of thinking in a cultural context where a daughter's birth is unwelcome. The same is manifested in his insistence upon an English education for her, in opposition to his mother's wishes. He says, "Let them learn good English. It is going to be more useful to them than being good Brahmins."[12] The father not only provides her with education, but also makes her see it as a means of life outside traditional roles which do not cater to the intellectual life of a woman. Jaya remembers later, what he had said to her, "... I, appa had said and I had agreed would get the Chatfield Prize, or the Ellis Prize, go to Oxford after my graduation ... you are going to be different from the others, Jaya, appa had assured me" (136).

Much of the dichotomy in Jaya's attitude arises out of the fact that the change initiated by her father in defiance of the system, cannot be taken to its conclusion on account of his early death. As the solitary link to a new identity snaps, she loses confidence and gives in to the pressure of expected norms. The possible price to be paid for daring to be different is evident in the father's own life, and becomes a deterrent to her own initiative in the direction provided by him. She knows that many of his attempts to break out of claustrophobic traditional mores had petered into inanity. The thwarted Gandhian dreams had to be replaced with a partnership in a small printing press. His literary endeavours had culminated in the mediocrity of his self-published poems, the copies of which lay strewn around the house. The recognition of his courage is always coupled with the knowledge of a life which was difficult, for it had no traditional buffers to fall back upon.

Jaya is scared of the struggle which involves standing alone. She knows that in saying that she was not like the others, her father had pulled her "ruthlessly out of the safe circle in which other girls had stood, girls, who had performed pujas and come to school with turmeric dyed threads ..., girls who it had seemed, asked for nothing more than the destiny of being wives and mothers" (136). Even though she knows that she could never be totally satisfied within that safe circle, she does not have the courage to stand outside it either. She tells herself, "I did not want to be different from the others. I wanted to be in that lighted room with them, not walking past, invisible, ignored" (136). Her unresolved confusions are reflected in her anger for the dead father. "It's all Appa's fault. I had thought bitterly ... for dying and messing up my life" (136).

The fear of being alienated for her difference, coupled with the apprehension of not succeeding in her endeavours against the flow, lead Jaya into building up a persona which contradicts the self, recognized and nurtured by her father. What Jaya fails to understand is that while her father's failures carried within them the strength of his convictions, her own flight from failure reflected lack of that conviction. She attributes to her husband, her tame submission to the identity of Suhasini, the mild mannered woman, who is content to be a mother and wife. She tells herself that she had no option but to give in to his demands of subordinating her natural instinct for writing, to a socially correct one of playing the role of a housewife. The latent discontent constantly manifests itself in the write-ups sent under a pseudonym, from Kamat's address, of which her husband is unaware. It is also reflected in the effort and exhaustion involved in the role playing she takes upon herself. The crises occurs when her husband's humiliating implication in a corruption case takes away the authority, which has all along been the subterfuge for blaming him for her own altered identity. The first step towards retrieval is to let go of the superficial identity she has cultivated for herself. The second which is the more crucial one; is to confront her own contribution to the formulation of that identity.

It is significant that in assessing her life from the crucial juncture of discontent, the father's presence is woven into the recollections and flashbacks, so that everything in her life is scrutinized from a perspective which originates in him, or in the orientations provided by him. She realizes that her father's presence continues to exist in the ideology he has bequeathed to her. The father's influence manifests through the substratum of her emotional and intellectual life. An important thing to be noted here is that the crystallization of those influences, and the complexes which thwart their realization, comes through Kamat, whose role becomes crucial in the revival of her connection with her father and consequently to her own self. Flashbacks to her life with her father, and references to the past, always run parallel to Kamat's presence and his mercilessly penetrative insights, thus establishing his importance as the link between the father's influence and its integration in Jaya's adult life.

The most significant of these coincidences is their very first meeting, when in explaining to him that she was no longer Jaya but Suhasini after her marriage, she elicits that caustic laugh, which for all practical purposes destroys Suhasini forever. It makes her face the absurdity of believing that one could change the formulating tenets of one's identity by changing one's name. She realizes then, that Suhasini's identity is a burden she carries because in denying it she elicited the husband's reproachful rejoinder "I chose that name for you" (15). Along with it comes the concrete awareness that "long before that Appa had chosen Jaya for me" (15). This clarifies to her, how severely she had impaired her own life trying to mould herself to the demands of others. The father's image returns to inform that at times it is necessary to be true to oneself, even if it is interpreted as self-centredness. The flashback to his seemingly selfish decision to go away from the family home and the incessant demands of the widowed mother, serves as a parallel to her own growing need to escape the burden of her husband's claims. Retrospectively thinking, she knows that she too would have to find her solution in the break from the norm as her father had done. "They called Appa cruel, but I understood why he had to go away" (29).

Once again it is Kamat who clarifies that the altered identity which she now professes to resent, has always had her silent assent and that she had resorted to it in order to find the easy way out. Chiding her for the hypocrisy of her martyred attitude he tells her "You enjoy making others dependent on you. It increases your sense of power" (84). The truth in his words stirs long dormant emotions, and brings her face to face with her own collusion in the circumstances, which now translate into the ennui and intellectual corruption which mark her life. That she needs to reach out to the father in the subconscious for seeking a solution is evident in the dream sequence immediately following the conversation with Kamat. The unidentified presence in the dream, which seems vital to her revived well-being, is obviously the father. His faith in the identity which she herself had relinquished, now seems to be the only panacea for her "paralyzed, aphasic" (86), state. "At first we are walking together. Then he goes on ahead and I am left behind. I am unperturbed and go on at my own pace; walking now between rows of houses so close to one another that there is a sense of claustrophobia … I do not know where I am, where I have to go and how I can find him, the disorientation is complete" (85–86). It is only when the unidentified image, obviously personifying the father, reappears that she finally feels that "my illness, my helplessness is gone" (86). He prompts her to hurry up and leave with him before it is too late, and as she runs after him in panic, there is the pervasive "it is my fault, all my fault" (86).

As we correlate Kamat's words and the dream sequence it becomes evident that Kamat has once again crystallized to her the fact, that living with a socially correct persona at the cost of the true self could only bring discontentment. Her retrieval lies in recovering her identity, aided by her father's understanding of her true self, even though he is no longer physically present to support her. Kamat also becomes the means of Jaya's recognition of the importance of faith in ones convictions, over security gained by intellectual compromises. This involves a vindication of her father's choice in spite of his numerous material failures. Her own partial commitment to her innate longing to write and the desolation at the constant rejection of her works, is mercilessly thrashed out by Kamat. In bringing her face to face with the reasons for her inability to reach up to her literary potential, he makes her realize that anything short of total conviction was bound to culminate in mediocrity. One could either commit oneself to one's true vocation at the cost of other losses, or live a life of compromise involving an emotional void at its centre.

The evaluation is triggered off when Jaya's story of a child widow, as told to her by her father, written under a pseudonym, and mailed from Kamat's address, is returned as not relevant to mainstream interest. She says, "This had been Appa's story …. It's rejection had hurt enormously" (146). In her anger and desperation she turns to Kamat and for the first time he makes her confront the confused priorities which prevented her from giving all of herself to what she wrote. He points out that her story could not go beyond insipidity because it lacked the passion of conviction, "There isn't even a personal view, a personal vision" (147). He brushes aside her attribution of this lack of thrust to the fact that as a woman she had constraints of time, opportunity and acceptability, saying "spare me your complexes" (148). Instead he ruthlessly brings her face to face with the fact that she had been evading commitment because she was afraid of failure. "If you don't commit yourself, you'll never fail" (15). For Jaya, this brings a changed perspective involving awareness, that while her father's failures carried within them the strength of his conviction, her own flight from failure reflected her cowardice. This realization becomes a crucial step, towards taking her role as a writer seriously. Thus, the movement towards self-actualization coincides with reconnection to the conviction which had been the hallmark of her father's life.

As Jaya finally comprehends in full consciousness, how she had chosen to give in to social pressures and the fear of failure, Kamat once again becomes the bridge between father and daughter. She shares with him her emotional turmoil at realizing what her father had offered in terms of his vision of her, and what she had lost in relinquishing her connection to him. In the course of sharing these raw emotions, it is as if Kamat and the father image merge into one. "I was crying and he was holding me .... It had been warm and comforting, like wearing Appa's coat on a chilly night" (156). The physical proximity to Kamat, and Jaya's momentary adult response to it, in continuity with the parallel she draws between him and her father, seems to establish the integration of the father's influence into her adult consciousness. The fact that this also happens to be the last time she sees him, indicates that his role is complete. When she next ventures to go to him she finds him lying dead and turns her back on him.

There is a deliberate consciousness, in her initiating physical intimacy with her husband that night. It is as though she is clarifying to herself the deceit inherent in a relationship, which rests on the denial of one's true self. It is also the beginning of awareness that instead of living with the "vitals-piercing knowledge of the blankness" (66), after Kamat's death or the "terrifying sense of emptiness" (66), after her father's death, she needs to replicate the honesty of those relationships in the other important relationships in her life. This she now knows, is only possible if she insists on being accepted for the person she really is.

It is through this recovered identity that Jaya finally finds the course for future. The alternative that she finally discovers again comes to her through her father. The Sanskrit words written at the end of his diary say, "*Yathecchasi tathakuru*" (192), which means, "do as you desire". These are lines spoken by Krishna to Arjun, when he tells him, "I have given you knowledge. Now you make the choice. The choice is yours. Do as you desire" (192). In this sense, it is the father image which releases her from the depressing inevitably of her situation and makes her realize that "in this life itself, there are so many cross roads, so many choices" (193). She chooses to reconnect to "the child, hands in pockets" (191), whom the father had introduced to the resources within. In the integration of this child with the woman, we see how the ideological strength imparted by the father equips her for making the most crucial decision of her life.

A Matter of Time is an interesting study of the diversity of paternal roles stretched across three generations. The parallels and contrasts provided by the relationship shared by Kalyani and Vithalrao, Sumi and Shripati and Aru and Gopal almost present a sociological account of the emotional and material implications of a father's role in the daughter's life. Since the story is inextricably woven with the past, in order to understand the protagonist's relationship with her father, we need to move back and forth, and unravel the many conditions which leave their resonance alive for future generations. What makes this novel different from the others is, that apart from recognizing the father's potential support, it questions the denial of that support, dwells upon the ways in which it can be proffered and then among other things, seeks it as a right. It also deals with the changing face of patriarchy in context of the daughters' search for self-sustenance and her attempts to extricate herself from her image of a liability.

The first link in the chain of father–daughter relationships is that of Kalyani and Vithalrao. It needs to be analysed in context of the fact that unless the paternal vision is coupled with volition and an assertion of the power vested in him by the patriarchal order, it is ineffectual in its collaborative aid to the daughter. The relationship here is one of affection and love, which nevertheless fails to retrieve Kalyani from the clutches of the patriarchal order, because Vithalrao fails to stand up to his wife who ironically represents that archaic patriarchal order. Manorama, a poor man's daughter, married into a rich family, is insecure behind her resplendent silks and diamonds, for she dreads a return to a life of poverty. This is evident in her total break with her family of birth. However, her fears return to haunt her, when after many miscarriages, and a daughter's birth, it becomes clear that she would not be providing a male heir to the family. Fear manifests itself into two forms. Her husband could marry again for an heir to the family. If not, the property could go to the family into which her daughter was married. Vithalrao, who sees no sense in either, considers his daughter an auspicious addition to the family. He nevertheless fails to stand up to the terrible determination unleashed by his wife. In collusion with the system, Manorama makes Kalyani a pawn in her power game. Vithalrao, who had wanted Kalyani to be the first woman engineer in the country, fails to prevent his wife from withdrawing her from school. He, who had dismissed the idea of leaving his property "to a stranger, to someone else's child, rather than to my own daughter"[13] watches helplessly as Manorama arranges Kalyani's marriage to her own brother, to whom she eventually wills the property. The writer tells us that "Vithalrao is unhappy about what his wife is doing, but knowing her determination, he has no choice" (21). Much later, when Kalyani talks of her childhood, the "stories concealed in the interstices of her silence" (121), speak of a loving but weak father, who could only revert to palmists and astrologers in hope of reprieve for the unfortunate daughter deserted by the husband, and mistreated by the mother. He eventually dies, leaving Kalyani with neither education nor assets and therefore with no alternative but to adjust to a loveless marriage with a reluctant husband.

It is against this background, that we need to study the relationship between Kalyani's husband Shripati, and their daughter Sumi. Shripati's life is one long reaction to the obligatory marriage, which thwarts his career and forces him into an unwilling relationship with a woman much younger to him in years. Kalyani's losing their only dim-witted son at a railway station, becomes the point of withdrawal and from then on Sumi's awareness of her father is defined by his unwelcoming demeanour in the one room on the top floor of the house, impervious to her mother's pathetic imploring and disinterested in any emotional connection with his daughters. Shripati's sense of duty leads him to perform all the functions allotted to a father. It is perhaps the consciousness of this responsibility, which brings him back to the family he has deserted. However his duties are not tempered with the joy of nurturance. He educates his daughters and tries to make them professionally qualified – Premi, the younger daughter is a doctor. Shripati has wanted Sumi, the elder one to follow his own career as a lawyer. It is he who arranges Premi's marriage to a qualified boy from a well-settled family. Though Sumi has rejected his choice of career and has opted to choose her partner in marriage, he is there to take her home when she is deserted by her husband. Yet, the very thought of their father instils desolation in the hearts of Sumi and her sister Premi, perhaps because Shripati's sense of responsibility caters only to the material and mundane aspects, which preclude the emotional sustenance which is vital to a parent–child relationship, and forms the basis of trust and security.

Among the two daughters, Premi submits to the dictates of the order propounded by the father, and accepts the peripheral relationship that he offers, which never goes beyond stiff formality. Surprisingly it is the rebellious daughter, frowned upon for breaking out of the patriarchal fiefdom by rejecting his choice of career and marriage, who finally constructs a changed father–daughter equation. The images of her mother's frustration as she deals with his rejection, and the recognition of the havoc it has wrecked on their lives, has made Sumi adamant about her refusal to exist in the parameters which enjoin such circumstances. The realization that this treatment has been meted out to her mother for having lost a son, instils in her a need to move away from all those constructs, which devaluate her as a daughter.

The basis for Shripati's changed perspective emerges out of these very attitudes, which makes him concede to her an equal and mature status. Sumi, deserted by her husband and left to shoulder the responsibility of three young daughters, is too self-respecting to replicate her mother's hysterical reaction, or to reduce herself to a liability. She decides to find her own ground, and seeks an independent life thus investing herself with a personhood, which even Shripati has to recognize. Sumi is surprised that the man who had never approved of her choice of friends, now wants her to invite them home. He, who had always made his daughters feel unwanted, is annoyed with Sumi for thinking of herself as a burden on him. He says, "... don't talk non-sense. This is your home. You belong here ... and don't speak of parasites. I would never encourage you to be one" (71–72). In fact, acutely conscious of his daughter's sense of self-respect and yet concerned about her needs, he offers her money as a loan, instead of giving it to her as charity.

We see a shift in Shripati's attitude to the father–daughter relationship, as he shares his own feelings and apprehensions with her. He surprises Sumi by saying, "I can't believe it myself that I am old ... Strange, how quickly it all happens – it over in a flash" (73). In fact, there are moments in their conversation, when it is Sumi who now offers her assessment and Shripati becomes a person assessed. "I suppose you think I am a stupid old man" elicits the response, "Old yes, stupid no" (73). The reversal in relational parameters is evident in the fact that instead of considering Sumi a liability, Shripati actually implores her to stay with him. It is also reflected in Sumi's fleeting reflections on hitherto taboo topics, like the possibility of her actually considering the paternal home as her own, in emotional as well as material terms.

If Shripati's attitude towards Sumi changes, Sumi too sees Shripati from a new angle. For the first time, she perceives him "as much a victim as Kalyani" (168). She recognizes his anger at the obligations which had forced him into an unwanted relationship and made him give up the ambition and career, which had been dear to him. For the first time; she understands that he had turned away from his wife and family, because "he was frightened of himself and of what he could do in his anger" (168). As a married woman, she also understands that in doing what he had done to Kalyani, he had also denied to himself the warmth and comfort of conjugai life. "He had given up everything and turned to solitude" (168). She makes the uneasy discovery that sins of patriarchy had affected his father's life, as deeply as they had scarred her mother's life.

The changed perspectives result in building a bond which perhaps both the father and daughter have missed throughout their lives. The new understanding reaches its culmination in that final moment when both Sumi and Shripati find themselves released from the compartmentalized roles they have assigned to each other. As she listens to his nostalgic memories of how he had chosen names for Sumi and the lost son Madhav, the reserve finally slips away. Instead we observe vulnerability in the brooding tenderness which precedes the accident, in which both of them die. In a way, Sumi's and Shripati's death at this critical moment of understanding becomes symbolic of the end of a way of life. The distanced, withdrawn approach born out of social and personal prejudices on either side, gives way to a connection in which the two find potential for true symbiosis. Shripati's room, which for Sumi had, "something guarded about it, an air of reserve, the very light in it being carefully doled out by the long narrow windows" (71), is now opened by Premi so that "the staircase is flooded with light, light that seems to bridge the room to the rest of the house" (243). We can see in this contrast, the writer's conviction that old prejudices will eventually give way to make paternal aid an effective instrument of change in the daughter's life.

Shripati and Gopal represent two contrasting embodiments of fatherhood. If Shripati represents awareness of responsibility bereft of emotions, Gopal represents nurturance and emotions divorced from responsibility. Both their reactions prove to be equally inadequate. Gopal is a father who participates as much as the mother, in bringing up and enjoying the children. To him, life is complete in "caring for my babies, tending them, caressing them ... holding the little warm bundles in my arms" (69). His life has never felt incomplete without a son and he has treated his daughters with the same joy and pride, as he would have treated a son. And yet, the same father first gives up his job for personal reasons, totally disregarding his responsibilities towards the family. He then leaves them to live an insecure life, claiming to have discovered that responsibilities of married life were not for him. The meagre assets which he leaves to them are enough to assuage him of the guilt, irrespective of the fact that he is actually leaving them with begging bowls in their hands and exposing them to shame, humiliation and deprivation in material as well as emotional terms.

Aru's attitude to Gopal represents the new equation among fathers and daughters, in an age where patriarchy stands weakened by female awareness, which now has legal props supporting it. Aru unlike Kalyani, refuses to accept her situation as her fate, and unlike Sumi, also refuses to quietly internalize the injustice. Gopal realizes this when Aru comes to meet him. "It was not only her question that daunted me, it was her look as well, the clear eyed, judging gaze of the young female, weighing me up, finding me wanting" (65). Unlike Sumi, whose mouth had always been covered by Kalyani's hand so that no sound of protest could escape, Aru is free and vocal in her opinions. Gopal's attempts at explaining his inadequacy at meeting the demands of family life, elicit the unsympathetic query, "why did you marry at all" (62)? She makes him listen to "the questions and innuendoes they have to face, the sense of shame and disgrace …" (62) and makes it clear that in doing what he had, he had lost her respect for ever.

It is through Aru's relationship with Surekha, the lawyer whom she meet through a women's group that the writer explores the legal options which make patriarchy less invincible and daughters less vulnerable. Aru discovers through Surekha, that born in her age and time she is as much a beneficiary of the rights once reserved only for parents, wives and sons. Surekha informs her that, "it's your father's duty and responsibility to maintain you and your sisters until you are married" (204). To Gopal's argument that "if you reject patriarchy, you must reject all the things based on patriarchy too" (214), Surekha's answer is, "… but until patriarchy is thrown out as a whole, we still need to see that the rules are observed" (214). Even Gopal concedes, "I think Surekha is good for Aru … if Aru is influenced by this woman, it won't harm her. On the contrary, I think it will help her" (220). Aru's relationship with her father remains open-ended. As Gopal returns to his daughters after Sumi's sudden death, and leaves again to immerse her ashes, Aru stands by her grandmother in the role of the successor and caretaker. The authorial privilege which provides us with a peep into the future tells us of her continuing preoccupation with issues like these, in her vocation as a lawyer.

The three relationships moving through their individual myriad situations thus show an overall change in attitude. The unspoken strain running through them is the reflection that the father's role can empower or impair a daughter. As the first male presence in her life, he can either equip her with material and emotional strength or cripple her with his own debilitated attitudes. Shripati, with his renewed awareness of this need to empower his daughter, shows the possibility of dynamism in perspective. In the fight against inequality emanating from the patriarchal system, the patriarch himself would be the most potent support for aiding the daughter.

The Binding Vine deals with yet another reflection of Deshpande's kaleidoscopic array of the possible manifestations of a father's role in a daughter's life. In the new rational world of gender equations, is there a possibility of an excess which leads to a woman's material and emotional empowerment at the cost of her emotional impairment? Urmi's relationship with her father, and the implication of his attitude on her life, takes the study beyond the simplistic construct of theory, to vital unaddressed aspects of changing social structures.

Urmi's father, an educated progressive man, makes no distinction between what he provides to or expects from his son and daughter. He expects academic excellence from both of them. He expects Urmi to show competence and to take up responsibilities. In fact he considers her more capable than the son and trusts her ability to deal with legalities pertaining to the family property. He also does not make any distinction between the two while willing that property. However, the tunnel vision with its keenness in making no distinction between the son and the daughter, also dismisses vital emotional aspects of a girl's life, which are linked to her emotional sustenance and contribute to her other roles in the social life. Urmi's father tries to empower his daughter by investing her with autonomy. Ironically, the son refuses to live up to the father's unrealistic aspirations and feels "he expects too much of us .... We've got to come up to his standards of achievement and that's expecting too much – at least of me."[14] It is the daughter who internalizes these expectations, thus constantly taking upon herself more than what she can cope with. Perhaps the desire to prove her potential is stronger in her because of the social image of helplessness, imposed upon a girl in her position as a daughter.

We find that right from her childhood Urmi accepts more than her share of responsibility, in the process compromising on her own emotional needs. Urmi's temporary shift to her grandparent's home is prolonged by her father, for the practical consideration of looking after her old grandfather. Her assent to the assumption of responsibility however dismisses as unimportant, an adolescent girl's need for emotional support and parental nurturance. The first childbirth, traditionally linked to the care of the maternal home is shifted to the mother-in-law's house due to Amrut's illness. Once again Urmi volunteers to facilitate Amrut's recovery, refusing to admit her own emotional needs. Close to his death, Urmi's father perhaps recognizes the emotional deprivation he has caused to her when he tells her, "We wronged you Urmi. No I shouldn't say 'we'. It's my fault entirely" (112). Urmi protests against his assertion of culpability, perhaps because she is yet to recognize the impact of this denial on a woman's essential need for connection to others.

A closer look reveals that assertion of her competence always runs parallel to indications of Urmi's struggle to cover up the emotional fatigue it induces in her. She refuses to confess her need to go back to her parents, lest it be interpreted by her father as her inability to cope. However, the fifteen-year old who volunteers to stay with her depressed grandfather with the brave declaration "we'll manage" (113), is haunted by the dirty behaviour of the servants she has to deal with, right into her adulthood. At the same time, her subconscious fatigue is symbolically represented in her perception of the train next to her grandparent's house, "It is climbing the gradient – puff puff – it sounds like a creature in distress .... There is a triumphant, strident whistle – HERE I AM … I watch breathlessly: what if the rails finally succumb and the carriages topple over …?" (12). The responsibilities keep on growing and accumulating and the persona keeps on hardening, its impact showing on her married life. Urmi decides that she can manage the house, children, mother, and career single-handedly, letting her sailor husband come and go at his own convenience. She never allows anyone to see the excruciating emotional deprivation which she undergoes in the process.

The superwoman who manages all this, unfortunately also loses her ability to connect to her own vulnerability, or to convey it to others, because of the innate desire to continually listen to the voice, which says, "Urmi so smart, Urmi so confident" (173). Her fear of vulnerability even prevents her from expressing her feelings of love to her husband, creating a distance between them, which threatens to destroy the very fabric of the relationship. Even when her young daughter dies, she claims that she is tough enough to manage the crisis all by herself. The facade remains impeccable, with frequently introduced comments like, "I am tough, you know that … I won't break down. I am in full control of myself" (20), "I don't need any one" (23), "I hate being fussed over" (25). However, the pent-up emotions seeking release get translated into psycho-somatic indications like the severe asthma attack. Her banging her head against the wall to find an outlet for pain, reflects the need for means other than competence, to deal with her situation.

The father's constant presence in Urmi's subconscious, his contribution to the expectations she has from herself, and her exhaustion with the role she has taken on, is symbolically portrayed in her dream preceding the asthma attack in the days after the daughter's death. "I am running along the sea. There is someone else with me – a someone, who is running besides me. I can hear the footsteps. I can hear the heavy breathing, but I cannot see, whoever it is" (16). This is followed by the awareness, "I have to keep running, and I go on … the invisible person keeping pace with me. Now it is becoming difficult; the sand, soft and squishy under my feet keeps dragging me down" (16). Her refusal to ask for help, coupled with the failure to cope, results in her inability to mourn her daughter's death, thus initiating the need to break away from that dominating influence which prevents her from connecting to her own inner self.

The realization unravels, with her involvement with the lives of two other people, both of whom cannot voice their respective stories of discontent. Kalpana, who lies in coma after being brutally raped and Meera, Urmi's mother-in-law whose attempts at verbalization lie shut in an old rusted trunk, in the form of her poems. In both the cases, we see Urmi's desperate desire to bring into open, all that had been left unsaid by these two women. In attempting to verbalize their experiences, Urmi is vicariously trying to bring her own latent emotions into open. This crystallizes in her conversation with Vanaa as she tells her, "They never had a chance it's not fair. It's not fair at all. And we can't go on pushing it – what happened to them under the carpet forever ..." (174). Urmi herself verbalizes her anguish for the first time at this point, and talks of all the times when she had taken up responsibilities, which she actually couldn't cope with. She also recognizes that each time the factor propelling her to do so was the fear of sounding incapable. She realizes now that in her race to become the superwoman, she had lost that vulnerability, which is essential to connect. She had never let her husband become a part of the real world, she could not connect to her mother, she could not grieve for the dead daughter. She knows that she would have to break through the image foisted upon her by her father, in order to live fully again. There is an understanding within her that one needs to create one's individual truths, shaped to one's individual needs, "in particular the need to be able to live comfortably with ourselves, with those we love and need" (55).

It is only when Inni tells her of her father's role in sending her to live with her grandparents, on a basis which shows a lack of compassionate wisdom in him, that Urmi finally breaks out of the invincibility of his image as an epitome of unchallenged authority. Just because Inni had left her with a trusted male servant for a few hours, she had been considered incapable of looking after the child. Urmi realizes that her father, whom she considered to be wise, was perhaps not always so. She also realizes that her father's expectations from her too could have been rooted in something lesser that the wisdom she attributed to him. For the first time, Urmi is unsure of her unquestioned faith in him. "I thought he was a just man, a wise man ..." (201). She recognizes the duality in people, which can make them wise and unwise, kind and cruel at the same time. She also realizes that one needs to draw one's own parameters of what one expects from oneself. Even a father, the primordial authority, needs to be tested by one's own discretion. It is the recognition of individual responsibility for the precepts one chooses, which makes her forgive her father. With it comes the liberation from his expectations. Thus, Deshpande dwells upon an unexplored but relevant facet of changing gender equations. Implicit in her rendition of Urmi's and her father's story is the need for change to be integrated with the intricate emotional pattern of feminine life. This is essential for emotional sustenance and balance in relationships.

Small Remedies also has a father figure, who with his unconventional attitudes inculcates in his daughter, attitudes and expectations which differ from the socially endorsed, discriminatory benchmarks for men and women. Madhu inherits from her father the belief that relationships rest on trust not control, that love transcends doubts to accept the person and not just the socially correct persona. However, she discovers that in her relationship with her husband, a transgression from the persona entails a collapse of all that she has invested into it. As she faces the crisis in her marriage, her thoughts keep reverting back to the relationship she had shared with her father. The honesty and integrity of that bond strengthens her belief, that a relationship devoid of trust is irrelevant, and that the responsibility of building that trust lies as much with the man as with the woman. As Madhu deals with the turmoil and eventually returns to the relationship on her own terms, we discover how the father provides the daughter with parameters, which help her to move out of stagnant social mores. Joe, her surrogate father proves to be prophetically right when he tells her after her father's death, "It hasn't gone anywhere, your life with your father is still there, it'll never go away."[15]

Madhu's father emerges as an unconventional man, whom she remembers as going his own way, uncaring of every one, except her. He had married Madhu's mother, an athlete fifteen years younger to him, and a Brahmin unlike him, after his first wife's death. The dignity of their relationship sustains years after her death from TB. As an only parent, Dr Eknath is exceptionally balanced. He leaves mundane issues to his trusted servants. To him, what is of primary importance is not gender delineation, but matters dealing with right and wrong, integrity and values. Thus, while Kaka tells the young Madhu not to run around in her petticoat, her father intervenes only when he finds the daughter being misled into stealing money by Munni, the next door neighbour. Even then the intervention is tactful not harsh. When he does intervene, the attitude is not one of coercion, but understanding. Madhu remembers that her father had never exercised irrational authority over her. In a way, he had always made her feel his equal. There are no arbitrary rules, no systems of discipline, which needs to be followed without a reason. If she is not allowed to go to the theatre, Madhu knows, it is because he does not like leaving her in confined crowded places. If he goes to listen to Bai's music without her, it is explained that she would not enjoy that kind of music. If he drinks and smokes, it is never hidden from her. Madhu remembers, "we were always comfortable and easy with each other. The space between us was not crowded with demands, doubts, assertions, or questions. There was enough air for us to breathe easily" (175).

It is this awareness of being equal in her relationship with her father, that makes Madhu secure. If there are things which lie outside the wholeness they share, they are immaterial. Therefore, when Munni tries to dislodge the trust by offering her the information that her father had a mistress, she thrusts it aside. "It had no place in our lives together. Child though I was, I had the wisdom to know that you don't need to know everything about a person" (175). Much later, when as a grown up person Madhu realizes how lonely her father had been, she thinks of the mistress to whom he had left half his property and wishes that it was not just a "purely physical thing ... I hope there was affection too" (174–175).

The discussion about father–daughter relationships in *Small Remedies* would remain incomplete if it left out the parallel description of Bai's daughter Munni, her relationship with her father Ghulam Sahib, and the contrast it provides to Madhu's relationship with her father. The two years which Madhu and Munni spend as friends, establish the difference in their attitudes in later lives, on account of their starkly opposite relationships to their fathers. If Madhu's father is the final authority in their household, Ghulam Sahib lacks authority in his relationship with Munni's mother, a strong assertive woman, who has made him subsidiary to her ambition and career. If Madhu's father is the focal point of Madhu's family life, Ghulam Sahib has only a supportive role in a household, which runs according to Bai's needs. Above all, in her refusal to marry the man through whom she had conceived this child, she divests him of the status of father and thus deprives him of authority over that child.

If Madhu's father represents social status and respectability, Ghulam Sahib represents just the opposite. A Muslim tabla player in a dubious relationship with a Brahmin woman, who has eloped with him from her married home, can only evoke social disapproval. That Munni is painfully conscious of this, can be traced back to the fact that she has spent a major part of her childhood in her mother's married home, perhaps because when Bai eloped with Ghulam Sahib, abandoning the one-year old child, the child was presumed to have been fathered by her husband. So, when she does come to live with her mother, Munni is well aware of the stakes involved in identifying herself with the respected Brahmin family of Pune, or the socially ostracized set-up of undefined relationships of Bai's home.

While Madhu revels in the security of her identity as her father's daughter, Munni leads the precarious existence of a child who is in denial and is constantly disassociating herself from the father, who reflects weakness and disreputability. She is constantly insisting that Ghulam Sahib is nothing to her, that her father is a rich respectable lawyer from Pune, who cannot come to take back her mother, because if he did, Ghulam Sahib would kill her mother. She tries to portray the gentle, kind Ghulam Sahib as a cruel, vicious, villain, who beats her up. Perhaps, like this, she validates her own denial of reality. The same is reflected in the deliberate shabbiness of her appearance, which is actually a ploy to disguise her evident resemblance to Ghulam Sahib. Her reluctance to defer to Ghulam

Sahib's timid overtures at disciplining her also reflects her refusal to accept him in a relation of authority.

The question which becomes relevant here is, whether reduction in a father's authority liberates a daughter. In Madhu's case, it is the paternal authority which without becoming suffocating, provides parameters of right and wrong, and helps her to take a stand for what she considers right in her future relationships. In Munni's case, the reduction of authority translates into waywardness as a child. Her exposure to adult emotions too early in life, her unmonitored interest in cinema, and the uncharted moral territory where she resorts to lying and stealing, indicates a lack of direction rather than liberation. We find in her, a destructive streak aimed at dismantling trust and relationships. It is visible in her attempts to control Madhu through the stories she makes up, which include misinforming her about adult emotions and scaring her through stories of a hostile stranger in the house. Her cold-blooded attempt at breaking the circle of trust between Madhu and her father by telling Madhu of his mistress, also reflects the same.

We are not informed about Munni's future relationships. What we do know is, that the denial which marks her childhood, eventually magnifies into denial of her identity itself. Years later, she refuses to recognize Madhu as they sit next to each other on a bus. The complete banality of her reincarnation as the middle class, mangalsutra wearing Shailaja Joshi, who refuses to accede her identity as Munni, makes one wonder whether the self-deception has percolated to other areas of her life. Her subsequent death in a bomb blast seems to depict the magnification of that destructive streak which was part of her make up as a child, and which increased in proportion to the negation of the self, finally destroying her completely.

The contrast between Madhu, who finds her way through fragile relationships to a more integrated self, and Munni who is symbolically destroyed through those deceptions, makes a telling comment on the father figures in their respective lives. It also brings up the crucial issue, whether the traditional feminist thrust towards dismantling the patriarchal fiefdom, of which the father is an important figure, is applicable from the perspective presented by Deshpande. Is it paternal authority which needs to be dismantled or the negative connotations implicit in it? In a cultural context where a father's authority has at times been wielded in socially regressive manners, change is required. But this change is to be sought, not in dismantling but in reframing that authority, and utilizing the power vested in it, in support of the daughter.

Moving On, the next novel gives primary importance to the father by making him that central point of reference from where the daughter learns to reconnect to herself and the world. The significance of the relational contribution lies in the fact that it arises out of the father's revision of his own role, as is revealed through the retrospective self-analysis in his diaries. Jiji's father discovers that autonomy for the daughter lies not just in equating her to a son, in terms of her potential to fulfil the parents' dreams, but also in allowing her space to grow as an individual. It lies in recognizing the many aspects of female identity, which are denied in deference to the unidimensional female role endorsed by social systems. It also lies in standing up for the daughter as she deals with the clash between her deepest feelings and the social disapproval against them.

Jiji's father has never been the distant patriarch portrayed in some of the earlier novels. He has enjoyed participating in the lives of his two daughters and never regretted not having a son. He makes Jiji capable and confident, making her assume responsibilities from an early age. However inherent in his pride at their camaraderie, is the expectation of total loyalty. Her decision to quit a career in medicine chosen by him, for marriage to Shyam whom he does not approve of, angers him. Tragedies arising from her decision alienate the two further. Shyam's illicit relationship with Jiji's sister, results in the birth of an illegitimate child and also in her sister's death. Her mother's harsh unrelenting attitude is unopposed, if not endorsed by her father. Torn between her loyalty to her family and her desire to give Shyam another chance, she loses both. Shyam commits suicide and her mother wastes away with disease before she finally dies. Burdened by the many guilts, Jiji lives with the feeling of her father's disappointment in her. The fact that before dying, her father wills his property to his grand-daughter rather than to her, intensifies her feeling of rejection and alienation. Her misgivings about his feelings for her, make her apprehensive of reading his diaries, which she fears might confirm his disappointment with her. The defensiveness makes her adopt an uncaring persona, which results in a withdrawal from participation in life. As she brings up her son and her husband's daughter born through her sister, she refuses all help from her father, and claims to have changed from the old loving and spontaneous Jiji, into an uncaring aloof one.

However, the misgivings give way as she brings herself to participate in her father's world by reading his most private thoughts, as penned down in his diaries. A whole new world of reconciliation emerges, providing a breakthrough in the emotional stalemate as she discovers the father's regret at his own response to the events in his daughter's life. His initial anger at her adamant refusal to continue with her medical studies, she discovers, had soon mellowed into a realization of his own attitude of appropriation towards her, "I made the mistake to shape Jiji's life ... I tried to make my beliefs hers ... I tried to make her take up my ambitions ... how could I have done it? My daughter, I thought, *my* child ... did that give me the right to take over her life? ... In my worst moments I think Jiji's actions were an act of rebellion against this, against me."[16]

Jiji discovers that the aloofness which she had attributed to his disapproval had in fact emanated from a belief that he had lost the right to reconnect to her, for not having stood up for her when she needed him the most. He regrets his inability to defend Jiji against her mother's disgust at her raw sensual passion for Shyam, which he knows was Jiji's attempt at connecting to the man she loved. He also regrets that he had not been more open-minded in his attitude towards Jiji, even if she had made wrong decisions. He writes, "to me, disobedience is not the original sin; in fact I do not see it as a sin at all. It is part of growing up, of moving on. Without the serpent, we would have remained forever, our child selves ... we need the serpent to keep the story moving" (205). His greatest regret however is his inability to stand up to his wife's hard hearted approach in dealing with Malu's illegitimate pregnancy. He cannot challenge her dismissal of Jiji's emotional pain, as she prevents her from forgiving Shyam. Malu's death, Shyam's subsequent suicide and the effect of all this on Jiji is palpable, and her father considers himself responsible for it.

If Baba's acknowledgement that he should have been more supportive, thaws Jiji's emotional alienation, his insights also help her to reconcile with her mother, who has inflicted hurt through her inability to adjust to any opinion other than her own. He makes Jiji realize that her mother's rejection of her is born out of what society had made her. The water tight compartments of right and wrong, in which she herself had existed, had made it impossible for her to recognize the vulnerability of spontaneous emotions. Jiji recognizes now, that in spite of differences, her mother had been pained at her suffering, and that she had never given up loving her. With this, Jiji's own defences weaken. Memories of her mother wasting with disease and death are enmeshed with Jiji's recognition of the many constraints of her life as a woman, dealing with her own complexes and unfulfilled desires. The father's influence thus brings reconciliation in other spheres too.

Jiji recognizes that terminal illness and proximity to death have invested her father with vulnerability, which is uncaring of social opinions. His reflections are the essence of his understanding of life. As she reads through them against the growing awareness of his unconditional love for her, they provide a direction to her own life. She discovers through him that either we believe in God, and agree that he is a power who will set things right for us, or we realize "there is no one but ourselves. We have to make the best of this life ... we are our creators" (304). This, she discovers, is only possible through a personal process of regeneration, by letting go of the past and move onto the future. Baba writes, "Grief shackles you to the past, it pinions you down to the moment of time, whereas happiness sets you free, it allows you to move on; Jiji has to learn to move on" (304). In a subsequent revision of the past, Jiji now gives benefit of doubt to all those who have hurt her. She choose to believe that Malu's relationship with Shyam had been born out of the same childhood desire to be like Jiji, which had made her stand in front of the mirror, copying her hairstyle and feeling thrilled that she looked "Jiji sarkhi" (328). She also tells herself that Shyam could not have betrayed her by killing himself, that he must have drowned in pitting himself against the waves as he had always done, in trying to exorcize himself of tension. She also recognizes that others too had forgiven her faults. Raja had let go of his anger at her relationship with Raman, and had moved on.

In a way, her father's writings also help Jiji to differentiate between independence and belligerence. Her defensive approach to being assessed, for how she could manage life as a single woman, has led to a retaliatory mood, in which she has for ever been daring others to question her rights and potentials. She is surprised to discover that her father had always admired her for her independence, that he had respected her for growing into an adult who took responsibility for herself. However, he separates for her this adult potential from the retaliation and hostility, which marred its worth. He hopes that she would relinquish the bitterness and that someday "the pointlessness and emptiness of her life" (304), would make her see the need to dissociate herself from the negativity, which had cost her so many emotional bonds.

As defences break one by one, Jiji understands her father's wish for her to reconnect to life. He makes her see that life can never be perfect, that we are all in the process of evolution, that wholeness can never be ours. Yet, this is no reason to stop living. In fact, the whole point is to carry on, to participate, to let go, to move on. Jiji lets go finally. The promise of a permanent bond with Raja, the camaraderie between B.K., Raja, and Sachi, Raja's and Jiji's sons' willingness to be part of this bonding, all contribute to regeneration, which is symbolically depicted in the flowering of the Brahma kamal in Raja's garden. Connecting to her father and participating in his self-assessment removes the burden of many guilts from Jiji's mind, breaks through her defences and paves the way not only for reconciliation with him, but also for reconnection to life. With this, her mask slips and she acknowledges that the reconstructed woman who wanted to stay away from all emotional involvements was only a facade, "the old Jiji wouldn't let go, she held on, clinging like an iguana to a rock" (245).

The father figures as sketched in *In the Country of Deceit* form the other end of the spectrum and remind us of the losses which could entail from the inability of the father to exercise his authority in the daughter's favour. Devayani's grandfather brings back memories of Vithalrao in *A Matter of Time*. A rich banker, he tries to impart education to his two daughters. However, he cannot quite stand up to the rigidly oriented wife, who can see at least one of them only as a burden, for being unfit even for a trophy marriage due to her epileptic fits. The father's guilt is reflected in a letter to a friend, in which he wonders, if he would have left the condition untreated, if the child had been a boy. The answer he realizes is in the negative. The property he leaves for her by way of assuaging his guilt comes late. The impact of his vacillating emotions is evident in the daughter's lack of confidence and timidity. Although, he shows some sensitivity in not trying to marry her off by offering a big dowry, the fact remains that her marriage to a clerk working in his bank, could have had better substitutes in making her independent in terms of money and education. Devayani's mother does get her share of her father's property, but only because there is no son to inherit it. By the time it comes, her life has already shaped itself in the deprived parameters where a husband who is a constant failure is construed by her as a knight in shining armour, because at least he has given her the dignity of being wanted.

Devayani's father on the other hand leaves his children permanently scarred because of his temperamental unsuitability to a provider's role. The memories of the losses in his ever changing business propositions and the precarious financial condition remain etched in their minds all their lives. Devayani cannot forget the "shabby home-stitched clothes and the let down hems showing, the secondhand books, the humiliation of being told in class that our fees had not been paid for months."[17] His fruit orchard, which never sees the day of life, the intellectual pursuits which peter out, the insurance policies he can never sell, the debts he incurs in the process, the abuses hurled at him by the moneylenders are impressed on the daughter's mind and she remembers him as a "… cliff hanger, hanging on to life by the tips of his fingers" (61). She understands the burden of having to live with a person who perforce is in a position of authority as well as responsibility, by virtue of being classified the head of the family, but who can in no way measure up to the role. She remembers, "… as things were, he lived with his problems and my mother, Savi and I had to live with him" (61). The fact remains that greater the authority vested in a social role, the greater is its potential for the enhancement or debasement of those who come under its purview. Both possibilities remain equally real.

An overview of the various paternal responses presented above provides us with the writer's ability to decipher the potential inherent in a father's position. *Roots and Shadows* provides the portrayal of a father's ability to provide ideological support to the daughter, thus aiding in a search for identity outside the prescribed role. In *The Dark Holds No Terror* we have a father who helps the daughter regain control by making her understand that her right over her life is greater than all the guilt inducing demands made by others. *That Long Silence* portrays a father who through his conviction in his daughter's potential, introduces her to an identity outside gender roles. Much later when he is no longer alive, his ideological convictions help the daughter to break out of a false identity and seek the true empowered self. *A Matter of Time* deals with a vaster framework depicting the process of change in attitudes. The emotional leap from a father's inability to stand up for the daughter, to a support which changes from obligation to genuine concern for her empowerment, is sensitively portrayed. It also deals with the vital new approach of a daughter's awareness of her rights and her demand for paternal support to move out of the constraints imposed by patriarchy. *The Binding Vine* deals with an altogether different facet, by dwelling on a father's attempts to empower the daughter by means which put at stake her emotional well-being. The daughter's eventual rejection of an empowerment which becomes another form of impairment, defines her as an agency with the right to decide what she needs by way of empowerment. *Small Remedies* on the other hand concludes that empowerment for women lies not in dismantling paternal authority but by reframing it, so that it aids from its position of authority. It also shows how a strong and balanced father figure invests the daughter with the strength to demand dignity in other relationships, while a weak father stripped of authority infuses the daughter with negation and denial. *Moving On* shows how the father helps in reconnecting the daughter to relationships, by reviving her faith in love and compassion. *In the Country of Deceit* shows the other side of the picture, portraying the dangers of investing the position of a father's authority in a person who is not equipped to handle it.

Thus, Deshpande's vast canvas captures the many facets of the issue at hand, analyses the possibilities inherent in them, dwells on the ways in which they can be useful and accepts the lacunas which might still prevail. Common to all possibilities, however, remains the fundamental presumption that autonomy "must develop from within social systems of interaction with others."[18] The father becomes the representative of that system, at times reaching up to the potential to become the instrument of change, at times failing to do so.

Notes

1. Catriona Mackenzie, Natalie Stoljar. "Introduction". *Relational Autonomy: Perspectives in Autonomy, Agency and Social Self.* Ed. Mackenzie and Stoljar. New York: Oxford University Press, 2000. p. 25.
2. Radhika Chopra. *Reframing Masculinities: Narrating the Supportive Practices of Men.* New Delhi: Orient Longman Pvt. Ltd., 2007. p. 4.
3. Shashi Deshpande. "Telling Our Own Stories." *Writing from the Margin and Other Essays.* New Delhi: Penguin Books India, 2003. p. 97.
4. Shashi Deshpande. "A Man of Integrity." *Writing from the Margin and Other Essays.* New Delhi: Penguin Books India, 2003. p. 43.
5. Shashi Deshpande. "In First Person." *Writing from the Margin and Other Essays.* New Delhi: Penguin Books India, 2003. p. 5.
6. Shashi Deshpande. "In First Person." *Writing from the Margin and Other Essays.* New Delhi: Penguin Books India, 2003. p. 5.
7. Shashi Deshpande. *Roots and Shadows.* New Delhi: Orient Longman. 1983. pp 74-75.
8. Shashi Deshpande. *The Dark Holds No Terror.* New Delhi: Vikas Publishing House Pvt. Ltd., 1980. p. 217. All other references to this novel are from this edition and page numbers are given in the text in parenthesis.
9. Kumkum Sangari. *Politics of the Possible: Essays on Gender, History, Narratives, Colonial English.* New Delhi: Tulika, 1999. p. 372.

10. Doreen D' Cruz. "Feminism in the Postcolonial Context: Shashi Deshpande's Fiction". <http://www. Murdoch.edu/Reading Room/Lit Serv/SPAN/Postcolonial Fiction.> p. 7/14.
11. Ibid.
12. Shashi Deshpande. *That Long Silence.* UK: Virago Press Ltd., 1988. p. 90. All other references to this novel are from this edition and page numbers are given in the text in parenthesis.
13. Shashi Deshpande. *A Matter of Time.* New Delhi: Penguin Books Ltd., 1996. p. 128. All other references to this novel are from this edition and page numbers are given in the text in parenthesis.
14. Shashi Deshpande. *The Binding Vine.* UK: Virago Press Ltd., 1993. pp. 52–53. All other references to this novel are from this edition and page numbers are given in the text in parenthesis.
15. Shashi Deshpande. *Small Remedies.* New Delhi: Penguin Books, 2000. p. 101. All other references to this novel are from this edition and page numbers are given in the text in parenthesis.
16. Shashi Deshpande. *Moving On.* New Delhi: Penguin Books, 2004. p. 241. All other references to this novel are from this edition and page numbers are given in the text in parenthesis.
17. Shashi Deshpande. *In the Country of Deceit.* New Delhi: Penguin. p. 60. All other references to this novel are from this edition and page numbers are given in the text in parenthesis.
18. Elizabeth Sperry. "Foucauldian Power, Relational Autonomy and Resistance through Friendship". <eministallies.blogspot.com/2006/.../relational-autonomy.html.>

7

Conclusion

Shashi Deshpande merits attention for exploring issues which look beyond the theories that initiate them. She chooses to interpret feminism from the point of view of the characters she delineates, keeping in mind their need to be part of the relational structures through which their identities evolve. Her approach towards female individuation is therefore integrated, with an understanding of the necessity of working upon it through the very relationships which hamper it. Her focus on male response is part of this concern with the context. It becomes a precursor to her exploration of the male psyche and hence of men's resistance to change. Through it Deshpande seems to be locating areas which hold the potential for a revised male outlook, enlisting a shift which could emanate from men's own interests as well. In doing so she seems to be assessing the possibility of creating traversable paths, on which men and women could walk together.

Nowhere does she imply that the perspective she adopts would ensure a smooth transition to new equations. Change in male attitude, when it is initiated, is usually constructed around conflict and emotional turmoil. However, it is this conflict which is shown as clarifying the forces which collide on its borderlines. What sets Deshpande's works apart is that she portrays the partial relational breakdown not as an inevitable outcome, but as a precursor to new more accommodating alignments. The possibility of a concurrent change in male response presented by her does not preclude the possibility of exceptions to it. There are no pretensions to clear-cut solutions. In fact, many of the works are open-ended, leaving one wondering what direction that response will take. Implicit in the eventuality of inflexibility of approach, is the possibility of regressive compromises or the break down in relationships. These, Deshpande would clearly wish to be the last options. She makes no claims to have reached any facile resolutions to the gender clash but she does provide an opening to the deadlock. The perspective emerging through it proposes that empowerment might be slow to come, but when it does relationships need not be a casualty.

Deshpande's contribution also extends to the development of a perspective which works through the premise that autonomy for one sex does not have to be sought in the alienation of the other. The comprehensive process of change suggested through her works involves its own difficulties and constraints, particularly in terms of the slow nature of its evolution. However, the eventual goal of restructured gender identities leading to a balance in gender equations, keeps the movement stabilized on a track which leads to a reconstruction of institutions and relationships. She also prevents the entire effort of altering the distribution of privileges and liabilities, from getting dissipated by the issues which would otherwise arise out of a parallel masculinist approach.

Deshpande's success lies in merging the distanced and intellectualized literary conceptions of the choices for women, with the social reality through which they need to function. In doing so she integrates the widely divergent yet overlapping issues, which make up the vast canvas of our social reality, into her own as well as the reader's consciousness. She entwines her perceptive abilities with the ideological peculiarities of her world and helps in building up a critical perspective suited to the real life needs of women in her milieu. Mary E. John, in her introduction to *Women's Studies in India: A Reader*, calls for a need to create a "Space of our own to further develop critical vocabulary, theories and methodologies ..."[1], for constructing the right tools with which to tackle the issues afflicting the female world in which we exist. Deshpande does exactly that. She relates her portrayals to what she actually sees in the world around her. Her stories are not about unusual, heroic or exceptional people but the average, common ones who look for workable solutions not iconoclastic ones. In this sense, fiction becomes her means of portraying sociological realities, life as it evolves in a particular cultural set-up over the generation and the shifts which work through its innumerable constraints. In this sense, she provides a perspective across disciplines, releasing real issues concerning women from their place in dull sociological data, to their analyses in the comprehensive and fulsome precincts of the living, mutating world of literature. In a sense, hers is a perspective across disciplines. She validates the view that a comprehensive and practical methodology in dealing with women's issues "will depend more than ever before on inhabiting multiple institutional sites and building links between them."[2]

A study on relationships can never be comprehensive and conclusive, because of the endless array of influences and the inherent fluidity of human response. This study does not claim to have covered the entire gamut of relational constructs, which could be studied under male response. Relational patterns change in varying socio-cultural constructs. Economic and cultural variations go into determining the complexities of gender dynamics. They structure the very world which men and women inhabit. Deshpande's chosen world is that of the educated middle class and this work has focussed largely on that. However, it does hope to throw open the possibility of a similar study in other socio-economic and cultural contexts, thus making men objects of interest, for those who hope to initiate sustainable gender formulations in real life situations.

Notes

1. Mary E. John. "Introduction." *Women's Studies in India: A Reader.* Ed. John. New Delhi: Penguin Books, 2008. p. 16.
2. Ibid.

Bibliography

Primary Sources

Deshpande, Shashi. *Roots and Shadows*. New Delhi: Orient Longman, 1983.

——. *The Dark Holds No Terror*. New Delhi: Vikas Publishing House, 1980.

——. *That Long Silence*. UK: Virago Press Ltd., 1988.

——. *The Binding Vine*. UK: Virago Press Ltd., 1993.

——. *A Matter of Time*, New Delhi: Penguin Books Ltd., 1996.

——. *Small Remedies*. New Delhi: Penguin Books, 2000.

——. *Moving On*. New Delhi: Penguin Books, 2004.

——. *In the Country of Deceit*. New Delhi: Penguin, 2008.

Secondary Sources

Amuta Chidi. Introduction. *The Theory of African Literature*. London and New Jersey: Zed Books Ltd., 1989. pp. 5–6.

Bharucha, Nilufer E. "Shashi Deshpande." *Dictionary of Literary Biography: South Asian Writers in English*. Vol. 323 (2006).

Bhasin, Kamla. *Exploring Masculinity*. New Delhi: Women Unlimited, 2004.

Chakravarti, Uma. "Whatever Happened to the Vedic Dasi: Orientalism, Nationalism, and a Script from the Past?" *Recasting Women*. Ed. Kumkum Sangari and Sudesh Vaid. New Delhi: Kali for Women, 1989.

Chopra, Radhika. *Reframing Masculinities: Narrating the Supportive Practices of Men*. New Delhi: Orient Longman Pvt. Ltd., 2007.

Daly, Mary. "Towards a Feminist Poetics." Quoted by Elaine Showalter. *The New Feminist Criticism: Essays on Women, Literature and Theory*. Ed. Elaine Showalter. London: Virago Press Ltd., 1986.

D' Cruz, Doreen. "Feminism in the Postcolonial Context: Shashi Deshpande's Fiction". <http://www. Murdoch.edu/Reading Room/Lit Serv/SPAN/ Postcolonial Fiction.>

Deaux, Kay. "Psychological Constructions of Masculinity and Feminity." *Masculinity/Feminity: Basic Perspectives*. Ed. June Machover Reinisch, Leonard A. Rosenblum, Stephanie A. Sanders. New York: Oxford University Press, 1987.

Deshpande, Shashi. *Writing from the Margin and Other Essays*. New Delhi: Viking, 2003.

——. "A Woman's World ... All the Way." Interview by Vanmala Vishwanathan. *Literature Alive* 1: 3, Dec. (1997).

——. "The Day of the Golden Deer." *In Search of Sita: Revisiting Mythology*. Ed. Malashri Lal and Namita Gokhale. New Delhi: Penguin Books, 2009.

Ensler, Eva. "Girl Power." Quoted by Chitra Subramaniam. <http://woman. In today.in/story.jsp.sid=6913> November 2009.

Felman, Shoshana. "Women and Madness." *Feminisms: An Anthology of Literary Theory and Criticism*. Ed. Robyn R. Warhol and Diane Price Herndl. 3rd ed. New Brunswich, New Jersey: Rutgers University Press, 1996.

Gilbert, Sandra M. "What Do Feminist Critics Want? A Postcard from the Volcano." *The New Feminist Criticism: Essays on Women, Literature and Theory*. Ed. Elaine Showalter. London: Virago Press Ltd., 1986.

Gokhale, Namita. "Sita: A Personal Journey." *In Search of Sita: Revisiting Mythology*. New Delhi: Penguin Books, 2009.

Gubar, Susan. "The Blank Page and Issues of Female Creativity." *The New Feminist Criticism: Essays on Women, Literature and Theory*. Ed. Elaine Showalter. London: Virago Press Ltd., 1986.

Hawthorn, Jeremy. "Theories of the Gaze." *Literary Theory and Criticism*. Ed. Patricia Waugh. 2nd ed. New York: Oxford University Press, 2007.

Heath, Stephen. "Male Feminism." *Men in Feminism*. Ed. Alice Jardine and Paul Smith. New York: Routledge, 1987.

Jain, Jasbir. *Gendered Realities, Human Spaces: The Writing of Shashi Deshpande*. Jaipur: Rawat Publications, 2003.

John, Mary E. Introduction. *Women's Studies in India: A Reader*. Ed John. New Delhi: Penguin Books, 2008.

Lee, Patrick C. Introduction. *Sex Differences: Cultural and Developmental Dimensions*. Ed. Patrick C. Lee and Robert Susan Steward. New York: Urizen Books, 1976.

Lipsitz, Sandra Bem. "Masculinity and Feminity Exist Only in the Mind of the Perceiver." *Masculinity/Feminity: Basic Perspectives*. Ed. June Machover Reinisch, Leonard A. Rosenblum, Stephanie A. Sanders. New York: Oxford University Press, 1987.

Mackenzie, Catriona, Natalie Stoljar. *Relational Autonomy: Perspectives in Autonomy, Agency and Social Self.* New York: Oxford University Press, 2000.

Meyers, Diana. *Gender in the Mirror: Cultural Imagery and Women's Agency.*<http://www.philosophy.uconn.edu/department/meyers/meyers. html.>

Miller, Nancy. "Plots and Plausibilities in Women's Fiction." *The New Feminist Criticism: Essays on Women, Literature and Theory*. Ed. Elaine Showalter. 4th ed. London: Virago Press, 1993.

Mohanti, Chandra Talpade. "Under Western Eyes, Feminist Scholarship and Colonial Discourses." *The Post-Colonial Studies Reader.* Ed. Bill Ashcroft, Gareth Griffith and Helen Tiffin. 2nd ed. Routledge: Oxford, 2006.

Moi, Toril. *Sexual/Textual Politics: Feminist Literary Theory*. 2nd ed. London: Routledge, 2002.

Mukherjee, Prabhati. "The Theory of Ideal Womanhood." *Hindu Women: Normative Models*. London: Sangam Books Ltd., 1993.

Pande, Rohini, Anju Malhotra. "Son Preference and Daughter Neglect in India. What Happens to Living Girls." <http://www.icrw.org/docs/2006_son-preference.pdf >.

Ramaswami, Vijaya. "Researching Icons, Representing Indian Women." *Researching Indian Women*. Delhi: Manohar, 2003.

Sangari, Kumkum. *Politics of the Possible: Essays on Gender, History, Narratives, and Colonial English*. New Delhi: Tulika, 1999.

Sattar, Arshia. "Sita: A Personal Journey." *In Search of Sita: Revisiting Mythology*. Quoted by Namita Gokhale. Ed. Malashri Lal and Namita Gokhale. New Delhi: Penguin, 2009.

Showalter, Elaine. *The New Feminist Criticism: Essays on Women, Literature and Theory*. 4th ed. London: Virago Press, 1993.

Sperry, Elizabeth. "Foucauldian Power, Relational Autonomy and Resistance through Friendship." <eministallies.blogspot.com/2006/.../relational-autonomy.html.>

Srivastava, Vinay Kumar. "Male Bias, Matrifocality and Family Dynamics." *Modernity, Feminism and Women Empowerment.* Ed. Abha Avasthi and A.K. Srivastava. Jaipur: Rawat Publications, 2001.

Stephen, Erick H. "Inner and Outer Space: Reflections on Womanhood." *Sex Differences: Cultural and Developmental Dimensions*. Ed. Patrick C. Lee and Robert Susan Steward. New York: Urizen Books, 1976.

Strathern, M. *Masculinity/Feminity: Basic Perspectives*. Quoted by Kay Deaux. Ed. June Machover Reinisch, Leonard A. Rosenblum, Stephanie A. Sanders. New York: Oxford University Press, 1987.

Termen, Lewis, Catherine Cox Miles. "Sex and Personality: Studies in Masculinity and Feminity." *Sex Differences: Cultural and Developmental Dimensions*. Ed. Patrick C. Lee and Robert Susan Steward. New York: Urizen Books, 1976.

Tharu, Susie and K. Lalita. *Women Writing in India: 600 B.C to the Present, Vol. II: The Twentieth Century.* New Delhi: Oxford University Press, 1993.

Turkman, Serap. "Identity in Colonial Land: A Critical Overview of Postcolonial Studies." *Alternatives: Turkish Journal of International Relations*, Vol. 2, No. 3 and 4, Fall and Winter (2003).

White, C. Sarah. "Men Masculinities and the Politics of Gender Development." Vol. 5, Number 2, June (1997). Quoted in *Exploring Masculinity.*

Index